PERSIAN DAWNS, EGYPTIAN NIGHTS

PERSIAN DAWNS, EGYPTIAN NIGHTS

J. Leslie Mitchell
(Lewis Grassic Gibbon)

Introduced by Ian Campbell

Polygon
Edinburgh

© The estate of J. Leslie Mitchell
Introduction © Ian Campbell 1997

First published in 1932 by
Jarrold Publishers (London) Limited

This edition published in 1998 by
Polygon
22 George Square
Edinburgh

New material set in Garamond by Speedspools, Edinburgh
Printed and bound in Great Britain by
The Cromwell Press, Melksham, Wiltshire

A CIP record for this title is available.

ISBN 0 7486 6231 6

THE OTHER GRASSIC GIBBON

Slowly, James Leslie Mitchell (1901–35) is emerging from the typecasting which engulfed him on his appearance in the 1960s from critical obscurity. The author of *Sunset Song* (1932), *Cloud Howe* (1933) and *Grey Granite* (1934) – together, the astonishingly successful *A Scots Quair* for which he is most remembered – was a writer who crammed many interests into a short productive life. As 'Lewis Grassic Gibbon' (an adaptation of his mother's maiden name) he had achieved considerable success as novelist of the Scottish renaissance, and seemed set to achieve more when his sudden death cut short a productive streak in spring 1935. As 'J. Leslie Mitchell' he was also becoming known, more perhaps in London than in his native Scotland, as a hard-working and successful journalist with a facility for turning his hand to many things – to film criticism, to general writing, to popular and often iconoclastic essays, to science fiction, to archaeological history, above all to writing about the theory of civilisation which fascinated him – the 'diffusionist' theories popularised in the UK by Grafton Elliot Smith.

Mitchell was an enigma in his time to many people, but he had a great gift of incorporating in his fiction parts of his life which would be hard to guess from those who know only *A Scots Quair*. *Persian Dawns, Egyptian Nights* may be the work of quite a different man from the familiar 'Grassic Gibbon', but it is that other Grassic Gibbon whose work, steadily being republished by Polygon, is now available to those who would like to understand him.

Persian Dawns, Egyptian Nights comes from several places in Mitchell's life. First, it comes from a close and personal acquaintance with what he would have called the Middle East, during military service in Persia and Egypt. Military service filled almost as much of Mitchell's life as did his writing period, but it is curiously little known and little has been made of its contribution to his output.

Mitchell was a crofter's son from the North East of Scotland, born in Aberdeenshire but growing up in Arbuthnott in the Mearns, unforgettably transformed to Kinraddie in *Sunset Song* and Segget in *Cloud Howe*, and curiously extended by his memory of the surrounding country and farmers in *The Speak of the Mearns*. The classic path of the clever Scottish country boy was through local school to local high school and university: the Scottish writers who preceded him had immortalised that path as the 'lad o pairts' in kailyard fictions without number. In reality, the 'lad o pairts' was no mere kailyard invention, but the factual experience of many who followed the path themselves, including the author of the most powerful realistic anti-kailyard novel *The House with the Green Shutters* (1901), George Douglas Brown.

James Leslie Mitchell himself was a classic case: from a bitterly poor background, recognised in Arbuthnott by his schoolmaster Alexander Gray, and 'brought on' for the Mackie Academy in Stonehaven with, doubtless, an eye to university in Aberdeen after. It was the kind of path he plotted out for his central character Chris in *Sunset Song*, and it would have surprised no one had the gifted, clever and sensitive crofter's son followed it himself.

Instead, Mitchell survived only one year in a school he found reactionary and unchallenging, then discharged himself in a scene he gleefully utilised in *The Thirteenth Disciple*, embarking on an extraordinary career which was to find some of its fruit in *Persian Dawns, Egyptian Nights*.

He tried journalism first – in Aberdeen, then in Glasgow. There he found an intense interest in the life of many social classes, strikingly so with the urban poor whom he had had little contact with in the Mearns, but who figure so prominently in his later Scottish fiction (above all, *Grey Granite*) and in the English city scenes of work like *Stained Radiance*. In Aberdeen docks and in Glasgow, he met arrivals from Russia and further afield, politically active people who opened his eyes to a wider set of values. Already in early manhood revolution fascinated Mitchell, and it never lost that fascination. When journalism failed for him – he was ignominiously fired after fiddling his expenses, even clumsily tried suicide – he was faced with a momentous choice. Either he surrendered the new found freedom and excitement of the cities to return to the life of the croft with his brothers, or – all but unthinkable to someone as lonely and fastidious in his habits as Mitchell – he could enlist in the forces. It says something about the firmness with which he rejected farming life (for all the aching nostalgia of *Sunset Song*) that he chose the forces, and in all but a decade of life in the Army and Air Force, most of it at private's rank, he combined his military life with travel, and with writing.

Persian Dawns, Egyptian Nights is the work of a close observer, a loner, someone on the outskirts of a life of teeming energy and chaos. Its conception is mirrored in the kind of scene Mitchell wrote as Chapter 3 of *Stained Radiance*, where a transparently autobiographical Garland types alone, aloof, 'The outside world had ebbed from Garland auricularly as well as visually'. For him, his book was a world to itself – and for his creator, his writing allowed him to live with the irritations of forces life.

The first half of this story cycle, the Persian tales, are supposedly the chronicles of an early Christian Bishop, removed by his office from the everyday reality of a world torn by war and invasion. The second half of the cycle, set in a Cairo which Mitchell visited and came to know quite well, is told through the medium of observers, people who are on the outside of both the English ruling class and the lower-class Cairenes themselves, in all their polyglot multifariousness. Mitchell could hardly help writing from this viewpoint. As Private Mitchell he was observer of the English officer class; as European, he was observer to the life of the streets and the rivers of the Middle East, while as Mitchell the student of archaeology and the history of civilisation, he was the fascinated spectator of the cradle of what he had grown up recognising as modern civilisation.

It is here that *Persian Dawns, Egyptian Nights* is an extraordinarily valuable aid to the study of Mitchell's whole span of work, not just the *Quair*. When J. D. Beresford writes an enthusiastic – and curiously unfocused – introduction to the Jarrold edition of *Persian Dawns, Egyptian Nights*, he reminds us that no lesser lights than H. G. Wells and Leonard Huxley had introduced and praised *The Calends of Cairo*. The influence of the East permeates short stories and novels alike, for Mitchell skilfully re-used scenes and characters in his haste to write and sell: he incorporated real life experience, and an omnivorous reading.

Wells was an obvious source of inspiration for the science fiction part of Mitchell's output – the novels, *Three Go Back* and *Gay Hunter* – and the science fiction arises from a fascination with the growth of the Western world Mitchell grew up in during and after World War One – revolution, World War, depression, the shadow of Nazism.

Diffusionist historians, maybe not many of them as articulately as Mitchell, saw in their times not the peak of modern civilisation, but its decay and imminent collapse. Like Wells' time traveller, diffusionists were aware of the price humanity paid for its temples and its technology, and they blamed 'civilisation' for enslaving a human race originally nomadic and free, without property and without fear, without religion and without shame, and making of them the factions of twentieth-century civilisation, rich and poor, exploiting and exploiter – civilisation, in short, led to the depression, the World War, the wearing-down of humanity into the grey anonymity, the spite and the class warfare Mitchell depicts in *Stained Radiance* and in *Grey Granite*. *Persian Dawns, Egyptian Nights* seeks to dip into the prehistory of 'modern' civilisation, using two of 'civilisation''s most notable achievements – religious systems and the city, both of them equally unnecessary and balefully hurtful in the diffusionist's eyes. Where Wells in *The Time Machine* travels to something of an apocalyptic future, Mitchell is content to start in the distant past, and move slowly to the present in the tale cycle.

Neesan Nerses, Nerstorian Bishop in the Persian hills in the thirteenth century, is Mitchell's fictive avenue for these Persian stories. For his chronicles, his life's work, are the absorbing passion which abstracts him from his diocese, his world, most of the time – till reality forces itself on him in a series of invasions, wars, personal crises of one kind or another which form the flashpoints for the stories told.

One of Mitchell's notable techniques here, and one which surfaced in *Cloud Howe*, is the almost amused detached use of the Christian myths and stories. Mitchell the artist knows them as historian but not as believer: Bishop Neesan Nerses is a believer in the context of his times, and the stories Mitchell makes him hear and record are an extraordinary blend of pagan and Christian, myth and sincere belief, the deliberate choice no doubt of an author like Mitchell who had lost his own Christian faith, but gained a fascination with the countries which fostered it, and had a historian's fascination with how stories arise and grow in the transmission. Mitchell is obviously drawn to the possibility that some of humanity's legends might be true – the lost race of 'The Last Ogre', the Wanderer of 'Cartaphilus', the Ancient Grove of 'The Floods of Spring'. Whether these are related to the creation story of Genesis, to legends of the Crucifixion or to prelapsarian humanity before Eden and The Flood hardly matters: the connection is there to be made, but hardly explicitly made by an author who would have regarded the Bible text as a fascinating historical document rather than a matter for faith or belief. In his other writing – *Three Go Back*, for instance – he was happy to play with the idea of Lost Atlantis, much more comfortably than he toyed with the crucifixion story in *Spartacus* where it has only the briefest place.

Mitchell deliberately, and skilfully, reins in the world of these stories to the confines of a monastery and a primitive Christian settlement ruled over by the Bishop-Chronicler: like many in his century, Neesan heard only what travellers told him, what returning warriors could recall of battles whose history would not be written for centuries (if at all), of distant races across mountains which could hardly be tackled without the near certainty of death. The Persian dawn is our millennium, and Mitchell catches uncannily the process of its early history as myth and legend shade inevitably into experience and first-hand memory: as the old man's life contracts, and his memories jumble, his chronicle blends all its sources into one, as we have received any of civilisation's legends which Mitchell the Diffusionist sees as wreckage in the 1930s. This is time travel of a special sort: the birth of a belief system which still exists today, and the inconspicuous but ceaseless application of the same irony as that other Gibbon uses in the *Decline and Fall* to question the authenticity of early Christian belief, and Christian history.

But it takes less of an effort at time travel to enter the Egyptian nights part of the book, vibrantly and almost shockingly alive at the time of publication, when Cairo was emerging into a metropolis of East and West, where asses and motor cars fought for the same road space, where the buried civilisations of the past were there to be uncovered by the casual spade and the impassive remains of one Egyptian civilisation looked down on the frantic scrabblings of its successor. Mitchell writes of this Cairo with what Jeremy Idle calls a 'brash uniqueness', born of a young man's willingness to experiment in style, and break new ground, even at the expense (as Dr Idle shows in his introduction to the short stories reprinted from *The Calends of Cairo*) of giving a picture clichéd from a Western perspective. By using a polyglot narrator (who reappears in *The Calends of Cairo*) *Persian Dawns, Egyptian Nights* goes some way to try to bypass the cliché identified for us by Edward Said: Mitchell interprets his Cairo through the double shifting mirror of memory, and of an only half-familiar consciousness to which the comforting familiarity of British life and British speech are more than half alien.

Sergei Lubow is the narrating voice as the Egyptian nights open: his fractured English, his mannerisms grate today, but he is a deliberate filter between Mitchell (who presents himself as a realist novelist visiting Cairo) and the Western reader.

Sergei is the teller of tales: he knows he is a teller, and takes pleasure in doing it well. To Mitchell he is the device to domesticate setting and unfamiliar language, to explain intimacies which a visiting European would probably be denied. The stories once under way, Sergei fades, and there is not even the pretence that we are following Neesan Nerses' chronicles: this is Egyptian life, mysterious, unmediated, direct. Some parts, no doubt, are direct from memory: the sound of the Nile at sunset, the jangle of traffic, the stench, the steady growth of a city threatening to obliterate its past. Some parts, equally, are obviously from Mitchell's fascination with epic and folk-tale. The Egyptian stories hover on the edge of magic, the unexplained; the quality of the stories matches the Western consciousness faced with the mystery of ancient Egypt, glimpsing a world which is incapable of being fully understood, even with an English-speaking interpreter.

This is, in the end, what *Persian Dawns, Egyptian Nights* is seeking to convey – the sense of a mysterious society, stretched over centuries of time, and deriving its origins from much further back, indeed back before the origins of what we would recognise as civilisation itself. *Persian Dawns, Egyptian Nights* transmutes its author's brief acquaintance with the Middle East to short fictions which would give some incomplete sense of the bafflement of the East: which would give him much-needed practice in producing publishable fiction, as well as much-needed income. When Mitchell noted at the beginning that the stories had appeared in the *Cornhill*, and that 'To its Editor more than the usual acknowledgements are due', he was thanking the editor for a breakthrough to publication. In republishing – recycling – early work, Mitchell was doing no more than underlining the business good sense his papers show all through. In creating the cycle *Persian Dawns, Egyptian Nights* Mitchell was coming to terms with a part of his past, while using it to explore another part of the present – our understanding of the past which shaped the civilisation of the 1930s he wrote in. *A Scots Quair* was part of the same search to understanding the unlovely present: he was still searching when he died.

Ian Campbell
Edinburgh

Jeremy Idle's introduction to the short stories from *The Calends of Cairo* reprinted in *The Speak of the Mearns* is essential reading (Polygon, 1994), esp. pp. 218–22.

Stained Radiance is available from Polygon (1993), as are the science fiction novels *Three Go Back* (1995) and *Gay Hunter* (1989).

Persian Dawns, Egyptian Nights has not been republished since the original Jarrold edition, the basis for this one.

For further reading on this part of Mitchell's life and work see D. F. Young, *Beyond the Sunset* (Aberdeen, Impulse, 1973), esp. pp. 154–7 on the short stories; and W. K. Malcolm, *A Blasphemer & Reformer* (Aberdeen University Press, 1984), especially ch. 3 'The English Stories', pp. 45–64. A specialised but valuable study is Uwe Zagratzki, *Libertäre und utopische Tendenzen im Erzählwerk James Leslie Mitchells (Lewis Grassic Gibbons)* (Frankfurt a.M., 1991).

GOOD WINE

A Foreword by J. D. BERESFORD

LIKE many old proverbs, that which says
'Good wine needs no bush' has little application to modern needs. There was a time when
connoisseurs knew where to find the right stuff, to
read or to drink. In the case of literature they
might be mistaken in their taste, since among
experts you may trust a judge of wine but not
always a judge of poetry. But those were the days
in which the world could maintain its population
in ease and security; in which a man went to his
inn to find good company and not to forget his
condition, in which books were treasures to keep
and re-read and not a mere diversion in idleness.

Moreover, and more appositely in this connection,
the recommendation of quality was then sufficient
to advertise the wares of the producer, whether they
were wine or books. Books were as few as good
wine was rare, and a local reputation would provide
for an author's necessities—with the help of his
patron.

In the world of to-day, the General Reader to
whom an author looks for his living has no con-
noisseurship and before he makes his dip into the
turbulent spate of fiction flowing in perpetual flood
through the circulating libraries, the recommendation of quality must be vouched for by someone
whom he regards as a competent authority. And
if this General Reader is not a member of the Book
Society, to whom shall he look for guidance?

Reviewer, publisher, library assistant, friend? Fallible authorities, all these, as he knows to his cost.

Which of them, for instance, will recommend the works of J. Leslie Mitchell? The publisher, of course, but you cannot trust a publisher's advertisements of his own wares, however honest the author of them may be. The friend is probably as unenlightened as the enquirer, since the friend of the G.R. is himself a G.R., and the difference of odds in favour of Mr. Mitchell's being selected increases only from about a million to one to a million to two. And I refuse to say a single word about the Reviewer or the Library Assistant.

Wherefore those who have some kind of belief in their own taste in literature come forward now and again to introduce an author whose work has tickled their educated palates. H. G. Wells and Leonard Huxley, for example, are my predecessors in answering for Leslie Mitchell's quality, both of them having put their names to a testimonial of his abilities in an earlier volume of his stories entitled *The Calends of Cairo*. Nevertheless, it was not through their recommendation nor through that of any one of the four other authorities cited above that I discovered him. It was, indeed, merely good luck—mine, not his—that sent me his novel *The Thirteenth Disciple*, and I am exceedingly grateful to the great god Chance—now being backed by the physicists for a high seat on Olympus—for sending me a book by a young writer who had something to say and knew how to say it.

But I do not propose to spend myself in collecting appreciative adjectives about the stories in this volume. When you, my dear G.R., Reviewer, or Library Assistant, have got so far as this, you will have my authority for going much further. I, in better company, have hung up a bush before Leslie Mitchell's door to apprise you that within may be found good cheer and a sound wine. Savour it well ; and if you do not agree with me, blame your own lack of taste, which will probably be due to a tired palate.

CONTENTS

PERSIAN DAWNS

EGYPTIAN NIGHTS

These two story-cycles have appeared in the Cornhill Magazine.
To its Editor more than the usual acknowledgments are due.

J. L. M.

THE LOST CONSTITUENT

I

MIRZA MALIK BERKHU was born in the hut of a Nestorian silversmith of Mu'adhan in the year of Our Lord 1200. Ten years after his birth he was sold as a slave to the Janissaries Regiment of the Pultow . . .

This is no tale of mine, you understand, but one transcribed and edited from the wordy chronicles of Neesan Nerses, sometime Nestorian Bishop of a long-vanished diocese in the Persian hills north of Sar-i-Mil. It is one of the earliest and shortest of his tales—those fabulous pseudo-histories leavened with ingenuous moralisings little to modern taste or the point generally. Living in an unliterary century—he began writing about the year 1245 in the Gregorian calendar, though twelve years earlier according to his Julian reckoning—he had no competitors to fear, and in his darkness of medieval ignorance knew nothing of the vivid phrase or the startling opening. No living reader but would skip the first three thousand words and fifty years of narrative to reach Baghdad of the year A.D. 1250, on a morning of the second date-harvest.

A city colourful enough that morning, as the Bishop paints it : banner-hung, crowded and prosperous, with its sheen of lacquered minarets and gilded towers, its Tigris a rippling scimitar in the sunlight. Half the palace guards had ridden out an hour before sunrise to bring the conqueror in from his camp beyond the Western Gate. They had ridden out, stout young men who had never known war, with much beating of drums and clanging of gongs, to the amusement of an irreverent populace already thronging the streets. The shouted advice and aspersions of the Baghdadese the Bishop records with unclerical zest, but the passage is best left untranslated, especially as it delays both the action of the story and the passage of the sleek and sulky guards. Men with grievances, the guards. They had ceased to count. They were out of favour, forsooth, because that unquiet fool Mirza Berkhu was returning from one of his wearisome victories.

Their private thoughts they appear to have kept to themselves, however, the while their captain spoke a long address of welcome to Berkhu at the head of his dusty and saturnine troops. Berkhu himself greeted the address with a sardonic grin. In chain-armour, six feet in height, mounted on a black Arab, his nose under the peak of his Christian hat looking more beaked and aggressive than ever, he rode beside the captain under the archway of the Western Gate. And there indeed he half-halted.

' What's this smell ? '

The guards' captain smiled sourly. ' Roses,' he said.

Rose-scent it was. The Baghdadese had surpassed themselves in preparation for the return of their hero. They had had camel-trains of roses brought from the surrounding suburbs, and with great blossoms, white, yellow, red, had hung River Street in scented curtains. Berkhu was almost startled, though he recovered quickly enough, and thereafter for nearly an hour rode forward between parallel banks of screamed approbation and showering favours, till his horse and armour were smothered with roses. Once he glanced up towards the gleaming heights of the Citadel—the palace where, as boy-slave to an entire regiment, he had been lucky to steal as much as three hours' sleep a night. . . . But God! how he had slept! Never such sleep as then!

Black faces, brown faces, small wizened yellow faces, even—those last the faces of little Hun traders from the remote north. So, amidst a kingdom of uplifted faces, rode Mirza Malik Berkhu, First General of the Caliphate, a Minister of the Divan, a poet, a heretic, and a notorious lover and wine-bibber. Fresh from the slaughter of raiders on the borders of Turkestan he came, and at either saddle-horn dripped a dozen severed heads: heads of hideous raiders whose kin would yet very terribly avenge them. But of that Berkhu suspected nothing. Nor would he have cared greatly had he done so.

Hideous heads. They might give thanks to God they were freed from the necessity of embarrassing their owners. Dead. They who had been quick now very slow. What had happened to them?

And, staring down at the trunkless dead, for the first time in his life he found himself thinking of life. He had been too busy living ever to think of it before.   Living—since those days as the slave-boy in Citadel. . . . Weariness and sleep, thirst and satiety, dust and boredom—unceasingly, unendingly. Life ; his life. All life ? Nothing else in it ? Or had he mislaid some ingredient that might have transformed the whole to a thing like—like a bugle-cry in a camp at morning ?

Sound without earache ? . . .

So, the bored General in fantastic speculation, he rides through the streets of Baghdad and the lengthy prosings of Neesan Nerses, who arrogates to himself considerable knowledge of the happenings inside Berkhu's head, and approves them not at all. They were, one gathers, wrong-headed.

The palace gates : Fanfare of trumpets, the carpet of state, dismounted procession. And there, within the great rooms, remote in that building like a worm remote in the woodwork of a cabinet, says Nerses, Berkhu came into the presence of the Caliph. A little, dried-up man, white-faced, the Caliph, and as Berkhu prostrated himself with clash of chain-armour he sat a long while considering his general. And Berkhu knew himself very near to death, and grinned sardonically in his beard, considering the floor under his nose. He had become too popular and well-loved in Baghdad. Besides, the mullahs had been at their work against the heretic.

Presently the Worm-King spoke, and at his words

guards and pages, saints and sinners, dwarfs and diviners who enlivened the lighter hours of Muhammud's successor, withdrew. Then Berkhu heard himself addressed.

'Rise, General.'

So they faced each other. The Caliph was blunt.

'I had no need of this victory or campaign. The populace forced it on me. Nor have I any need of you. So you do not return to your army.'

Berkhu laughed. It was characteristic of him, this unseemly levity, says Nerses. 'Not even my head?'

Now those two had once been friends—long before, in the days when a gallop across the sands and the strife of spears was like wine in the mouths of their youth. And they peered at each other in that dusk and scented room, and the Caliph sighed.

'O Malik, we've come far, you and I, since those morning rides to Baqubah. What have they given you, all those years that have passed since then?'

'Fools to fight and much weariness to endure,' said the heretic General, and also was blunt. 'But not so much as they have given you.'

The dried-up little man who ruled Islam nodded. 'That is true. Now the weary should rest. For me there is none, but for you——'

And again he considered him, and Berkhu thought amusedly of the dripping heads waiting outside on his saddle-bow. But that memory of the Baqubah rides had disturbed the Caliph's intention.

'You will retire to your palace and garden on Tigris-bank. There you will remain until I give you leave to come forth.'

Thus the little Worm-King, looking in Berkhu's mocking eyes. Then the General made another prostration, rose, and passed from that room— passed, indeed, from all the colourful life of Bagh-dad, and for ten long years, in macabre pursuit of life's own secret, was remote from it as the dead.

II

But that pursuit began not at once. The first few months of exile merely accentuated his boredom— though Nerses gives it a more theological name— to an agony almost unendurable. Wearied though he had been of camp and field, his army and com-mand, never had he known such weariness as that endured, day on day, in the great blue-painted rooms of the Tigris-bank palace. They were set with gilded screens of fine mushrabiyeh work, those rooms, hung with Persian cloths, their floors mosaic'd by the cunning hands of Shiraz workmen. In one of them multitudes of chryselephantine statuettes, idols of pagan gods and spoil of a raid on raiders of the Hindu Tiger King, stood to peer unholily from floriated niche and lacquered pedestal upon the flowing of the Tigris. Fountains sprayed in the inner courts—fountains in eternal cannonade of besieging legions of lilies through the early summer and of roses and mimosa in the intenser heats. The garden-scents haunted Berkhu even in the remotest cellars to which he betook himself.

But he also wearied of wine very quickly. He wearied of the innumerable palace women, their squabblings and their lusts. In his library, unrolling from their scrolled silver cylinders the tales and romaunts of Arab imagination, he found no surcease. Rest from himself—there was none. What rest indeed had any man ever found from himself except in the blind restlessness of youth?

So for three months, while in Baghdad the indignation and curiosity over his dismissal began to die out. Within six months, his army dispersed to the limits of Iraq, he was forgotten as hero and conqueror. Over-clouding that once burnished reputation arose another.

The heretic General was engaged in sorcery.

III

It was a common enough pursuit in that age and country and the word covered a multitude of darksome activities. What led Berkhu into his quest of the life-essence Bishop Nerses—who at this point mysteriously abandons the narrative and involves himself in an entirely irrelevant denunciation of the Latin Rite—only hints at in a belated and hurried aside. It was a devil-inspired memory of the dripping heads that had hung from his saddle-bow and the aching speculations they had aroused.

Life, this burden and weariness of days and years
—yet if a man could re-live it deliberately might he
not search out some secret certainty and splendour
to light the years as with a torch ? If youth came
twice . . .

Slowly the hope kindled. At first his studies
were little more than an amusement—a bored
amusement. He had a great Riverwards room
sealed to his own exclusive use, and there immersed
himself in such Satanic literature as was then
available ; and might never have passed beyond
such harmless whiling away of time but for the
fact that a Greek slave from Istambul, newly come
into his possession, discovered himself a chemist of
some little note and considerable pretension.

Instantly he was impressed into the service of
Berkhu's private room, absolved from all other
duties, and promised his freedom when, by creation
or rejuvenation, they had run to earth the life-
formula.

Abiogenesis was as favourite a dream of the
pseudo-savant of that time as it is of his successor
of this. The Greek's private opinions are not
recorded. Probably they were highly sceptical.
Nevertheless, he taught to Berkhu all he knew, and,
having been wrung dry, found himself relegated
to the position of sweeper-up and bottle-washer
the while his amazing pupil went on into mysteries
the Greek had never essayed—not even with the
aid of the still-unproven algebra.

Days swept seaward on the southern flow of the

Tigris, according to the poetical but unastronomical bishop. Weeks followed them into months, into years, and remote, unapproachable in his palace-wing, Mirza Malik Berkhu, once the first soldier of Islam, still climbed and adventured unceasingly amidst the ghoul-haunted slopes of sorcery.

What he had begun as an amusement, a relaxation, had become an obsession—a fact which tempts Nerses into a lengthy disquisition, unnecessarily Freudian, on the psychology of the Devil. The quest of youth, the life-essence, the life-formula had beckoned him through experiment after experiment. Gradually the immense treasure accumulated during forty years of campaigning was largely dissipated, though the Tigris-bank palace continued to house some hundred women, guards, slaves, and parasites unclassifiable. The Greek assistant had died and his place been taken in rotation by innumerable others, drawn to Baghdad by rumour of fabulous reward. One by one they had been tested, found wanting, and dismissed—renegade mullahs, shamans from the far North, even, according to Nerses, Buddhist priests from remote Thibet. Their promises and formulæ wilted under performance, for, however otherwise changed, Berkhu remained disconcertingly practical even in his sorcery.

He had had an immense furnace installed in the room of the chryselephantine statuettes—heat being a natural corollary of hellish studies, according to his chronicler—and appears to have gathered together a laboratory equipment of tanks and test-tubes and coolers extraordinary enough for his day. He had progressed from his first crude experimentings with the bones and blood of this, that and the next animal to the attempting of more complex syntheses. The furnace would whoom, the retorts bubble reddishly, and the sorcerer and his assistant of the moment pore over charts and diagrams the while some new concoction—the brain of a slave, the poison-sac of a cobra, poppy-essence, mandragora—seethed to an odoriferous spume. Then would come the testing of its efficacy : Berkhu had strong belief in testing the results on his assistants, and the emetics of the time, much in demand after each test, were crude and forcible. It was seldom an assistant stayed for a second experiment.

But Berkhu went on undiscouraged, through list after list of unhygienic recipes, the mildest ingredients of which seem to have been the livers of wolves and the hearts of bats. Until that phase passed also. The ingredients fined down. The sorcerer General was on the track of the simple, elemental things, amazed that he should have neglected them.

He had great bouquets of flowers brought to him for dissection. The laboratory was turned into a hothouse for the forcing and observation of innumerable seeds which sprang overnight, strangely manured, into sudden plants. And these, in turn, were culled and ground and pounded into nauseous mixtures which sometimes maddened and sometimes slew. . . . And still the secret eluded him.

Yet, looking back over his experiments, a strange conviction grew upon him.   Again and again, by a score of different routes, he had neared success in manufacture of the life-essence—but for the discovery of a single constituent.   Mysterious, unnamed, unsegregated, this lost ingredient slipped betwixt the bars of formulæ and tests.   Again and again . . .

In research a forerunner of the moderns, he abandoned his furnace.   He had a new laboratory built on the roof of his palace.   There, in the blaze of the sun, great crystals were erected to concentrate light into pools of wine and water and oil and liquids unnamable.   Sometimes the wavering gleams from the palace roof would scare the strayed stranger in Baghdad's streets at night, the while Berkhu experimented with the radiance of the full moon.

And still the secret eluded him.

And outside Baghdad advanced the Mongols.

IV

But Berkhu was deeper in the devil's toils than ever, says Nerses.   He cared nothing for Mongols, but only for his search.   A long-forgotten figure began to appear in the streets of Baghdad, to wander the heat and dust and din of the daytime bazaars, the soqs of the cameliers who came from the Gulf of

Ormuz with pearls and sandalwood and outrageous travellers' tales, the quarters of the Persian poets, the kennels of the Somali dervish-troupes. At night the drowsy mullah would start at sight of that wanderer on the floor of his mosque, some ghaffir shrink into his doorway at sight of that beaked, thin nose and sardonic, searching eyes. The heretic General had abandoned his palace roof and gone out into the world in quest of the lost constituent.

If neither in blood nor bones, drugs nor scents nor sunshine lay the secret towards which he had struggled by so many roads, might not the ultimate bridge to it, this last evanescent ingredient, abide in some creed or phrase or stanza, all unwitting its own power?

But neither in fable nor fantasy, incantation nor dogma, the droning of the mullahs or the screamed revelations of epileptic dervishes could he find a clue. Nor by purchase of Christian scripts and long poring over the forgotten creed of his childhood did he find it. For, as Nerses sententiously points out, he sought not life eternal but youth on earth. His was the quest not of the humble heart but the golden grain—to recapture the years of the slave-boy in Citadel and with that as beginning upbuild a life full, perfect, unhaunted by a mysterious weariness and frustration.

And then a dreadful fear came on him and all one night he tramped the palace roof-spaces in agony— albeit a questioning, sardonic agony still. How if the lost constituents of the life-essence he sought and the life he had lived were the same? He himself—perhaps it was he who was at fault. . . .

He fell to a night-long examination of himself, under the circling stars, with far lights twinkling meaninglessly on the Persian hills and once or twice vexing him from his inquisition. What did he himself lack that the life-essence eluded him? Except youth, he had everything : Courage, strength, passion, ardour even yet, wit, fantasy, invention. Love he had known, hate he had known, fear, exaltation, hope. . . . Everything. What dream or desire in the minds of men had not been his?

Women?

Next morning he abandoned his hermit-existence. He emerged into the life of the palace again—a procedure which struck the palace with the amazement due to a divine advent—had his principal wife garrotted, the rooms cleansed of her lovers and favourites. Then, in this last pursuit of the lost constituent, he indulged in such debauch as the palace had never known even in its heyday. He clad himself in fine robes again, feasted on delicate foods and wines, and sent out his steward to the slave-market to purchase women. There was less selection than of old, but they brought him gorgeous creatures still—white Circassians, damask-skinned Persians, dusky and sly and spirited women of the mountains. And in their arms, in wine and laughter and song Berkhu still searched unavailingly for the golden grain.

And the Mongols drew ever nearer.

V

They were battering at the gates. They brought up great Chinese bombards and hurled jagged rocks into the city. Their battering-rams clove in the Western Gate and they poured in and swept the Janissaries back. Then the Worm-King, roused from his half-life in the Citadel, fled across the Tigris and across the desert. Mutinous, disordered, the Janissaries made but a half-hearted defence against the attacks of the yellow plainsmen. Then, in that hour of desperation, says Nerses, the populace remembered one who would surely save them, one who had been the Lion of Iraq, greatest of generals.

Their shouting filled the streets below his palace and he awoke from a long meditation and went to the wall-parapet and looked down. At that the shouts redoubled. ' Berkhu ! Berkhu ! The Mongols—save us ! '

And Nerses tells that they swarmed into the palace, kneeling in desperation and entreating him, and slowly, coming out of his dream, he listened and understood.

' The Mongols at the gates ! God, why was I not told ? Go back, you scum, go back and hold them. I'll follow ! '

He drove them from the palace, all except a young captain of Janissaries who stayed to guide him. Then he turned and shouted for his attendants. But the palace had emptied overnight. Men and women, lovers, lackeys and favourites, they had fled across the Tigris in the wake of the Worm-King. All except one old woman, toothless and bent. She heard his shouting and came, bringing him food and clothes and armour. The Janissaries' captain had vanished down a corridor to watch from a window the swarming tumult by the Western Gate. And as Berkhu buckled on his chain-mail with the help of shrivelled hands his heart rose high and singing within him. He glanced at the face of the woman and dimly, hurriedly, tried to remember that aged, rheumy face.

'I do not remember you,' he said, snatching the scimitar from her hand.

She raised her head and looked at him, and, strangely halted, he stared back.

He remembered her then. He had thought her long dead. She was a Caucasian slave, the first woman he had ever possessed. . . . Years before, in the dawn of time. How she had hated him, how loved! That he recalled, and himself of those days, and suddenly, says Nerses, some sealed and secret chamber seemed to crumble within his heart.

'Do you remember those years, Saith? I—' he heard himself, an unwonted liar, with amazement— 'have forgotten them never, nor all the wonder you gave me then——'

The Janissaries' captain was at his elbow. 'My lord, my lord, the defence is broken again!'

Half-blinded with a strange emotion, the old General found himself with the young man at the palace gate. There he had sudden thought and gripped the Janissary's arm. ' See to her—that old woman who tended me.'

The Janissaries' captain stared. ' What old woman ? *It was some young maid.*'

Then the tumult of the street-fighting came up towards them, and Berkhu rode towards it, wondering, and took command of the flying Janissaries, and hurled the Mongols back. But behind, at three different points, their horns were blowing and the fires rising. Twice was the Western Gate cleared only to glut again with the ingress of fresh hordes, and Berkhu knew that he and the city were doomed. He drew his cavalry together and charged once more, still brooding, and then, says Nerses, in that final mêlée some realisation seemed to come upon him. He half-wheeled round, the old Lion of the River, back towards his palace, as though some secret amazing were revealed to him at long last. He shouted incomprehensible words.

' O God, the lost constituent ! '

And then the charge of the invaders swept over him, and the Mongols slew him and planted his head on the Western Gate. And they took Baghdad and slaughtered therein for many days.

II

THE LOVERS

OF all the voluminous chronicles of Neesan
Nerses which lie still unedited and untran-
scribed in the archives of the Monastery of Mevr,
one caught my attention and held it so that I went
back to it again and again, savouring its flavour,
puzzling over it, this footnote to those fabulous
annals of a fabulous century. Through that recorded
clamour of war, controversy and wild adventure,
with background unceasingly the arrow-hail of the
Mongol bowmen, it sings with the sweet, bitter
voice of the pipes of spring, unforgotten in a
haunted wilderness. As I think Bishop Nerses
himself could never forget, looking out at evening
from the palace windows of that long-vanished
diocese of his above the hills of Persia.

For his diocese of Alarlu is as vanished as his
century and Nestorian Mevr, kindly, indifferent,
stacks the records of the lost historian in crumbling
confusion with unread medicinal tracts, treatises
on mountain devils, horoscopes, monkish diaries
and the like. From the heights of Mevr you can
see far off at dawn the glint of the hills amidst
which Nerses ruled that pocket of Christian
Assyrians so long ago—those hills across which his
son came riding that afternoon in the year 1260,
across which he watched that son ride out again

and vanish for ever before the passing of another nine months.

1259 : Twice that year the Bishop rode out at the head of the Assyrians and beat off marauding stragglers from Hulagu's army. All one night he lay and watched across the desert, from an eyrie in the hills, the flames of Baghdad light the sky. For men who were devils were ravening there, as he knew, and with heavy heart he went back to his fortress-palace in the dawn—to hold early Mass and tend the sick and superintend the clipping of goats and ache for news of his son.

And presently his daughter Amima—sixteen years of age, with her mother's flaming darkness of hair and eyes—came treading through the byres, seeking him out and storming at him because he had neglected to change from his night-soaked riding-gear. The Bishop smiled at her, guiltily.

' I forgot. I was thinking of the goats,' he confessed.

Amima stamped a small foot.

' A goat never forgotten—yes. You were thinking of Hormizd.' And then softened, perhaps at sight of the misery in Nerses' eyes. ' There's no news of him ? What kept you out on the hills all night ? '

' The barbarians have fired Baghdad,' said the Bishop, ' and Hormizd was in the Caliph's guard.'

' Then Hormizd is safe,' averred Amima, flippantly, ' for he said before he went that the horses of the Caliph's guard were chosen for their fleetness in running away. . . . . He'll be here to-morrow.'

But to-morrow passed, weeks and months went by, and no news came of Hormizd, the Christian mercenary. And, as he tells, what had been a vivid pain settled to a dull ache in the heart of Nerses, and more and more in spare hours he shut himself up in his watch-room above the palace, penning his record of the times from the varied information that ebbed up to Alarlu with wandering mercenaries, starving pilgrims, Arab brigands, lost Moslem mullahs—the flotsam and jetsam of a continent in travail with history. He built up those records, I think, as a barrier against that ache, and Amima rode the Assyrian boundaries and kept the peace, as he realised with a dull gratitude. And Hulagu swept north again, he and the loot of Persia and Iraq, and Paschal brought one white morning its driving snows to the Persian hills, and through those snows——

Amima saw the coming of them, went out, accosted them, came racing back on her Arab pony. Up the ringing stairs to Nerses' tower she ran and burst in on the Bishop deep in his *magnum opus*, that laboured dissertation on the Latin Rite which lies unread and unreadable to this day.

'Father!' she panted, and sank at his feet and shook him. 'Hormizd has returned!'

'Hormizd?' He stared at her, for a moment

unable to associate the name with anyone he had
ever known, as he tells. Then he got to his feet,
trembling. 'Hormizd——'

Hormizd and no other—tattered as a beggar,
minus his gay silver helmet, his chain-mail hanging
in ragged links from his shoulders, but his eyes as
restless and eager as ever. He was waiting in the
central courtyard, he and his companion, and
Nerses heard his laugh as he went down the stairs.
Then, at sight of his father, the laughter went from
the Christian mercenary's face. He knelt for the
Bishop's blessing and then was in Nerses' arms
the while the great Balkh wolf-hounds clamoured
around the two of them, and Amima, booted,
spurred, the small warden of Alarlu's marches,
confronted Hormizd's fellow-rider—a pallid-skinned
giant, bearded and moustached as were no southern
men, clad in leather, with a great horn bow slung
at his back.

'You are a Mongol?' she demanded, staring
up at the tip of the bow above the immense
shoulders.

The giant glanced at her gravely, indifferently,
stroking his beard. 'I am a chief of the Outer
Hordes.'

'A heathen?'

'Leave be, Amima,' said the Bishop, loosening
his arms from about his son, while Hormizd
scowled at his sister and turned to the giant, the
eager impatience passing from his face into such
look as made Nerses catch breath.

'Father, this is my brother from the horse-tail Hordes whom I have brought to the refuge of Alarlu.'

II

All that night the snowstorm raged, and the Assyrian herdsmen drove the goats into the byres, and kindled at Nerses' orders a great flambeau of pitch-soaked wood to flame on the palace roof, a guide to the lost and perishing in the wastes beyond Alarlu. But in the great guest-room, with the brazier's glow ruddy upon the whorling inscriptions of the ancient walls, none thought of sleep for many hours the while the story of Hormizd's adventurings in the plain was told, now by Hormizd himself, now by his giant blood-brother.

In stumbling Persian, beard in hand, staring at the brazier, the giant. 'I am Gezir Noyan, from the Plains of the Outer Wastes. We dwell on the edge of the world, far to the north. In the long seasons there is no darkness in our nights, and up in the great rivers at dawn the ice-islands clash as they go north over the edge of the world. . . .'

One's imagination touches in that scene in the Alarlu guest-room, though Nerses' record attempts no such limnings : Hormizd, despoiled of his battered armour, lying full-length on a goatskin rug, his eyes on this pagan blood-brother of his ; the brazier's light jerking from dour neutrality of tint wide red-specked patches on the leather jerkin of the giant himself; Amima kneeling with chin hand-cupped. Nerses himself that brazier which burned seven centuries ago probably showed robed and bearded, ensconced in his high chair, his long, curling black hair already streaked with grey, his eyes wandering continually to the face of his son. . . .

And the tale of Gezir Noyan :

'Now the spring came and with it messengers from the Great Horde, the yellow men who had brought us into alliance in the time of the Khakan Genjis. The horse-tail banners were out and the great khan going south to the conquest of the followers of the Foul Prophet. So I gathered my bowmen and rode to join them.

'Beyond Kara Kum we marshalled and news was brought that Persia lay undefended. So Hulagu led us west and south, leaving a little force to vex the Persian borders from the north. And one morning the breath came pantingly in our throats and men fell and died. For we had come to the great poison desert of Kizil Kum.

'And this for eighteen days, with no taste of water and drinking the milk and urine of mares, we crossed, holding to the south-east and bursting at length on the green plains. Merv Hulagu fell upon and devoured and I plundered with the others, yet was sickened with slaughter after the first two days. So I withdrew my gurans from the city, and would have marched north again, abandoning the horse-tails, but that Hulagu sent a cloud of spearmen to stop the way, and for the time we surrendered and consented to march with him again.

'And we came to Baghdad, dragging with the Hordes great bombards from Khita which hurled rocks and levelled the walls. Of that tale you have heard. On the third morning of the fighting I reached the gates of the Citadel and there found the horse-tail standards had already broken through, despite the desperation of such of the Caliph's guard as had not fled with their master across the river.

'And in a corner of the great courtyard, half-choked with smoke, while Hulagu's Mongols smote off the heads of the dead and wounded guards and flung them into carts to be taken to build the great skull-pyramid without the city, I came on five of the yellow men attacking this my brother Hormizd. He was singing and laughing as he struck down one Mongol after the other, and they drew back, as they had reason to do, and shouted for bowmen to shoot him from a distance. But in that moment he staggered and fell and I saw that he had a great leg-wound. The attackers shouted and made at him again. But I put them aside.'

'Why?' It was Amima's clear young voice in the semi-darkness. 'How was Hormizd more to you than any other stranger whom your barbarians were murdering?'

Hormizd jerked to angry attention in the brazier-glow. 'How can a woman understand?'

'Nor can I understand.' The giant's face turned

from one to the other of them. ' More ? I do not know. But I knew him for my friend. So I bandaged him and bore him out of the burning citadel, and prevailed on a flying citizen with a mule to carry him out of Baghdad to some place of safety where he might recover——'

But it was Hormizd's turn to interrupt, leaping to his feet.

' God, with what tongue of a colic-stricken camel is he afflicted ! Heed not this tale, my father, else in a moment will it appear that it was I who saved *his* life, not he mine. Now listen to the truth of it——'

And Hormizd's truth was indeed a jewel with different facets from Gezir Noyan's. There had been no casual, unhindered rescue of Hormizd in the blazing courtyard of the Citadel. Instead, Gezir had killed two of the attackers and held the others at bay till some of his own men from the Outer Wastes came to his aid. With their company he had made his way out of the Citadel, carrying the wounded man, fighting every inch of the path, for the news of this attempted rescue of a guardsman had spread, and Hulagu's orders were being defied. And this casual tale of finding a citizen with a mule—it had been done only after a long period of desperate search, through streets swarming with plunderers who not infrequently had heard rumours of the rescue and sought to stop it. Then, finally, on the outskirts of the city, Gezir had indeed prevailed on a fleeing refugee to carry away the

wounded guardsman, while he himself turned back
to face the wrath of Hulagu——

'And what happened then?' questioned the
Bishop, while the whoom of the snowstorm came
to them from outside the palace of Alarlu.

'Ask not of him, else will he say that the Khakan
embraced him and wept on his shoulder in admiration. This happened: He was overpowered by
the foul horse-tails, dragged to the great square
next morning where Hulagu sat sharing out the
plunder among the Hordes, and there accused of
saving the life of an enemy. And Hulagu ordered
that he should be impaled upon the walls, and he was
hurried away to the western gate, and there would
have been tortured and slain but that Hulagu heard
that the men of the Outer Wastes would revolt
again if this was done. So he sent a fresh order
that Gezir was merely to be stripped of his rank and
titles, enslaved, clad as a woman, and given in chains
and under stripes the foulest tasks of a camp-
follower.'

Even Amima stirred a little at that. But Gezir
Noyan merely smiled into his beard, though his
face twitched a little.

'It was a just sentence. Indeed, a merciful one.
I had saved an enemy from the pyramid of skulls.'

So, reviled, spat upon, avoided by his own
followers from the Outer Wastes, he had been set
to the vilest tasks in the great Mongol army which
still lingered amid the smoking ruins of Baghdad.
Till one day in the litter of the horse-lines, raising

his head he had seen a man limp past, and had
thought little of it, bending to his task again.
Then the limping leg had passed once more and a
little sack had been dropped into his hands. He had
concealed it without attracting notice and in the
moonlit squalor of the slaves' quarters opened it
that night, discovering it to contain a small file
and a stabbing-knife.

For Hormizd, guided out to Baghdad's suburb
of Baqubah—still intact, having fortunately made
no resistance to the invaders—had lain recovering
from his hurts and wondering as to the name and
fate of his rescuer. So soon as he could he had had
enquiries made through Assyrian merchants trading
in the Mongol camp. And at last he had learned
the full facts. The stranger who had befriended
him, whose memory and face haunted him, was a
man degraded and ruined, doomed to the foulest
tasks in the Mongol camp.

And, hearing the news, Hormizd had cursed his
wounded leg and lain making wild plannings.
Winter was coming on and the march of the Hordes
back to their plains about to begin. How to rescue
the giant?

A plan came to the Christian mercenary. So
soon as he could walk again he had one of the
Assyrian merchants engage him as a camel-driver
in bearing provisions into the encampment of
Hulagu's army. Once within the lines, stretching
mile on mile to the north of Baghdad's ruins, he
had sought out the degraded chief of the Outer

Wastes and left with him that tool and weapon
which Gezir uncovered in the moonlight. Next
day the camel-driver had passed near the giant
again, dropping him a little bag of food, and the
giant had raised his eyes and recognised the other and
whispered a promise to have his irons filed through
in readiness for escape before another nightfall.

So he might have done, and Hormizd conveyed
him safely outside the Mongol lines. But next
morning Hulagu's army had begun its long northwards trek. On its flank, among a medley of other
followers, rode Hormizd on his stolen camel;
in its centre, his chains filed almost to breaking-
point, trudged Gezir Noyan. Under the shadow
of the Alarlu plateau they had passed, the Hordes,
and Hormizd had glanced up longingly at the far
heights where a band of rescuers might have been
gathered to make a sudden descent on the straggling
army with the horse-tail standards. But there were
other means of escape to hand.

The Horde of the Outer Wastes, sullen and
mutinous, still held to the great army, but many
of its members no longer avoided their disgraced
chief. But for the terrible vengeance Hulagu
would exact should he discover any of them
attempting to free Gezir they would have had little
hesitation in striking off his chains. And at length,
again obtaining direct contact with Gezir in a pass
of the mountains, Hormizd had put their hesitations
to use.

Under the lee of the Kablurz Beg one stormy

night the giant succeeded in filing through his chains and creeping to the limits of the camp. There, at the point guarded by his own following, he was given a horse and leather coat, a bow and the vowed devotion of that following, and passed out into the night. And in the night beyond the light of the camp-fires was awaiting him that stranger for whom he had suffered so much, the stranger who in turn had sought to defeat an army for his sake.

'Where now, brother?' Hormizd had asked, when they had kissed. 'Your followers say they will still receive you as chief in your own land. Let us ride there.' And he had turned his mount round towards the northern passes.

But Gezir had caught his arm. 'That journey is one of months and you would ride with a wound half-healed. It would be death. Also'—as Hormizd laughed at this prophecy—'there would be no safety for me in the north. I would live in Persia henceforth. Let us ride to your home in this Alarlu of which you have told me. It is near?'

'Very near,' said Hormizd. 'Yet——' Then he had turned about slowly, with a last glance at the stars above the northern mountains, and stretched his hand to Gezir in the darkness, and guided him back on the road to Alarlu.

III

That winter of 1259 lasted scarcely a month in the Persian hills. Presently the spring was with them at

Alarlu, the grass green in pasturage for the great
herds of goats, the snows melting and waving their
feathery bands of vapour down over the deserts
of ruined Iraq. Bishop Nerses rode at the chase,
trying out the Mongol bow of horn, and once, far
up towards the Kablurz Beg, slaying a lion with it,
as he tells with some pride. He had a multitude of
duties in that dawning of the hot weather—mar-
riages, baptisms, riding the marches and beyond
to find out what government, if any, he would have
to treat with in the interests of his Nestorians ;
judging, meditating, escaping Amima's candid eye
and tongue when he had forgotten to change from
a soiled robe ; continuing his great work on the
Latin Rite. But he was not too busied to watch
the fortunes of his son Hormizd and the barbarian
chief Gezir, nor slow to apprehend that since their
coming to Alarlu each played a rôle for the benefit
of the other. Lovers at first sight they had been,
inseparable and passionate friends they had grown,
yet both hid their inmost thoughts and desires with
such skill that neither suspected the other. But
Nerses, uninterfering, friendly to both, watched the
tragi-comedy played with a tightening of his heart-
strings.

Hormizd—Hormizd, still young, son of a wayward peasant mother, brother of Amima whom the
Assyrian community regarded with mingled pride
and horror—he was a prisoner in Alarlu, feeding
on dreams that he might forget the horizon-beckon-
ing realities. Stupendous dreams he would recite

to his father in that watch-tower above the Persian hills—a mission to Rome; a league of Nestorian bands throughout Kharismia to seize the land and defy Mongol and Moslem alike; manufacture of that fire-powder which the Mongols had brought against Baghdad. . . . Nerses would sit and look at him and listen to him, while the Latin Rite went unconfounded, and remember his own youth. There were wider lands than those beyond the deserts to explore, as he tells he might have told that son of his : the wonder countries of meditation and contemplation, of knowledge and belief and faith. But he kept the knowledge to himself because the spring was crying out there on the hills and he remembered his own youth.

And his dreamings, it was soon obvious, Hormizd himself regarded as but dreamings, not to be mentioned in the hearing of the grave Gezir. For not only was Alarlu the only safe refuge for the latter but it seemed he had settled contentedly enough in that refuge. He was, indeed, a warrior and wanderer only by necessity. He averred a grave interest in all things Persian, in goats and olives and camels and the cultivation of millet, a fondness for palm-wine—that wine which had earned for the Nestorians of Alarlu the worst of reputations among the surrounding Moslems. He made proposals for the breeding of other horses than hill-ponies, for manuring the fields with the dust of powdered bones in that fashion of agriculture which the Mongols had learnt in the conquest of Kin. Except in the matter of Christian observances he played the part of the Alarlu-born Nestorian to perfection.

And Hormizd, putting away his dreams with his battered armour, tried to model himself in like pattern, blindly unapprehensive that Gezir Noyan in his secret soul loathed the life of the Persian hills with such loathing as few exiles had ever brought to those hills.

He hated the endless rise and fall, heat-haze and mirage-sway, glister of distant desert and undistant sandstorm which made up the scenic phenomena of the land he had adopted for the sake of Hormizd, believing Hormizd would perish on the journey to the north, or in that north grow weary for his native Alarlu. He hated the braziers and scented woods, the bell-ringing, the spiced dishes, the bright, fervid air and unending heat. Inside the palace walls he went with the air of a proud, trapped animal. The wide and stream-flecked plains, bright with tamarisks, the long, unending nights of the northern summers haunted him night and day, says Bishop Nerses, with a lover's memory and a lover's passion.

But he never talked of them except in moments of self-forgetfulness, and then to Nerses alone, in the watch-room above the palace to which he would sometimes climb to tell of the gods of his people, of the great Northern trinity of Esegé Malan, Mandiu, Hotogov Mailgan—gods from belief in whom the tolerant Bishop made but little attempt to convert him. Squatting in that tower of Nerses, the giant, great beard in hand, would pass from memories of the gods to memories of their worshippers, to tell of the land of freezing colds and great herds, the winding tracks of tribal migration across unending snows, the far roaring of the sea northwards, in winter, at the world's end, when the banners of the Golden Roan waved in the midnight sky. Sick with nostalgia, he would tell of those things. . . . Until they would hear ringing steps come up the stairs and Hormizd would burst in upon them, seeking his brother, and the giant would cease his tale the while those two looked at each other like the fools and the lovers they were. . . .

Then they would go down the stairs together and Amima, chance-met, would still her singing to scornful silence at the sight of the detested pagan. And the Bishop, with the threads of the tangled skein ready to his hands to untangle, with vision of a Hormizd lost to him for ever, would bury his face in those hands in an agony of indecision.

IV

And then one of Hulagu's lieutenants took a hand in the matter.

In Baqubah he heard of Alarlu, as the Bishop tells, and the odd little community of Assyrians that had sheltered there from time immemorial, tolerated as peaceful subjects by the Caliphs. But peacefulness in his subjects held no appeal for the Mongol. So he sent an embassy up into the hills and they encountered on the lower slopes a shepherd whom they questioned. He answered them civilly, and turned, offering to guide them. Then, in sport, one of them shot him through the back with a barbed arrow, and they left him screaming in a pool of blood and rode casually up the hill roads till they came to Nerses' palace.

The Bishop came down from his manuscripts to receive them. There were some half-dozen in the embassy, true Mongols, not such strangers as Gezir Noyan, and their thin moustaches drooped across flat, yellow faces. Their demands were brief and casual, and their leader spoke them in a singsong chatter, looking round the crowded courtyard as he spoke. Half the Alarlu herds and fifty virgins under the age of sixteen were to be driven down to Baqubah at once. . . . The spokesman broke off and, still with an expressionless face, reached out, gripped Amima by the shoulder, and swung her into the hollow of his arm.

' This maid can stand surety for the other forty-nine. See to the orders of the governor, slave.' And he turned away, preparing to mount, while the rest of the Mongols, after a hungry glance around, were already in their saddles.

For a moment the Bishop and his followers alike were speechless. But only for a moment. A roar of indignation arose, someone strode past the Bishop and next moment Amima was reeling away, freed, while her captor, still expressionless, dropped senseless from his saddle and Gezir Noyan unclenched a bruised fist. . . .

The other Mongols were dragged from their horses and disarmed, and the Bishop held an anxious conference with Gezir and the elders of the community. Release those men they must, else the Hordes would come up from Baqubah and destroy them utterly.

But while they sat in debate they heard a wild shouting and a sudden, piercing shriek of grief from a courtyard. They rushed outside and found confronting the Mongol embassy Hormizd Nerses with the body of a dead Nestorian in his arms. It was the shepherd whom the Mongols had shot and whom Hormizd, out hunting, had come upon just before he died. . . .

The cries of rage died down. All looked at the Bishop, waiting for him to speak. Amima hid her face. And Nerses, as he tells, braced himself to pronounce the dreadful words.

'Let these men be taken outside the courtyard and shot to death with arrows.'

It was done. Nerses heard the thudding of the arrow-heads as he climbed uncertainly to his room. And Alarlu cleaned its hunting spears and all through two long nights the smithy furnaces flared the while Gezir Noyan, a skilled maker of arrow-heads to fit the short bow, beat out bolts to arm the Assyrian bowmen against the coming invasion.

Come it did, more quickly than they expected, though not in such force. The news from Alarlu appears to have reached Baghdad at the very moment of the recall of Hulagu's lieutenant. He had no time to send a strong expedition against the Christians in the hills, but on the northwards march detached a complete guran, eight hundred strong, with orders to raze Alarlu to the ground, pile the heads of the men in a pyramid, and drive the women out in the wake of the Mongol army. With them, dragging it across the desert, the guran took a bombard, one of the terrible engines brought from China.

Amima was the first of the Nestorians to take the field. She was down in the plains, in the first lightening of that morning, on a ride in search of buzzard. Two Mongol scouts rode round a shoulder of the foothills. One, failing to see in Amima a woman and fit matter for other diversion, hurled a javelin. Amima ducked, avoided it neatly, and raced her pony up through the gorges to Alarlu. There she turned round her panting mount a moment and saw the Mongol guran a moving blotch like the shadow of a sandstorm upon the desert— a shadow that rapidly neared the foothills.

Now, Gezir Noyan, tells the Bishop, was that early dawn engaged at the head of the gorge in planting a new millet patch on which Alarlu was to try out the Kin notions of manuring. The Bishop's daughter came pelting across the patch on her pony, glanced over her shoulder, glanced impatiently at the giant and his two Nestorian helpers.

' Back to Alarlu ! The Mongols are in the foothills.'

Gezir dropped his implement and ran to the edge of the gorge instead. There he saw the Mongol guran, with the remembered horse-tail banner of Chépé, already beginning the climb to Alarlu. It would reach the plateau long before defenders came from the palace. Gezir turned to the Nestorians.

' We have hunting spears. We must hold them until Hormizd brings your brothers.'

Two miles away, while Hormizd shouted and mustered the Christian levies, while Amima rounded up stragglers from outlying fields, while Bishop Nerses, as he tells, struggled absentmindedly to fit a coat of chain-mail over the robes in which he had just celebrated Mass—they heard an appalling sound. It was the Chinese bombard.

Halted half-way up the gorge the Mongol captain, standing impatient witness of the fight waged on the dawn skyline between his advance-guard and a handful of Christians, had had the piece levelled and fired. Spinning clumsily in its flight, the great stone ball fell in the midst of the attacking Mongols, rose again, killed one of the Nestorians, narrowly missed the head of Gezir Noyan, and ricocheted into the new millet-patch. With a roar of laughter the attacking Mongols who had survived the descent of the bombard's projectile flung themselves upon the two surviving defenders of Alarlu's Thermopylæ, and a moment later when the racing Hormizd and his levies burst in view of the millet-patch they found it already aswarm with yellow plainsmen. . . .

Three times the Nestorians charged and three

times were beaten back. Then suddenly a thunderous explosion shook the hills. A bright light rose and flared like a geyser. The Mongol guran turned back on itself in wild confusion, and Hormizd rallied his men and charged again. . . .

Bishop Nerses, galloping across the plateau a few minutes later at the head of reinforcements, abruptly halted those reinforcements and pointed. Like the battle-figures on a wind-shaken tapestry, remote and unreal against the fervour of the sunrise above the darkness of the Alarlu gorges, the remnants of the Mongol guran were already streaming down the hill-side in wild rout. The blowing up of the bombard had both killed their captain and shattered the morale of the attackers. Behind them, slaughtering without mercy, went Hormizd and his levies.

But at the foot of the gorge Hormizd abandoned both the pursuit and his followers and rode back at breathless speed to Alarlu, with sudden memory upon him of Gezir Noyan. Beyond the lip of the plateau, wending towards the palace, he came upon a procession of Nestorian wounded. And in a litter in the midst of that procession, unconscious, hacked and bleeding from a dozen wounds, lay the giant of the Outer Hordes.

v

For a little it seemed to the Bishop impossible that the man could live. Nevertheless, he had

Gezir borne to his room in the palace and his wounds cleansed and bandaged. Then he drove out the stricken and helpless Hormizd and summoned a Nestorian woman to act as nurse.

But this order was unexpectedly countermanded. Next morning, when Gezir regained consciousness, he stared over the Bishop's shoulder in surprise at the Bishop's assistant.

' It is not seemly that your daughter should tend me.'

' It is not seemly that a heathen should die in Alarlu palace,' said Amima, also addressing her father. Nerses, as he tells, stared from one to the other of them in some bewilderment.

Hormizd found himself as a pariah in the great house. Only by stealth could he obtain converse with Gezir alone, as he complained to his father.

' You are better, my brother? Amima heeds to you ? '

Gezir would groan and toss. ' As though I were a sick calf. . . . And a heathen calf at that. God of the Golden Roan, if I could but see the skies again ! '

VI

Summer aflame over Alarlu, deepening into the wild russets of autumn Persia, with the millet standing dark brown and parched, ripe for harvest. They set to gathering the olives—a great crop that year, and one that sold at price in the famished towns of Iraq. Gezir Noyan still lingered in his sick-room, progressing but slowly, all unaware the remarkable result his illness was producing outside the range of that room.

For Hormizd, robbed of his companionship, yet tied by his presence to Alarlu and its lands, had begun to discover in his blood something of which he had been never before aware—that aching land-love inherited from generations of hillmen-peasants, that love which could lure Neesan Nerses from the most absorbing of travellers' tales, the most clamorous point of a theological treatise, out to the wonder of burgeoning or corn-laden fields, of ripe orchards of olives. Hormizd discovered it with characteristic enthusiasm.

' The fool I have been, my father! I who longed to wander in far lands when I might have gathered olives in Alarlu! I'll never take armour or bow again unless other raiders come against us. Gezir and I will make this the granary of Persia.'

He set to work as a peasant in the fields, stealing indoors occasionally, much begrimed, and wary of discovery by Amima who was as irreverent towards his land-love as all his other passions, to talk enthusiastically in Gezir's room. And the black-bearded giant would listen and assent, then turn his face to the stone wall, as though seeking sleep. . . .

The olives had been gathered and the tiny flails were pounding the millet in Alarlu village when Gezir's relapse took place. All one night he raved in delirium, crying out in his old passion of home-sickness for the wind-swept plains of the north, held down and tended by the scared Hormizd, summoned to Amima's assistance. . . . They did not wake the Bishop and by morning the giant was quiet again.   Out on his usual early ride Nerses came on his son staring northwards towards the dim bulking of the Kablurz Beg.   Only then did he learn of the happenings of the night, and Hormizd broke off abruptly, clenching his hands.

' Prisoner !   Why did he never tell me he so hated Alarlu ?   I thought him a contented guest. . . . If he should die here, far from those lands he loves——'

He laughed strangely.   His hands were shaking. And because this love of a man for a man was something that the Bishop knew in the bitter silence of his own experience, he looked at his son and ached for him, saying nothing.

' Amima quietened him, at the last.   He saw her while he raved in the devil-fever and thought her some woman of his Horde.'

The Bishop started a little at that.   ' And what did Amima do ? '

' She kissed him and made pretence to be that woman, and he fell asleep in her arms.'

VII

It seemed that night had been the turning-point. Thereafter Gezir began to mend rapidly.   Soon the bandages about his great limbs could be dispensed with, and, propped by servants, he could totter out to the sunshine of the courtyard. Thereat the Bishop, with a sigh of relief, closeted himself with a wandering Buddhist monk from far Cambodia and for a week, as he tells, forgot Alarlu and all its problems in debate of the life of Sakya Muni and its likeness to the later incarnation of another Master. Then, with the departure of his guest, he descended from his tower one afternoon and came on an unexpected idyll, and at the sight thereof stood as surprised as many a father before and after him. And the sight was his daughter Amima in the arms of the pagan giant of the Outer Hordes, standing together under the sun-awning of the inner court.

For a moment he disbelieved his eyes and then, as he tells with a touch of sad whimsy, he saw that the two were not kissing each other, as would surely have been seemly. They were deep in debate. Amima in her giant's arms had not ceased to be Amima.

'But you are a heathen, a worshipper of devils,' she was saying, and Gezir Noyan was frowning at her perplexedly.

'I worship the same trinity as yourself, though under different names. And your Isho—who is he but Uha Soldong, the Golden Roan of heaven, though with us no helpless babe? He rides the skies in our northern lands, Amima. . . . What thing have I done now?'

'You have blasphemed,' she said, and put his

hands away, and turned from him into the palace. Yet, going, she glanced back at him, secretly, anxiously, as the Bishop noted. Gezir stared after her, smiling. . . .

He started as he heard the footsteps of Nerses, and for a moment they looked at each other. Then Amima's father also smiled.

' I think Alarlu will have none of those gods of yours, unless you worship them under the names it knows—though those names may be but names.'

At that invitation and acceptance of himself the giant flushed a little, tugging at his beard. ' Of those names you will teach me, father of Amima.' He turned and looked out over the Persian lands with such contented glance as the Bishop of Alarlu had never yet seen on his face. ' For even home is called by many names.'

VIII

Bishop Nerses sat long in his tower in idle, happy thought that evening, watching the sunset colours turn to darkness and that darkness pale in the coming of the star-rise. So the skein had unravelled itself, Gezir and Hormizd alike had found content by ways unforeseen, and Alarlu would keep them. . . . He turned to his scripts light-heartedly.

And, while he sat and wrote, his son Hormizd, grown strangely self-absorbed of late, was riding back through the starlight from a two-days' expedition into the plains. . . .

Nerses heard the sound of his arrival, heard him hand his pony to a palace servant. But he did not ascend to the tower immediately. It was nearly an hour later, as the Bishop noted by the notchings of his candles, before footsteps came up the stairway and Hormizd asked permission to enter. Behind him bulked the giant.

'Father, I've come to pray that you give me leave to go from Alarlu again—with my brother Gezir.'

'Go?' The Bishop stared at him, and knew at once what he meant, knew at once that this was no planning of a casual expedition. 'Leave Alarlu? But you've loved it of late.'

Hormizd laughed with a strange gaiety, avoiding his father's eyes. 'That was but a passing fancy—and oh! there are other lands to see before a man dies. There isn't a Mongol guran on all the borders, the road to the north is clear, and Gezir and I would take it—back to his people in the Outer Wastes.'

And then, his face as pale as death, Gezir Noyan made a despairing gesture as Neesan Nerses' eyes turned on him.

'This is no plotting of mine, Bishop Nerses. I have told Hormizd he will die if he never again sees Persia—for there will be no returning. And I— I have no desire to go. I have grown to love— Alarlu.'

Hormizd's laughter rang out.

'Listen to him, my father! So he still dares affirm to us, who know his hunger for the northern

lands, who've heard him raving of them in dreams—
dreams wherein he mistook my sister Amima herself
for some lost love of his!' The giant started.
Hormizd turned from both of them, and Nerses
saw his hands shaking again. ' I die ? I've always
longed to cross the deserts to the wild lands. It is
I as well who would die here in the littleness of
Alarlu, as my father knows, who will give us leave
to go. . . . And then—the road to the skies where
rides your Golden Roan, my brother ! '

' Ah yes, the Golden Roan,' said Gezir, dully.

IX

The whole of Alarlu palace and village turned
out the evening of their departure, and Nerses saw
already on the trees the dark, bitter green of winter.
And, amazed and stricken, yet with pain stifled in
exhaustion, he watched the two young men. Amima
alone was absent from the throng of farewell-
makers.

Two baggage-mules, loaded with the provisions
and weapons the travellers were to use on their
thousand-miles journey into the darkness of Asia,
were brought out. Gezir Noyan, gigantic and alien
again in leather jerkin and hauberk, more pallid than
ever, knelt for the Bishop's blessing, and stood up,
and looked round about him half-desperately.

' The Lady Amima——' he began, and stopped,
with words stuck in his throat, looking down at her
father.

And the Bishop tried again, knowing the useless-lessness of his urgings. ' Then why leave her ? Hormizd is doing this only to pleasure you. Tell him you do not want to go.'

The giant shook his head and turned away. ' Already I have told him, but he laughs the louder each time, believing me a liar for his sake. Were that all, I could stay, but—do I not know this son of yours ? There is joy and fever in his blood to see far lands, and I go with him, for he is my brother.'

The crowding Nestorians drew back. Then Hormizd knelt also for blessing, and stood up, and embraced his father, both knowing they would never meet again. And Hormizd swung into his saddle and bent from it his gaily helmeted head.

' I'll come back again—if ever the deserts and years will give me passage, my father.' He laughed with stricken face ' Think of me sometimes in those northern lands—here, when the olives ripen in autumn.'

' But there's no need to go. Gezir would stay. He would marry Amima——'

Hormizd laughed again, turning his face from his father's. ' He is a prince of liars and a prince of brothers. He would swear for my sake that the burning pains of hell were pleasant and agreeable. Amima ? He has pined this year with memory of some woman of the north—her of whom he raved in dreams.' His horse leapt forward under the touch of sudden spurs. ' Ready, my brother ? '

And when next Bishop Nerses raised his head he saw the darkness come raining from the east over the deserted hills.

X

One pauses above the last crinkled leaves of the ancient script to hear far across the centuries that remote piping of resentment and bitter pain in hearts long powder and nothing on the winds of forgotten days; to watch those two who had ridden into Alarlu nine months before ride out again, following and misjudging each other in a passionate obstinacy of love; to start in sudden, puzzled wonder, as did Bishop Nerses himself that night at the words spoken to him by Amima when she climbed to him in his tower.

'Fools? They were wise at last, each for the other, as only lovers might be.' She hid her face and then looked out into the starred silence, her breath coming in a sob. 'Oh, I *knew*, my father, I who loved them both. Always I knew, even while I hoped. . . . Each sick at heart himself and wise for the other—*for to the end it was Gezir's Hormizd who was the real Hormizd, Hormizd's Gezir the real Gezir.*'

THE FLOODS OF SPRING

I

IN the library of the Monastery of Mevr one turns the crinkled pages of the *Chronicles* of Neesan Nerses with careful fingers, lest presently those pages crumble into so many handfuls of dust. They are bound with rotting sinews, there are dark stains across the last third of them, perhaps the blood of some lost Nestorian priest; one corner of the bundle has been scorched with fire—a relic, that, of the Turki invasion that depopulated Alarlu long after Bishop Nerses had ceased to rule and write there. And out of those ancient pages the eye brings sudden phrases unexpectedly homely or inexplicably alien, for the Bishop mingled in a cheerful amalgam record of Alarlu's life and Mongol morals, Nestorian rites and denunciations of the Roman Church, beggars' tales and Persian legends. All was grist to his mill, and he wrote with an omnivorous disregard of plausibility and stylistic criteria that in happier times might have earned his writings fame and fortune from many a groaning printing-press.

But it was not until my second week in the Monastery library, bending in some weariness over the long, looping scrawl of the Nestorian script, that I came on this tale of Zeia and Romi which I have called the Floods of Spring. It bears no title at all in the Bishop's record. The sheets on which it is written lie crumpled betwixt a treatise on goat-breeding and a dissertation on demonology—and whether this is their appropriate placing by the Bishop himself, or but the chance cataloguing of later ages, I found it impossible to guess. The story had been begun and left off several times. On the margin of the first page, indeed, is scrawled, as though in irritation : 'But surely this was only a dream that came to us at Bushu. . . .'

One visions the Bishop hesitating above his script, frowning at it in indecision the while the daylight waned from the hills of Alarlu. Dream or delusion—how else explain that double avatar and immolation in the ruined lands of the Bushu Nestorians ?

II

It was 1262. The Mongols had gone, leaving Baghdad smoking and desolate, and its few surviving inhabitants free to creep starving from well and cellar to gaze on that desolation. Gone also, never to return, in the company of his Mongol friend and lover, was the Bishop's only son. Winter closed in on the upland plateau of Alarlu, kept by its Nestorian farmers, and Nerses retreated to his high tower and his writings the while the cold grew more intense, though across the waste lands of Iraq the sun heats burned fierce and vivid still. Out of that burning desolation, penetrating up even to the Bishop in his tower, came presently rumours and tales of the mangled world the Mongols had left behind. Amima Nerses came back one day from buzzard-shooting in the foothills, her bow slung across her back, on her pony a dying woman who still clasped the skeleton of a child in her arms. She had had no food, the woman, for many days ; there was no food to be found in the plains, nor any prospects of it, for not only had the Mongols destroyed the crops—they had broken down the ancient irrigation system, smashed in the dams and flooded the cornlands. . . . The Bishop heard the story, fed the woman, saw her die, and went back to his tower to write that fierce pacifist diatribe which reads as incongruous to his century as a treatise on psychoanalysis. The plains and their horrors—thank God for Alarlu and the safety of his Nestorians !

But there were others of his creed remote in those plains. They had heard of him, though he not of them, and, journeying across a land of famine and murder, they arrived at Alarlu late on a raining night in January.

Amima, bursting into the Bishop's room, brought the news of them.

' Six of them—marshmen from some place on the Euphrates called Bushu. They have already eaten three ducks and all to-day's loaves.'

' We must not be inhospitable,' reproved the Bishop, ' seeing especially that they are of our Faith.'

' It was only with the eye of faith I could grasp that my loaves had gone so quickly,' said Amima, flippantly. ' Their leader, Kalaitha, is now mourning over a marrow-bone and Mesopotamia. He prays that you will see him.'

So the Bishop went down to the great room where the brazier burned and the six Nestorian tribesmen sat at meat. They were tall, gaunt men, members of a Christian pocket in a kink of the Moslem Euphrates country, and their leader, the white-bearded Kalaitha, laying aside the marrow-bone reluctantly, rose and kissed Nerses' hand and explained his mission.

' The Mongols came, burning and killing and breaking down the dams. So we fled to the marshes and there hid until they had gone. But our priest fled not, and him they killed. Now we have returned to our homes, and are a people lost, being without a priest.'

' Have you repaired your dams ? ' asked the Bishop.

' No,' said Kalaitha, ' for a madness of sloth has fallen upon our people, being without a priest. So we six elders——'

The six, abandoning for the time a tribe mysteriously beyond their control, had journeyed to Amarah, seeking to induce the Nestorian Bishop there to send them a priest. But the Bishop was fled. Scared and horrified at the sights of the maddened country through which they passed, Kalaitha and his companions had yet ascended the Tigris to Baghdad, in quest of *its* Bishop. But the Bishop was dead. Turning southwards again one

of them had halted and pointed to the far loom of
the Persian hills.

' There, it is said, a Christian Bishop rules in the
mountains. The Mongols may have spared him.
He will give us a priest.'

And now here in the mountains they were. Nerses
was unsympathetic.

' It is an engineer rather than a priest you want,'
he told them, disregarding Kalaitha's shocked look,
' seeing you have not yet repaired your dams. . . .
And I have no priest to give you. There is none
other here but my chaplain.' He thought for a
moment. ' Who rules now at Bushu in your
absence ? ' he asked Kalaitha.

The delegation glanced one at the other with an
odd unease. Nor did Kalaitha seem more assured
than his followers.

' It is the no-rule of Zeia.'

' No-rule ? Zeia ? '

' He is a stranger who came to us from the
marshes. He makes no claim to rule, yet the
people follow him, though he speaks of our customs
as folly. He laughed at this mission of ours in
search of a priest.'

' Then he is a man of sense,' said the Bishop.
' See now to this. Return to Bushu and take to
Zeia my message that he himself is to journey up
here to me in Alarlu, where I myself will question
him and ordain him as the priest you lack.'

Two of the delegation grinned. Kalaitha stroked
his grey beard and shook his head.

' He will refuse.'

' Refuse ! '   It was a century when Christians did not balk at a Bishop's commands.

' So he will do.   For it is he who has led the people into the madness of sloth, preaching—he and his woman Romi—that the earth is for the pleasure of our lives, not our lives for the slavement of the earth.   Also, he says of priests that they must be either children or fools, or more often both.'

This lunatic-sceptic of the marshes sounded not uninteresting, thought the Bishop.   He walked the room, meditating the matter, watched by the marshmen.   It was a difficult matter.

' To-morrow I will decide what to do for you. Meantime, you shall stay here and eat.'

' We have been much anhungered crossing the plains,' agreed the grey-bearded Kalaitha, brightening.   ' Our stomachs being saddened by memory of Bushu, whose people are without a priest.'

III

Half that night the Bishop walked the room of his tower, listening to the late winter rain sweeping over Alarlu.   A mission of folly if he went on it, yet— escape from these rooms haunted by remembrances of his lost son. . . .

In the morning he called up Amima as she was mounting her pony in the courtyard, preparatory to riding out on her usual rounds of the plateau boundaries.

' My child, almost you rule Alarlu as it is. Could you and Eidon, the chaplain, heed to it between you for a month ? '

' For a year, if need be,' said Amima, thoughtlessly. And then was startled. ' But you——'

' I am going down to the plains with Kalaitha and his men to see to this madness in Bushu.'

IV

He has left but scanty record of that journey across the ruined lands to the southern Euphrates. I think they took the eastern road, skirting Baghdad. At least, the Bishop comments on the plentitude of game in the Persian foothills, and, later, of a man who was reputed to rear serpents in a hidden farm near Baqubah, and sell their eggs at profit. Almost, one can believe, he felt inclined to abandon his mission and turn aside to investigate the activities of this unorthodox poultry-farmer. Near Eik a band of robbers rode out and assailed the Nestorians, and the Bishop shot two of them with arrows from the Mongol bow his son had brought to Alarlu. Kalaitha's companions fought valiantly, putting the attackers to flight, but Kalaitha vanished and was later found hidden in a nullah, combing his beard thoughtfully, peering from behind a tussock of grass, and declaring that courage went from a people that lacked a priest.

' It is better to lack a priest than to lack life,' said Nerses dryly.

' So declares Zeia,' said Kalaitha, shocked.

' I will have somewhat to say to this Zeia when we come to Bushu,' promised the Bishop, taking the lead again.

And at length, after venturings bloody and fantastic enough from our view-point, but so commonplace to the age and country that the Bishop but notes them in passing, they forded the Tigris at a spot somewhere below the modern Kut, crossed the lands between the two rivers, and late one evening reached the eastern banks of the Euphrates. Beyond the River was a brown, dusk land, and even in that dim light it was possible to see on the far bank the heaped and crumbling ledges where once the dam of Bushu had stored the River waters at time of flood. Now the River ran shallow and muddy, too low in its bed to reach the dam-points even had they been operable. . . . Nerses' party had been sighted by the Nestorians of Bushu, and presently a round, flat-bottomed bellum was being poled across the River towards them. But the Bishop's attention was elsewhere, held by an unusual phenomenon in that treeless land.

' What is there ? ' he asked, pointing beyond the dam ruins and the brown cluster of huts huddling beyond the dam. Against the evening's encroachment on the remote marshes to which the Nestorians had fled at the Mongol invasion a little gathering of plumed titans watched the coming of darkness.

' It is the Last Grove, my lord,' said the grey-bearded Kalaitha, indifferently. He rubbed his stomach, and watched the languid approach of the bellum with impatience. ' Surely it will be they have prepared a kid to feast us.'

' Last Grove ? ' queried the Bishop. ' Of what ? '

' Of the Ancient Garden,' said Kalaitha. ' So were we told in the days when we were a people that lacked not a priest.'

v

Next morning the Bishop rose from his bed in the guest-hut at the first coming of the light. Bushu still slept. A little unplanned grouping of huts, odoriferous and insanitary enough, one imagines, even in the white wonder and stillness of the morning. But the Bishop tells nothing of that : he lived in an unfinicky age. Wearied no longer, for he had taken no part in Kalaitha's feast and retired early to the guest-hut on the previous evening, he walked to the verge of the village. A marsh bird wheeled over his head. Around, in the lush grass, fed straying goats and kids. Bushu lay before him, with its flood-ruined lands. Behind, in the sunrise, was the soft sweep of the Euphrates waters.

Now the Bishop saw that there had been two dams—the main-feed from the River and the long storage-dam. Midway the latter, a half-submerged islet, had stood the Last Grove. Then the Mongol guran had descended on Bushu, smashed in the river flood-gates and the gates of the feed-dam,

allowed their cumulated waters to pour into the
storage-trench, and seen the ancient banks of the
latter melt and crumble in an avalanche of mud.

So it must have been. Now, viewed from this
lower side, the bottom of the storage-dam was but
a wide swath of grass encircling the shining
tamarisks of the Last Grove—a swath of vivid
greenness in those landscape browns and greys that
were as yet unstirred by the black loam prickings
of re-cultivation.

All this the Bishop noted, and then he saw something else—a woman coming towards him from
the direction of the tamarisks. She walked dreaming, with unbound hair—a free, sweet·walk, says
the Bishop. Presumably, unlikely though it seemed,
there was some bathing-place beyond the grove
which accounted for her lack of costume. He would
have retired discreetly enough, but that it was too
late. She had raised her head and seen him. She
came forward, embarrassed not at all. She stood
in front of him, smiling at him—smiling down at
him, as he realised with a little shock, from her great
height.

'You are the priest from the mountains ? '

Her voice seemed to the Bishop as sweet and alien
to a Nestorian woman as her walk. He had thought
her young, but now he was uncertain—uncertain
as he was of the colour of her eyes and skin and hair
—a magnificent mane, this, garmenting her deep-
breasted beauty not ineffectively. Young eyes,
gay eyes—and yet within them a heart-breaking

tiredness. . . . He tells how he shook himself to sternness.

'I am the Bishop Nerses. Is it customary for the women of Bushu to greet strangers—so?'

'Custom?' The great eyes opened puzzledly. Then lighted with the sun in them. The woman laughed. 'I do not know.'

He had an inspiration. 'You are the woman Romi—the wife of Zeia?'

'I am Romi—for so was the child called who slept and slept in my arms and would not wake.' There was no gaiety at all in her eyes for a moment, but only tiredness. 'As for Zeia, he also sleeps.' She sighed and laughed in a breath. 'He was always a laggard.'

She turned away from him lightly. Her action had the discourtesy of a child's. He stared after her frowningly, and then for a moment suffered from a brief hallucination. Almost he started forward with a cry—

That walk of hers—it had been his wife's. So the mother of Amima had once walked, her, and no other woman in the world.

VI

Three hours later, goes on the Bishop, a score or so of the Bushu Nestorians, headed by the grey-bearded Kalaitha, gathered on a riverward space outside the village to listen to him. This was the purpose of the gathering, Kalaitha told him, and

Nerses regarded the unauthentic venerableness of the headman in some perplexity.

'But what am I to tell them?' he asked.

'That I do not know, my lord. For we are a people without a priest.'

There was little help to be had from this bending reed, the Bishop decided, and looked upon the gathering without enthusiasm. Less than a score out of a village population of over three hundred!

'Where are the others?' he asked Kalaitha.

'They would not come,' said the headman, 'being busied eating or sleeping or lying in the sun.'

The sun-bathers were everywhere obvious. They trooped in pairs towards the tamarisks of the Last Grove, or lay, like beasts themselves, among the somnolent goats of the herbage stretches; reclining in the shallows of the River, their voices came down to the gathering. It was indeed madness that had come upon Bushu.

Then, as the Bishop looked round him with dark brows, two figures emerged from the huts and approached him.

One was the woman Romi, clad now in an incongruous brown cotton garment. The other was a man, gigantic, bearded, with tousled hair and garments that appeared to have been assumed in the utmost absentmindedness. As he walked he rubbed his eyes and yawned. In sight of the gathering he stopped, regarded it surprisedly, and then, followed by Romi, walked to the front of it, inspected the Bishop with lighted curiosity, and sat down. Romi sank beside him, deep-breasted mate of a sleepy Titan. The Bishop stared at the two of them, startled. For a moment he had seen flicker in the giant's face the likeness of his own son's. . . . Was this a fever that was coming upon him?

He addressed the somnolent gathering.

'Your headman came to the hills, seeking me, that I might provide you with a priest. I think he did ill in the venture. Priests do not grow on the Persian hills, even as they do not grow by Euphrates, for the plucking. Moreover, it were better to have seen to the rebuilding of the dams. How have you managed to live since your return from the marshes?'

A sleepy voice said: 'We had stores of grain hidden under the huts which the Mongols did not find.'

'And when you have eaten this stored grain—what then?'

There was silence—an undisturbed silence. The Nestorians sat and stared with bovine eyes. Romi, dreaming, looked into the bright sunlight. Zeia appeared on the point of falling asleep again. And Nerses tells that he felt anger stir within him.

'Have I come to address those bereft of their senses?' He pointed to the man beside Romi. 'You, Zeia, you have misled this people. Why?'

The giant started, yawned, stared, spoke drowsily.

'The spring comes again, O priestman. So we two heard, and came also.'

'And is not the spring the time of labour?

Is there not ploughing and planting to be done, lest famine comes ? '

' So we two also believed in the foolish dream we dreamt. But there are better dreams. There is sleeping and love and the sound of birds ; there is noon and sun and cool grass wherein to lie when the wind comes through the trees ; there are stars and the coming of the moon to watch.' He raised great grey eyes upon the Bishop. ' Ours is the older dream.'

Then the Bishop knew it was a sorcerer with whom he dealt, for under the stare of those eyes strange dreamings arose in his own brain. He crossed himself.

Romi laughed. And, laughing, Nerses saw that she wept.

VII

It was February. The Bishop walked up to the ruined dyke and considered the brown flow of the Euphrates. In a month at most the floods would come, would go roaring down to the Shatt el Arab, leaving the River at its usual level, the dam empty, Bushu doomed to starvation—if this madness still persisted among the people.

Now Nerses was no stranger, in the readings of his Church's fortunes, to the vagaries of Abelites, Abraham-men and the like. Every catastrophe brought them wailing and naked across the face of whatever land catastrophe fell upon. And, sooner or later, time gathered and destroyed them, even

if their fellow-men gave them welcome and tolerance. So it would be with this Zeia and Romi, the
bringers of madness to Bushu.

But when? And whence had those bringers come?

Kalaitha, questioned as to their origins, had told
a simple enough story. They had been encountered
in the marshes. They had come walking out of those
marshes, naked and yawning, one morning while
the refugees from Bushu were debating the safety
of returning to their ruined village. Then a woman
had recognised Zeia.

' He is my cousin whom I have not seen for years
—my cousin Zeia from Shim'un.'

Shim'un was another Nestorian community, far
down the River. Undoubtedly Zeia and the woman
were fugitives, and still dazed, for Zeia had neither
denied nor admitted the relationship. Instead, he
had waved aside those crowding about him.

' We return, for the way is open again.'

But Romi had knelt and fondled an abandoned
child, one whose mother was dead and itself close
to death from starvation. And Zeia, impatiently,
had waited while Romi lifted the child and bore
it with her. Together they had held eastward, and,
moved by a strange instinct, the Bushu tribesmen
had followed.

Nor had the instinct been at fault. Bushu they
had found deserted and the Mongols gone. . . .

And soon it was like to lie deserted again, the
Bishop reflected. Here before another spring would
be famine and death, here, where a sorcerer lunatic

of the marshes had outfaced and outfought a
Christian priest. Unless——

Nerses turned from the River dyke and went
down to the village. And that evening he com-
menced his campaign.

From hut to hut he went, taking with him
Kalaitha as secular authority. To each individual
he gave the command that on the morrow he was
to join the others, with spade and mattock, by the
verge of the ruined feed-dam an hour after sunrise.

The Bishop, as he tells, had expected resistance,
if not point-blank denial of his authority. But
opposition was of the feeblest. Toil was engrained
in the natures of these peasants, and, sun-weary
of their lunacy, they had but required the voice of
decision to rate them out of it. By midnight of that
February day in the year 1262 the cowed Nestorians
of Bushu were pledged, one and all, to attend the
dam-construction of the morning.

But for two exceptions. The hut of Romi and
Zeia had been found empty.

' They walk often in the night hours,' explained
Kalaitha, and would have ended with his unvarying
formula but that Nerses interrupted him hastily.

' And ye have been unable to prevent them, being
a people without a priest. Let be. The mad go
unconscripted, even in such times of stress.'

But, falling asleep an hour later in the village
guest-hut, the Bishop heard a sound that made him
rise and look through the hide-shielded cavity that
was the window. It was the time of the moonrise,

a still hour of fleeting shadows and the dance of pale ghosts on that Euphrates land. And the sound drew nearer, and the Bishop saw the cause of it.

It was Zeia and Romi returning from their mysterious midnight excursion. Naked, crowned with flowers, their voices lifted in a low song that had neither words nor melody, yet it seemed to Nerses that he had heard it often, that so the winds sang round Alarlu, that he had heard it in the laughter and agony of many men. And with that song and the singers was a companying terror that made the Bishop reach back into the darkness by his bed, in quest of the Mongol bow.

Behind the singers stalked a lion—a great, black-maned brute of the swamps. The eyes in its swaying head glowed in the moonlight. And, as it walked, a slobbering chant came from its hanging jaws.

Then, on the verge of the village, Romi turned about and spoke to the beast. And it lifted its head as though listening to her, then turned about and padded away into the dimness.

So they came and passed, the two sorcerers and the beast, and the Bishop closed his eyes and crossed himself—and then looked again on the pallid moonlight and wondered if he had but dreamt.

VIII

Dawn—a spring dawn, fervid and eager, as though it were the soul of Iraq herself in swift expectation of seed-time and the coming of the tiller. But all over the land where there was already famine the dams stood as heaps of rubble and charred beams, the soil lay waste and untouched, for there was no grain for food, far less for seed. Except, the Bishop noted grimly, at Bushu.

Seed here in plenty—but was there time now in which to plant it and ensure its fructification by the River?

The main-feed dam was a jumble as though a great Titan had trodden down all its landward bank. The locks which had connected it with the Euphrates lay buried under some fifty tons of shale and sand. The deep channels of the main distributaries had been smeared into faint traceries by the flood unloosed by the wrecking Mongols five months before. . . . And the spring floods were not more than a fortnight distant.

' If only I were an engineer ! ' the Bishop groaned, and for the first time in his life regretted many hours spent in poring over the esoteric cults of the ages. Better he had kept to Archimedes. ' Who tended the dams before the Mongols came? ' he questioned Kalaitha.

The headman brought forward two men—stolid, unenterprising labourers. They had indeed done no more than tend the old-time irrigation system. They had shored and delved and repaired with diligence enough, perhaps, but theoretic questionings of pressure and resistance had vexed their lives but little. The dams had functioned from time immemorial—or rather, from the time of that first Sargon to whom the Bishop, in another text, refers with unintentional humour as an 'ancient devil.' But Sargon's engineers were long dead, and in their place a Nestorian Bishop who was an authority on the Latin Rite and the Buddhist penetration of Fusang had to grope out method and formulæ for himself.

A third of the Bushu tribesmen he set to planting, a third to re-digging the distributaries. The remainder was impounded for the heart-breaking task of clearing the feed-dam.

All that day they laboured, and Nerses, surveying their work in the evening, saw that they had made little or no impression upon the ruins. His heart sank as he thought of the short time they had before the floods came.

Next morning he withdrew half of the workers from the distributaries and joined them to the squads labouring in the dam. It blazed a red heat that day. Far off, as the afternoon drew on, Romi and Zeia were seen to stroll from the village towards the green coolness of the Last Grove. A little growl of anger went up, but the Bishop stayed it.

'Do ye grudge the demented their diversions?'

There was laughter at that—a shout of laughter that for some reason fell to a shamed silence as they watched that unhasting twain against the trees in the bright weather. Reasonlessly, Nerses felt the shame no less his. He doffed his robe then, to the wonder of Kalaitha, and joined in the task of

F

filling with earth the great skin sacks which toiling
ant-trains of women and children bore upwards
to the rim of the dam.   Unhasting as Romi or Zeia
the sun passed across the heavens.   But at nightfall
half the rubbish had been cleared from the floor of
the dam.

They toiled until after sunset.   Then, setting a.
guard upon the place, the Bishop went to bed, and
in the early hours of next dawn was back at the
excavations.   There the guard greeted him with
unlooked-for news.   A boat going down the
Euphrates in the night hours had hailed the Nestorians with the news that the floods were earlier
this year, owing to the intense heat of those spring
days.   The snows were already melting in the
Armenian mountains.

' How long does that give us ? ' the guard had
called to the River sailors.

' Two days, O unbelievers.'

IX

Two days—and still half the dam to clear and the
River lock to unearth.

They began work in search of that lock.   The
massive gates lay smashed and buried, as has been
said, under many tons of sand.   At length, and with
care, they were unearthed and brought to the
surface—they, together with an ancient implement
of copper and the skeleton of a girl.   Some time in
the ancient days a blood-sacrifice had taken place

here. But the Bishop, for once, was in no mood for archæological enthusings.

'We must have timber for new lock-gates.'

'There is no timber to be found in this land,' said Kalaitha.

Nerses pointed to the shining standards of the Ancient Grove. 'Is there not wood there?'

Kalaitha blanched. 'The Ancient Grove stood untrodden for generations until the Mongols burst the dam. Nor would we harm it now. For it is the last of the ancient Holy Places, as we were told in days when we lacked not a priest.'

'Then ye were told lies,' said the Bishop shortly. 'Call the village carpenters.'

So they were called and assembled and the Bishop put himself at their head and descended on the Grove. It was but the tiniest plantation, as he discovered, unremarkable but for its lack of rotting timber. Counting the tree-rings as each tree was hewn down, Nerses was confirmed in his belief that the grove's antiquity was but a fable. Less than a hundred years had elapsed since the trees were planted. . . . He counted again, and a little chill of fear came upon him. *Less than two score years had passed, yet Kalaitha and others spoke of the Grove as unaltered since their childhood.*

x

Late afternoon. The Ancient Grove was a tree-less desolation. Looking down from the banks of the main dam the Bishop could see the heaped tangle of splinters and boughs he and the carpenters had left behind. The axes, gripped in terror-taut hands, had ceased to ring there. Ceased also was that demented wailing—like the crying of lost and tortured children—which had burst on their ears in the early hours after noon.

But memory of it, as they worked to bind the tree-trunks together in the form of a new lock-gate, was with Nerses and the others still. They had paused and listened to it with blanched faces, seen in the blaze of sunlight the running figures of Romi and Zeia disappear in the tangle of the Ancient Grove, heard the wailing die to a moaning whimper that yet seemed to go on and on, far down the Euphrates country. . . . Silence since then. And now another sunset was near.

Suddenly the Bishop became aware of Kalaitha and the carpenters, halted in their tasks, staring at the River.

' What ails you ? ' he asked the headman, and then saw himself.

The Euphrates mid-channel stream was flowing brown with silt. Far up the ruined cornlands of the River a giant beast with crested head roared and quested southwards. This was the signal of his coming, and, unused to such signal, the Bishop stared a moment appalled.

' The flood—it is coming ? ' he demanded, and then, as Kalaitha and the others bent guiltily to work, realised that they had but seized an opportunity to rest their aching muscles.

'Always is there a day's warning,' said Kalaitha. 'It will not come until noon to-morrow.'

XI

Two hours later exhausted Bushu went to bed in the darkness. Before them, in the Bishop's calculation, was some three hours' toil next morning ere they clove a way through the Euphrates' bank and laid a new channel to the new lock-gates. Little time to spare, but time enough.

A sickle moon came out and rode the sky that night, and in the air, says Nerses, there was a moistness he had never met before in the ancient lowlands. Despite the ache of all his bones from days of unaccustomed toil, he could not sleep, and lay wakeful for long in the dimness, in uneased tiredness. Near the time of the moonset he fell into an uneasy doze and was startled out of that by the murmur of voices near the guest-hut. As once before he raised the hide-curtain of that window, and, as once before, saw Romi and Zeia alone together in the night.

'It will be here before the dawn—quicker than they have ever known it come.' It was Zeia's voice. 'This ancient folly it will sweep away—it and the priestman. We did not dream this spring.'

So the Bishop heard, then a lower murmur of voices, then, amazed, he saw that the woman Romi was weeping.

'O my children, my children! Toil and war and

death, toil and death and famine—and how may our coming end them? We are no more than a dream they dare not dream. . . . The priest is right. They would starve and die if they followed us. We must rouse the sleepers.'

' Rouse them? It would not help. In a moment it will be darkness.'

And Romi's voice: ' That is no bar to us.'

Zeia's laughter belled across the moonlight. Then the Bishop saw Romi's hands upon his shoulders.

' So once before you laughed, at the dream of another spring which passed. . . . And some time—oh, some time our dream will come again, no dream, for us and all the world. But now——'

They stood and looked at each other in the waning moonlight. Then Zeia laughed his drowsy laugh again, and nodded, and hand in hand they turned about and passed out of sight, hastening. Of what had they talked?

And then, suddenly, in the dawn darkness, realisation burst upon the Bishop. The spring floods!

XII

He dragged on his robe, tore open the door of the guest-hut, ran up the village street and began to beat upon the door of Kalaitha's house. But already the watchers of the dam, standing in the dim radiance of the time between moonset and sunrise, had heard afar off a low murmur that grew to a throaty baying, that grew to the roar of a thousand wolves in pack-cry. They knew the sound for what it was, and cried their fear, and fled undecidedly towards the village. And, running, they met—or dreamt they met—two figures, naked, gigantic, racing from Bushu towards the abandoned dam.

They crossed themselves, the dam's guardians, and yelled, bursting into the village and adding fresh confusion to that already created by Nerses' eviction of Kalaitha from his bed, and Kalaitha's voiced conviction that he was being assaulted by robbers. Then, disentangling recognitions, the awakened Nestorians of Bushu heard the news brought thus pantingly. A groan of despair arose.

' Too late ! '

Another cry followed : ' The sorcerers bewitched us from our work. Where are they ? '

' Zeia ! '

' The harlot Romi ! '

' Kill them ! '

They broke down the doors of the alien hut. It was empty. In the eastern sky a pallid, tentative hand touched the blinds of darkness. The Bishop at length made his voice heard above the uproar.

' Who will come with me to the dam ? '

' Too late ! '

Now from Bushu itself they could hear the sound of the coming flood, and, slowly, the hand poised in the heavens drew wider the curtain of the day.

With that filtering of light a strayed dam-guardian came stumbling into the village street.

' The sorcerers—the dam ! '

The cry brought silence. The Nestorians wheeled River-wards and looked.

Against the promise of the sunrise, in the dimness that was almost dawn, two Titans laboured upon the ridges of the dam. Under their hands the black wall to the River melted away to right and left in showering curtains of sand-spume even as the Bishop watched. And the howl of the nearing flood rose and rose.

They saw it then. The dark Euphrates banks glowed grey in a reeling tide of suds, and in that moment the dam-channel miraculously cleared clove through to the River ! A boiling yellow torrent of water poised, hesitated, whelmed leftwards, burst through the new lock-gates, flooded and spun and mounted till it brimmed the dam.

Then the gates closed and the surplus of water swirled outwards to the Euphrates.

XIII

' The sorcerers. . . . '

The words rose in a long sigh. The boiling flood had come and gone. Now dam and channel alike glimmered lifeless in the light of dawn.

A man near the Bishop gripped his arm and pointed.

The morning had hesitated still in the sky,

strangely. Then, slowly out of darkness, that grey shape like a clenched hand grew to clarity again. From its midst a long red beam of sunlight traversed the sky, quivered, hesitated, acquired hilt and guard, became a sword, and twice, gigantic, arc'ed across the sky.

Nerses crossed himself and prayed, his mind a tumult. And when he raised his head again day had come upon the land.

IV

THE LAST OGRE

I

SPRING in the uplands of Alarlu in the year 1263 of the Old Calendar. Un-dreaming a new one, Bishop Nerses, all the long winter days and nights, had so busied himself with that stupendous *Contemporary Chronicle* that the contemporary life of his diocese had almost escaped his notice. The snows of winter shivered and silted against the horn panes of his tower window as he sat and wrote far into each night, perched high above the Persian foothills and the lightless deserts of Mesopotamia. Eidon, his chaplain, young and vigorous and confident, saw to the spiritual needs of the Nestorian farmers of the Alarlu plateau ; Amima Nerses, confident, vigorous, young, saw to the physical needs and necessities of the same community, organising the winter-time hunting and meat-curing, gathering and staffing the great annual caravan which descended on the southern lands to dispose of Alarlu's surplus products, tending the sick, brow-beating the bullying, carrying out a multitude of duties as the warden of the plateau. . . .

Sometimes of a winter morning, his window opened to the frosty fall of sunlight, himself apace in search of the ideal word or phrase, the Bishop would glance out and see Amima, young face grave and composed, a Mongol bow slung at her back,

ride forth on this or that expedition amid the sleeping fields. . . . An ideal daughter—if she had but
been a son, as the Bishop records he thought,
wryly unhumorous.

And, almost abruptly, the Bishop was aware of
the coming of the Spring. Sleet no longer pelted
his tower. Of a night it would be either a moon-
lighted, soundless world without, or the dark
alive with the soft, fresh hiss of rain. Sometimes,
writing far into the dawn, and rising in weariness
and opening those windows, a smell of greenness
and growth would flood his tower chamber,
moistly, confusingly, so that Neesan Nerses would
stand and dream and forget his *Chronicle* and the
urgencies of history the while the Persian uplands
wheeled eastwards into the sunrise and the cocks
began to crow in Alarlu village. . . .

And across that beginning of Spring seven centuries ago, green and ablow with new leafage and
pasturage, Amima comes riding young and restless
and rebellious, so that one stares at her in the
dusty pages of Nerses' *Chronicle* with a sudden ache
of wonder and recognition. So, indeed, the Bishop
himself seems to have stared. The Spring and a
maid. . . .

Restless and strange and wayward, no longer the
plateau's grave, competent guardian. She quarrelled
with Eidon over a detail of Mass, egged on the
laggard peasants of Alarlu to absent themselves
from early devotions, and might well have created a
fresh Nestorian schism but for the intervention of

the Bishop. Her singing was heard no longer;
slim and dark and bored, clad in that male attire
of boots and jerkin and bonnet that still occasionally
shocked the Bishop's notions of propriety, she
lounged in the halls of Alarlu palace, eating sweet-
meats she was wont to scorn, teasing the great
Balkh hunting hounds, intractable and impossible.
Or she would climb to the Bishop's own room with
unwarrantable frequency and prowl amid his
manuscripts, and peer whistling from his window,
and prowl again, softly, slim shoulders a-droop,
padding like a restless panther.

' Amima.'

' My father ? '

' Come here.'

Standing in front of him, warily, restlessly even
while standing, the Bishop would see in her,
startled, with a wild pang of pain for forgotten
Springs, himself of other years and all the quests
he had once sworn to lead and all the questionings
to answer . . . before his life had been snared
by a room in a tower and the scripts of ancient un-
wisdom.

But Amima was a woman. There need be
neither quests nor questionings for her if the plain
and obvious need could be supplied. The Bishop
sighed. That need was a husband—and where
might such be found in these wild lands and
times ?

I think he fell into a puzzled day-dreaming then,
the while she stood and faced him. But his mind

leapt to startled attention on realisation that she was speaking to him, and realisation of the purport of her speech.

'Father, I wish to go hunting in the Kablurz Beg.'

'Eh?'

She nodded, holding his eyes steadfastly, her hand knotting and unknotting in the leathern horse-thong she had brought up to the tower. Nerses stared at her astounded, as he tells, and then himself looked through the open window, across the afternoon sunlight peace of Alarlu, at that dank, craggy toweringness on the north-eastern sky—the bastions and ramparts of the desolate mountain-jumble that crept upon Persia from out the wild wastes of Baluchistan. Perhaps twenty miles away—though, lagging behind the times, Nerses still thought of distances in parsangs—those mountains rose to his gaze. They seemed nearer in the sun-haze, shining blue and immediate on the upper summits with unmelted and unmeltable snows. Save for the scarce and wary trapper unchancily snaring and hunting its fringes it was land unexplored and unknown, the great range of the Kablurz Beg. Land once demon-haunted and of ill repute, as legend had told to the sceptical Bishop. . . . Demons there were, but their hunting-grounds the canyons and dark corridors of the human heart, not of any mountain range, as the *Chronicles* record his own heretical convictions. . . . But for Amima to hunt there . . .

'You may hunt the plains—as you do—for buzzard, our uplands for deer. What more do you seek?'

'I wish to hunt in the Kablurz Beg. Oh, my father, I am so weary of the little life of this little place! I want to see other lands if but for a day, if but at a distance of twenty miles from Alarlu. . . . You will let me go?'

She had dropped on one knee then, her hands on his knees, the rebellious restlessness for a moment transmuted into something else, and her eyes, dark and deep, smiling up at him. He stared at her troubledly. A maid and the Spring.

He said, slowly, 'To-morrow I will ask Eidon the Chaplain to gather a hunting-party for the waste lands of the north. Will that content you? There are lion there. But the Kablurz Beg'—and he looked away from that stark gaze of hers to repeat with due gravity what he himself believed to be but the fuddled imaginings of work-weary peasants—'it is said that a great grey monster, as in ancient times, haunts the passes near to Alarlu.'

'I also have heard of the Grey Beast. I do not believe it is a devil. Only some bear.' She had stood up. Her eyes were defiant now. 'My father, I wish to go hunting in the mountains.'

'And that I forbid—or any thought or intention of such hunting. You understand?'

She nodded. She knelt and kissed his hand, formally. She turned and left him, and the Bishop, with a sigh of relief and impatience, went back to his scripts, hearing as the night came on the moan of the Spring wind sweeping Alarlu from its icy birthplace on the mountain ledges of the Kablurz Beg.

II

And next morning Amima was missing, and all that day, and all the night that followed, and there was a ringing of alarm bells in Alarlu heard far down in the deserts, and a wild drift of rumour and surmise from peasant hut to hut.

Youthfully and very coolly and unexcitedly Amima had calculated the consequences of her act : twelve hours of anxiety for her father and then a rating and punishment for herself when she returned at dusk. These could be borne. But not the challenge and wonder of the unexplored mountains.

So at dawn she crept out from Alarlu palace, taking the Mongol bow that had been her brother's —a bow of overlapping plates of horn, a magical instrument with a flat trajectory and a mighty twang in the loosening—and a bag of dried fruits and a hunting-knife. These she bound to the saddle of her pony and led him softly from the courtyard. It was but barely dawn. She mounted on a path that ran betwixt the little millet-fields of the Nestorians, and glanced back once and blessed her father, gravely, for she loved him, and turned her eyes to that shadow against the morning that was her planned hunting-ground ; and set her pony at a sharp trot to the brink of Alarlu plateau.

On that brink, at the edge of the pass that led down to the plain, almost she halted and turned back for a cloak, for the wind was bitter. But down through the morning mists she saw the desert-lands already gleaming cobalt in the sunshine. . . . And she would be back in Alarlu before the night fell.

Two miles away, round the far shoulder of the plateau, she turned her pony's head towards that far glistering splendour that a few moments before had been a dark matutinal indecision. Now, sun-kissed, pinnacle after pinnacle betook to itself an icy corona. The pony trotted forward into the tundra country, and Amima unslung the horn bow in readiness and at length was out on that expedition that had haunted her imagination all through the dark winter months.

III

It was a desolate land, neither desert nor herbage, but a treeless waste of thin bushes, ungreen, un-rustling in the morning heat. Nothing lived or moved, it seemed to the Nestorian girl, but the pony and herself. The air, not yet the usual dank stagnation of the plains, tasted like warmed moun-tain ale. Amima shook her pony into a trot, into a gallop that was presently, her mount entering into the spirit of the hour, a wild flight across the waste lands, their centaur shadow in pursuit. When at last she pulled in the pony and glanced back

towards Alarlu she gave a little gasp of surprise.
The plateau had dwindled to a dot on the
horizon. . . .

The sun climbed; the bushes acquired shadows
jet as ink-nut juice; the pony trotted perspiringly,
once stopping gladly and with heaving flanks to
plunge his muzzle in a little spring that rose in the
tundra in one spot and dwindled to a seeping extinc-
tion a few yards away. It was while she bent over
her mount, allowing him to drink sparingly, that
Amima heard a rustling in some bushes in front.
She raised her head and simultaneously was aware
that her pony had raised his, had ceased to drink,
and was trembling as with grass-ague.

A great, black-maned lion had risen and stopped
to sniff the air and cast an incurious glance at pony
and rider before turning about and padding off,
at an unhurried lope, towards the two-miles distant
spurs of the Kablurz Beg.

For a moment, one guesses, Amima's heart stood
still. But the moment passed. Not without result
had she been reared in a time of wild alarums and
wilder essays; and the Spring was with her; and
never before had she hunted lion alone. . . .
She strung the Mongol bow, bending the shining
plates of horn to thigh and knee, and fitted a
steel-tipped arrow, and lashed the pony into
pursuit.

The lion heard the beat of their coming, and
faced round and growled, amazedly, warningly.
The shivering pony slowed down to a canter;

halted. Amima rose in her short stirrups, and levelled the arrow of the flat trajectory sweep, and felt her mount quiver beneath her as the bow-cord twanged like the plucked string of a Titan lyre. . . .

Thrice she succeeded in dragging her pony beyond reach of the lion's squattering charge. The third time, charging, it broke its bound in mid-air and squatted on the ground, tearing at the arrow in its chest. Amima strove to loose another arrow, and at length succeeded. But the quiverings of her mount flung the projectile wide of its mark, singing over the head of the clawing, spitting beast she hunted. But at that sound and arrow-impact in the ground so near at hand, the lion crept to its feet, turned tail, and fled. Amima thrust the pony again on its track, and raised her eyes, and saw with amazement the walls of the Kablurz Beg, long desired, attained at last, towering almost overhead.

IV

They rise cragged and bushless now, treeless, a wildered jumble of naked escarpments serrating the far sky-line from the roof of that Monastery which houses unread and forgotten the *Chronicles* of Neesan Nerses. But seven centuries of suns and winds and the rains of denudation have played on those mountain masses since Amima Nerses, hot on the trail of the wounded lion, entered the range through a bush-choked gulley and found herself in a maze of canyons and corridors patterned and choked in the surge of a cold, jungle life. Conifers dropped lianas across the pathless path ; ferns, rank and gigantic, scraped the sides of her mount. Torrents droned in unseen caverns of the rock. High above this green, tenebrous world the sun played on the frozen points that crowned the scarred cliff-walls.

The lion seemed to have vanished. Then she saw him again, going very slowly far up a bush-strewn slope She urged the pony in pursuit and for a little, because the quarry went draggingly, gained on him, crossing the slope briskly. But its farther side shelved more steeply than the portion she had ascended. The pony hesitated, then floundered downwards, snorting and unsure of foot. It was deeper there, the cliff-walls curving over-head.

And at that moment the lion sprang.

It had crouched behind a lichened boulder. Leaping, arrow in chest, it screamed a fraction too soon for fruition of its purpose. The pony, over-nervous already, swerved and dipped, dragging the bow from Amima's hand with the saddle-peak, flinging Amima herself far among the boulders. Rolling, she flung her arms across her throat and face, as she had been warned to do if ever she lay at the mercy of the great carnivores. She heard the lion roar again, heard a wild clatter of hooves, and then ceased from hearing anything.

V

When she awoke the sun stood overhead. But for the unceasing shrill of mountain streams the jumbled, lost valleys of the Kablurz Beg drowsed undisturbed in the seep of sunshine. It was very warm. The rocks against which she lay seemed to perspire moistly. She dragged herself, achingly, to her feet.

Near at hand lay the lion, dead. There was no sign of the pony. Alone and weaponless she was left in the heart of the haunted mountains.

But that strange, insolent courage that is of youth and no historical epoch did not wane from her at all. Very thirsty, she sought out a pool and drank there and laved her face, and loosened her hair about her shoulders for comfort, and wept a little, not from fear but vexation for that lost pony and bow. Then she went and stood in the rill-haunted silence of the canyon and looked in some pride at the lion. If she could but carry him back to Alarlu !

But that was impossible. She would have task enough in transporting herself thither. She set out.

At first the way was clear enough—the slope over which she had galloped, the gulley she had descended. At the top of the latter a black panther slipped past her, cat-like, with suave grace. She sprang aside with a startled cry ; but the beast paid no heed. A little shaken, she turned again to resume her journey out through the mountain bastions to

the tundra-land. Strange that the way showed no
mark of the pony's passage.

VI

The sun was low in the sky. Heat had departed
from the dark inlands of the Kablurz Beg, and a
grey fog crept and frothed and poured in soft,
soundless billows through the boulder-strewn
canyons. And through those canyons, stumbling
now and then, Amima, hopelessly lost, still sought
an exit to the world beyond.

She sat down and thought. In less than an hour
it would be sunset and darkness. Unless she
found some shelter from the night, from beasts
and . . .

She sat, very tired, watching the light die from
the blue peaks overhead. At her feet a little stag-
nant lake shimmered and rippled in the half-twilight.
Beyond and around, crystalline, gigantic, the
canyon cliffs pierced upwards to peer in the face of
the dying day.

Day that was yet upon Alarlu, kindly and secure,
sleeping in the loveliness of a springtime afternoon. . . .

But of that she would not think—of neither that
nor the horrific tales of the peasant huts : of the
beasts and worse that ravened here at night.

She raised her head. It had grown darker even
while she sat. She stood up and looked round her
bewilderedly. And then, across the little lake and

far down a narrow corridor in the cliffs, she saw a light pringle to being against the coming of the night.

VII

It was no cave from which the light emanated, but the merest fault in the rock-surface that left a triangular cleft there, some twenty feet deep. And midway this cleft burned, unattended, the fire.

Amima crept into the cleft and warmed herself at the blaze. Outside : the night-fretted silences of the Kablurz Beg and its winding mazes. Inside : nothing but the crackle and hiss of the dried bush-branches, no mark or indication of him who had kindled them.

But the light grew, and at the far end of the cleft she saw a thing that seemed not of natural formation. She went towards it, cautiously. It was a kind of nest, built of twigs and long grass, and, bending over it, Amima Nerses started back with a cry that echoed far out the cleft and was caught and reverberated away and away and back again, rock-impelled, unendingly.

For in the nest lay dead a thing that might have been a human child but that it was a Grey Demon of the mountains : No lie, no old wives' tale as her father had taught her to believe, but a loathsome reality.

She would have turned and fled then. The echoes of her startled cry had died away. But now she heard them replaced by another sound. It drew steadily nearer and nearer, a horrid, baying cry, the weary cry of a tortured animal, a snarling, moaning gibberish. Nearer it came and, looking out, for a time the girl could see no cause of it. And then she saw.

By the mere of the lake the Thing came bounding into the fire-radiance. Neither upright nor on all fours it came. Its skin gleamed a hideous, dead grey. It dragged a great club behind it, snuffling up the slope to the cleft. Its head and face came in view then and as she saw them, Amima, lost far from Alarlu and its shelters, heard wrung from her lips such cry of horror and disgust as would surely echo to the plateau itself.

VIII

Many parsangs away in the sunset at that moment Bishop Nerses and Eidon the Chaplain were camping the main body of the search-party under the outer walls of the Kablurz Beg.

'It may be my daughter has found shelter in some cave of the mountains. We can do no more for her until the light comes again.'

Eidon the Chaplain shook his head. 'By the claw-marks on the pony's saddle it seems that some wild beast seized her.' He glanced fearfully towards the dark, sky-towering walls. 'Or some devil of the mountains.'

But even at that moment he found his Bishop as heretical as ever. 'Demons there are—but in our

hearts, Eidon.   Pride and Fear and Hopelessness
are the devils that cry in the night.   All else are
phantasies.'

'From antiquity our Church has believed in the
existence of demons.'

'From antiquity our Church has suffered from
the existence of fools.   Heed to the men, Eidon.
I would be alone.'

It was dreadful in those night hours.   What from
cold and fear the shivering Nestorian search-party
slept but fitfully about its camp-fire.   Nerses himself sat unsleeping, head in hands, listening to that
far, attenuated twitter and rustle in the darkness-
shrouded mazes of the mountains.   One of Amima's
hounds crept up to him and thrust a cold nose
against his cheek, and sat with him listening.   A
pony stamped and whinnied, smelling the prowlings
of some great cat.   The stars came out and glittered
and wheeled down into the west.   And at last the
Bishop saw the fires dying, and that it was dawn.

Blue-tinted and cold, sharp-edged, the near
peaks stood out as the details of a slip-painting
against the copper bowl of the dawn.   Remote on
the tundra-fringe the jackals were baying.   But, as
the little expedition from Alarlu rose and shook
itself and mounted, one of the great Balkh hunting
hounds broke loose from its lead.   It capered for
a moment, stood hesitant, then, nose to the
ground, headed up the nearest passage into the
mountains.

Nerses stared after it, glanced at the ground near

the canyon entrance, and turned to Eidon. 'Loose
the other hounds. We will follow them.'

Loosed they were and went baying up the rugged
track that still, in its soft parts, bore marks of a
pony's hoof-prints. They were on the trail of
Amima Nerses.

IX

That trail had long been lost on the banks of a
stream that at length ceased from being and vanished
roaring into a cliff-side vault. They were many
parsangs deep in the mountains' heart. Overhead,
the morning that had been a promise was now a
skyey fulfilment. The hounds squatted panting.

And then, while they stood by that stream at a
loss, and the Bishop, as he tells, at last gave up hope,
Eidon the Chaplain called to him, and called the
Alarlu men to silence, and all of them listened.

It was the sound of a voice lifted, singing. Far
away, eerily, wonderfully, the singer sang in the
morning hush, and Neesan Nerses felt an icy hand
grip at his heart. The Chaplain Eidon crossed himself and the pallid peasants of the search party
shivered, clutching their bows.

'It is the lost and wandering ghost of the lady
Amima,' Eidon whispered by Nerses' shoulder.
'Look.'

The hounds had ceased to squat, tongues lolling
out, in lazy enjoyment of the halt. Now they
cowered under the feet of the ponies as though seeking protection from a nameless, bodiless terror;

and as that far singing ceased the beasts lifted their muzzles, whimpering. At that, says the Bishop, his own frozen fear went from him. He remembered only that vivid presence defying him in the palace tower of Alarlu. . . .

'Drive the hounds across the stream.'

So it was done, and, with some urging, the beasts again picked up the trail and followed it subduedly, halting every now and then to whimper and cringe. Behind, splashing through the dark waters, went Neesan Nerses and his company.

Penetrating from the south, they were in a wilderness of closed valleys. Ahead gleamed a dark lake. But minute by minute it brightened with the diffusion of light from those sun-warmed upper reaches of the air. And suddenly the singing, the singing of a Nestorian hymn, in a voice sobbing on the verge of exhaustion, burst forth again, very near at hand. The Balkh hounds stopped and backed away, and no urging would compel them forward again. But the Bishop had ceased to heed them. He drove his mount forward betwixt cliff and mere and burst in view of that cleft where Amima Nerses had sighted the fire in the sunset dusk of the previous day.

x

The fire a smoke-spiralling heap of embers in the grey of that mountain morning; Amima Nerses in the arms of her father; Eidon, bow bent and taut, glaring towards the mouth of the cleft;

the peasants of Alarlu staring with protruding eyes ; the devil . . .

He had crouched and snarled and backed away at the clatter of their coming ; he had caught up from behind the fire the hideous miniature replica of himself, and, shielding that, splayed himself back against the rock, moaning and snarling. And the scepticism of Neesan Nerses wavered and sank, looking over the bowed head and hysterical weeping of Amima at that frightsome caricature of men.

Great and squat and naked, browless and chinless, with an arching neck and massive, down-thrust head, it crouched blinking, facing them ; it was matted in a growth of red-grey hair ; it stared forth at them wildly, glazedly, trying, the Bishop realised, to raise in challenge the great malformed head overarched by the brutish neck. . . .

The peasants, a Bishop to lead them, the Church to defend, were half-recovering from their fright. Nerses was aware of a bending of bows under the direction of Eidon. So aware also was Amima. She broke from her father's arms.

' Do not loose, do not kill ! It has not harmed me. . . . It has but grieved above its dead while all night I have sung——'

And then, says the Bishop, an unpremeditated resolution came on him. He waved Amima to silence, waved aside the threatening bows, and, his hand aloft, walked forward towards the Thing.

It snarled, blood-curdlingly, with a tightening of pendulous lips. For answer the Bishop made the sign of the cross and halted not three feet away from its threatening presence.

XI

. . . A race of demons, forgotten by God, abandoned by nature, lost in forgotten mountains of the world; retreating and fading to the waste lands of the earth, leaving behind a rumour and memory of ogre and devil to startle and bemuse the human cohorts out on their mission of conquering the earth. . . . Dim age on age, with the closing in of that alien, hostile world about their last retreats, the demons staring their wonder and fear of it from mountain-eyries and darkened forests as the fires of humankind lit up the nights. . . . Uncomprehending, forgotten, discarded in God's vast purposes as yet might be their own conquerors in the deeps of unborn days. . . . Dwindling to a score, to a last prowling hunter of the twilights, the last of his young clasped dead in his arms.

So, tells Neesan Nerses, he dreamt or visioned or read in a last flame and flow of broken images in those glazed, brutish eyes of the Thing that fronted him that morning in a cul-de-sac of the Kablurz Beg. No noice came from it, but in the hideous eyes dawned a look that spoke and wrung his heart. He raised his hand and again made that sign of an Agony he believed would yet salve and transmute all agonies, human, demoniac, bestial, the world had ever known. And the eyes of the Grey Monster, it seemed to him, lighted for a moment. It half-uncrouched and rose towards him.

High in the morning air rose the twang of the bowstring of Eidon the Chaplain.

XII

And the Bishop mounted his daughter behind him, and drove the white-faced Nestorians from that place, and without a backward glance rode behind them out through the maze-like gulleys of the Kablurz Beg for many parsangs ; and behind them the dank jungles closed and left no trace ; and they came at last to the plains and the Spring sunshine again. Strangely silent, unfrightened, wide-eyed, with meaning at last in her Spring, in the blowing of its every bud, went Amima. And they rode out from the mountains into the sunlight, all of them, into the sunlight and brightness of their days and years, and the darkness that closed on them long centuries ere we were born.

In front of me, transcribing to our alien script and speech this tale of Neesan Nerses, lies portrayed by the hand and imagination of a modern artist the probable appearance of that strange precursor of Man, the inhuman monster who left his bones and fire-sites and clumsy weapons in Spy and Gibraltar and the caves of Palestine, who perished from the earth in the fourth of the glacial ages—all, it may be, but stray packs of his descendants who hid and fled and dwindlingly survived in the mountain chains that branch from the Roof of the World. A raving thing of lust and blood and brutishness he glares from the artist's page, this Neanderthal Man.

But I remember that last monster that wept its dead in a cavern of the Persian hills, and with Nerses grope through pity to a clearer understanding— even, it may be, as the charitable of some alien species will do to our last descendants if we weary God and He put us aside.

CARTAPHILUS

I

THOUSANDS of words have mouldered into illegibility on the fringes of that manuscript record which Neesan Nerses of Alarlu penned seven centuries ago. He called it his *Polychronicon,* and here and there even yet are colours that shine undimmed from phrase and phantasy. But the years have done more than dim the record : they have rendered long stretches of it unreadable. One turns page on dusty page of the crabbed Nestorian script, dull, alien, incomprehensible, beyond the enthusings of such mere raider in history as myself. They go back to the shelves of Mevr's Monastery, there to await the coming of that inevitable German, bespectacled, perspiring, who will read them and love them for themselves and print them all at Stuttgart in ten fat folios with footnotes. . . .

It was towards the end of my stay in the Monastery, and I sat reshuffling the pages hurriedly when a word glanced up at me from the scuffle of the yellowed sheets. It glanced again. *Cartaphilus.*

I remembered that section—such of it as I had persevered to read. I had halted midway the first three thousand words, resolute that Matthew Paris's Latin had told the tale better than ever Nerses' Persian. And how many the variants of the tale that had drifted east and west in that century of theirs ! It had blown up suddenly, a great smokecloud of tenebrous legend out of the past when

Rome ruled the world. It was a story that haunted the thirteenth century, till everywhere men talked of it and debated it and looked on each straying tramp and Jewish pedlar with a wild surmise. Impostors innumerable had risen with claims that doctors disputed in council. Singers had sung that story, in Europe, in Syria, in the Crusaders' camps, in the Christian-manned galleys of Baber—half-fearful, half-desirous, singers and hearers, that a step would sound and Cartaphilus himself come shuffling in out of the night.

And then I found I was deep in the later half of the record I had passed by in such impatience. Sîs—Evid—Lur's olive groves in autumn—the Figure at Mailapur—a Christian refugee with a tale from the slave-pits of Baghdad; what had these to do with that tale that haunted the world?

II

This, tells Nerses : On a winter morning of the year 1250 King Haithon of Lower Armenia had a message despatched to every guard-house in and around the city of Sîs. The knight Baisan Evid, wherever found, was to be apprehended and brought to the palace in chains.

Baisan Evid ! The news sped beyond the guard-houses to the quarters of the women, the kennels of the lackeys, the Templars' barracks. Evid the young, Evid the cruel, Evid of the shining sword and graceless speech—Evid the palace favourite !

That buzz of thirteenth-century gossip and surmise rises fresh and vivid enough from the Bishop's pages. Presently that buzz was one of delight. It had been discovered that the favourite's paramour was—in another sense—the king's favourite !

Grinning messengers whispered it and licked their lips. For the tragedy to the actor was the comedy to the spectator in bloody Sîs—and indeed in all that world where a madness of new-learnt cruelty moaned and whimpered in the footsteps of new-learnt knowledge. Evid and Miriam—they had vanished into the mountains for a day. And when they returned——

That they did at nightfall, carelessly enough, pleasantly wearied from their riding the mountain bridle-paths. High up at one point, late in the afternoon, Sîs gleaming below them like a garnet in a crystalline cup, Evid had drawn rein and laughed, breathing the air greatly into a young, strong body.

'Ugh ! Good to smell clean air after weeks in that rat-run. . . . Could not we stay all night ? '

Miriam shook her head. ' The rat would scamper in our tracks.'

He laughed again. The breath rose in a little cloud from their halted horses. He put his arm about her, carelessly, haughtily, as were all his actions. ' The knight who robbed King Rat ! '

She sat very silent in the afternoon sunlight, still and silent, as he was afterwards to remember: Haithon's mistress, the king's paramour whom he had stolen. But presently, not looking at him, she spoke.

'"King Rat"—cruel and mean and dull. But still a king. And, in his foolish way, he has loved both of us.'

He raised fair eyebrows at her, pale Greek face— for he came, says Nerses, of the family of Baz, claiming Byzantine descent with better warrant than many another claimant—amused and indifferent above the green samite cloak he wore. 'Are we to waste the day brooding on the virtues of Haithon?'

'Evid, have you never in your life pitied anything or anyone?'

'Pity?' Spurring his horse down the path he stared back at her puzzledly, haughtily. 'Pity? What need have I of pity?'

III

And at the gates of Sîs they took him and chained and tore the green samite cloak from his shoulders. Miriam vanished from his sight. He was urged on foot through the mired streets to the palace gates, thrust roughly within them, and led to the presence of the ancient king. Wizened and wrinkled and old, his hands yet shaking with rage, Haithon peered up from his cushions at that haughty Greek face fronting him.

'Now you will tell of that which has passed between you and Miriam,' the King whispered.

And Evid said nothing. Then the King raised his hand, smiting with a wire whip that lacerated the haughty Greek face. And Evid said nothing. And the King whispered again : ' Now you will tell.'

But Evid neither spoke nor moved, chill and contemptuous. It was evening by then. The shadow of the old King flung from the wall-cressets was like that of a gigantic toad as he levered himself to his feet.

' Bring the prisoner.'

So they took him from out those gay and painted halls, golden and blue, hung with ancient tapestries from the times of the Sassanids. They took him down a little stairway that wound and wound far in the heart of the living rock. To Evid, fearless yet, yet strung and quivering with expectation, a curious illusion came : it was as though he were being led into the deeps of his own heart.

Never such darkness. And as they went lower and lower the chained knight heard on either side lethargic scufflings and the slow clank of fetters trailed in the night-blinded gropings of chained and hidden men. Now, says Nerses, they came at last to a chamber of torment.

' Here you will speak,' the old King whispered.

IV

He had spoken. Remembering that, he lay and raged with shame in the darkness. So, it seemed

to him, he had lain for week on week of shame and
bodily agony.   At first he had believed himself
blinded, but as the days passed he had come to see
the charcoal blackness of his cell faintly sprayed as
with a ghostly snow of light.   Ghost : ghost of that
world above, where the sunshine raced on the long
Armenian roads to the still beauties of sunset, where
mountain-shepherds drowsed at noon, where the
hot lists clanged in the wheeling practice of the
Templar knights.   Sunshine and day that he would
never see again——

And then he would move, and his body seem as
if afire, and he would bite his lips and groan—but
silently, lest some spy of Haithon's listened still.

If he were but whole and free again ! If Haithon
were in his hands, that shrivelled throat in his
hands——

And then he became aware of another, one who
seemed hardly to breathe or move, who shared
that darkness-shrouded dungeon with him.   A
faint clank of a chain, a deeper blackness, a shadow
in darkness would sometimes move at the far end
of the cell.   He called to it between his teeth.

' Haithon's spy !—or are you also a prisoner ? '

There was no answer.   But it seemed to Evid
he heard a sigh.   He cursed the sigher, and ground
his teeth again because of the pain of his tormented
body, and fell and fell into abysses of sleep from
which fresh onslaughts of pain uptore him.   Awake,
he found a hand upon his brow, soothing him—a
hand rough-fingered but strangely gentle.   And

for the first time since childhood, says Nerses, he wept.

'Who are you?' he asked.

But he was answered again only by that sigh. The other prisoner had moved away. It seemed that his chain reached far. Could it be that he was dumb—some mutilated palace victim? Evid called that question, but heard no answer. And a strange tide of angry compassion flooded his haughty heart.

'Hear me, friend: If I win free but an hour—terribly will I avenge both of us!'

But neither was that answered. Evid fell back on elbow, and then, says Nerses, was suddenly vouchsafed a terrible vision.

For he saw all the prisons of the earth, and the maimed, forsaken multitudes prisoned therein—longing as he longed for star and sun and the kiss of the wind, guiltily guiltless as himself, men who had loved and feared, laughed and wept and known surcease of sorrow, men who had dreamt their shining dreams. And all his own years of easy life and facile lust and unthinking cruelty men in the dungeons of Sîs had lain unpitied by him in such agonies as his own body knew at last. And, like a great beast squatting against the sun, he saw that unthinking cruelty for the monster that ruled his world, terrible, implacable, unsated. . . .

Why then did the Christ delay that Second Coming of His that was to crumble away prison and palace alike like the wrack of a dream?

V

They are ablow with flowers this time of year, the mounds that mark the city of Sîs, where Baisan Evid lay and questioned the darkness with despair seven centuries ago. But that question of his, old in his age, has echoed fresh in agony down to this. Nor need we, with Nerses, presuppose miracle for that vision that came to the young knight in the cells below the palace of Haithon. Youth, edged steel-keen with pride itself, it was that had smitten through to searing vision of that horror he had gone unheeding. . . .

In an agony he called aloud to the silent other who shared his cell :

' O friend, I am fearful and forsaken. Tell me your name.'

And then at last that other answered him, in a low, still voice, sweet and full, burdened with a sadness that yet seemed undespairing :

' Men call me Cartaphilus.'

VI

Cartaphilus ! Baisan Evid shrank and quivered in the darkness. Pity and compassion at last his heart had reached through its own pain. But now came fear.

Cartaphilus, the Jew who had mocked the Passion of Christ, and because of that mocking still wandered the world unresting and undying ; Cartaphilus the

Denier; Cartaphilus the forsaken of God and men. . . .

Not for a moment, it seems, did he doubt the identity of the other. For who but the accursed himself would claim to be that Cartaphilus on whose name even the paynim Muslim spat? And all Armenia was filled with rumours of his sojourn in the land, though it was said the horror of that unaging body and face went cloaked and hooded perpetually from the eyes of men. . . . Evid heard a question quaver again on his own lips:

'How came it that Haithon prisoned you?'

There was no reply. Himself shrinking from speech, shuddering at memory of the contact of that hand, Evid lay and brooded in the darkness. And presently neither sleeping nor waking, solution of the world's salvation burst and flowered in his mind as a lambent flame. That vision of the world of evil and the Christ Who delayed His Coming inexplicably—— Yet inexplicable no longer. *For still the Wandering Jew denied his Master.*

Still, century on century, that Master awaited acknowledgment from him He had set to wander the earth. Still, in the dust and din of the rushing years, He waited for that cry of belief that would rise to Him as the trumpet-call for His return——

VII

He started awake with a light flashed in his eyes and a rough foot touching him. He started up, his fetters clanking, memory of the dream that was no dream vivid upon him. The two gaolers who had come for him stared stolidly, but he cared nothing for their starings, himself peering into the far corner of the cell. And then a cry burst from his lips :

'Cartaphilus! Where have you taken Cartaphilus ? '

He struggled and fought with them, a madman, as they dragged him from the cell, and they were men astounded, for none before had ever shown reluctance to leave the dungeons of Sîs. But he was weak and impotent enough in their hands as they took him to the upper air again, bathed him and clothed him and told him his fate. It was banishment.

'And a fate you've to thank the Caliph's wines for,' grunted the head gaoler. 'They softened Haithon. He sent back the slut Miriam in payment and ordered your release. Well, have you no message of gratitude ? '

But they saw then that he had gone mad in the torment and darkness. For he heeded nothing to their talk, only babbled unendingly of that other who had shared his cell with him, babbled still as they thrust him out of the prison gates.

'What have you done with him ? In the name of God tell me what you have done ? '

The head gaoler banged the gates. 'No prisoner but your idiot self has been released. Stay—one stout clown there was, sold as slave to a merchant

from Kin or Ind.' The man grinned. ' So get
you after him thither if you will!'

VIII

It was spring. The roads were alive with a motley
processioning—those roads that bestrode 'twixt
sunrise and sunset the mountains of Armenia.
Camel-trains with grain and fodder, trains of asses
with wines and spices, trains of young ponies,
half-wild, laden with hides and furs, driven by the
yellow plainsmen of the north—they passed and
counter-passed through the rugged defiles that
guarded Sîs. And amid them, tramping with staff
and wallet into the east, went the mad knight Baisan
Evid.

A merchant from Kin or Ind with a new slave in
his train ? Some laughed ; some cursed him and
rode on ; some picked up staves to beat him away
from the gates of their encampments and then
dropped the staves and grew quiet at sight of that
look on his face. Merchants ? Merchants innumerable. But stay : one such as he named had taken
the roads to Baghdad. . . .

Questioning no more, hirpling long leagues till
his body recovered its strength again, the prisoner
from the dungeons of Sîs followed the merchant's
tracks. Storms of rain and sleet raged up from the
plains ; he tramped them unaware. To left and
right towered the mountains, poising above him
each freezing nightfall as if to fall and crush him

while he slept; but his sleepings were few.
Mountains? They would dissolve away as a mist
and a spume, they and all the world of cruelty and
shame, when once he had knelt beside Cartaphilus,
pleaded with him, heard rise to the lips of the Forsaken that Name that would bring in splendour and
flame the Second Advent.

Wolves in packs ravened on the slopes beyond
Lake Van. A terrified caravan of Basrah traders,
barricaded from the beasts, saw the long figure,
white-faced, black-wrapped, hatless, of one who
came striding down a mountain path at sunset
with score on score of wolves at his heels, snarling
and whining. Heedless of either men or beasts,
encampment or coming darkness, the man went by
and vanished into the eastern night, as one trader
long afterwards told to Nerses of Alarlu. 'Some
thought him a mountain devil, but I saw his face,
young and white and sealed with the madness of
God, and knew he had come unharmed through
the wolf valley because he walked both unfearing
and unseeing.'

So, through that hasting spring of shining days
and aurulent nights, set with stars that he might
not stumble, Baisan Evid crossed the wild lands,
unharmed, unquestioned, up through Erzerum,
into the country of the Comani where league on
league lay the cobalt deserts, overhung by blood-
red suns, haunted by the foul avigi-birds. Still the
merchant eluded his pursuit; still, where others
failed or perished he pressed forward, crowned and

guarded in the garment of his purpose. Bandits besieged the city of Mosul; he walked through their ambushments unharmed and undetected, the first stranger from the outside world since the siege had begun. . . . So they told him, the Mosul innkeepers, staring at him askance. But he found they lied or had been misinformed—one other had come from the west, a prison-exile who had gone on towards Baghdad. A little Christian trader told him this, two days after his coming to Mosul, peering fearfully to left and right the while.

'I myself was told of him but an hour ago. They say—but I do not know—they say it was the Wandering Jew himself!'

Cartaphilus again! How had he freed himself from slavery? But that question could abide Baghdad. Ragged, shoeless, unlingering, Evid took the southern road to the city of the Caliphs, and a little Christian crowd gathered at the southern gate and stared and gestured after him.

IX

The Golden City of the River rose before his eyes, its minarets blinding blue, mosaic'd with Koranic texts, dazzling in the hot sunshine. High in air, as though hung from the fabled gardens of that mythic Babylon that mouldered in dust and legend beyond the river, uprose palace and tower and citadel. And Evid stood and looked at the city,

says Nerses, with wonder for its fairness and foulness. For at the great gate men hung dripping from
brazen hooks set in the walls, crying in day-old
torments. So were the city's malefactors executed.
And something rose hot and stinging in the heart
of the lost, mad knight. For a moment, in the
hearing of those agonised moans, his quest blurred
and shrivelled like a mirage-picture, his lips opened
to cry the people of the earth themselves to end this
shame and horror. And then his head drooped,
he went by with hasting step and averted face.
God's messenger to the Forsaken—how dared he
delay fulfilment of that search that would end all
misery for ever?

In a little Nestorian church, half-hidden in the
stews of the slave-quarters, he questioned a sleepy,
heat-lazy priest.

'An escaped Armenian slave? And why come
here? Is he the Wandering Jew himself?' added
the priest, in jest.

And then, observing better the white, haggard
face and mien of his questioner, something of the
lazy indifference left the priest's eyes. He quailed
and shivered strangely.

'You have followed this brother of yours from
far?' he asked.

'I follow him to the ends of Ind if need be,'
answered Evid, and turned and left that place and
spent a day in swift searchings from bazaar to
bazaar, in the slave-crowds that jostled with the
coming of evening, in the camel-trains that swung,

bell-ringing, across the bridges to the deserts of
Arabia. And suddenly he heard a voice cry his
name :

' Evid ! O Evid ! '

It came from a passing litter, negro-guarded. A
hand had thrust aside the curtains. Evid raised his
head and looked into the eyes of Miriam.

Haunted eyes of fear lighted by an impossible
hope she bent upon him, and he understood. She,
the slave-gift of Haithon, was being carried to the
Caliph's palace at last. . . . Miriam, once closer
to him than breathing, Miriam of the shining body
and sad-glad soul-- —

He sprang forward with upraised hand, and a
black eunuch cowered aside. Then the hand
dropped. What part had he with love or hate ?
—he, whose Message to the Wanderer would bring
the Christ in the flame and thunder of his Second
Coming.

Unheeding the cry that followed him he plunged
with averted head into the evening throngs. That
night he slept in a hut on Tigris' bank, and at dawn
resumed his searchings. . . . And, as once before,
creeping up like a little wind mysteriously born,
mysteriously ablow, he was aware of a drift and
tangle of rumour of the one he sought. One—it
was whispered Cartaphilus, the Wandering Jew
himself—had passed through Baghdad, vanishing
eastwards in flight to the haunted lands of
Ind.

X

And eastwards on that trackless pursuit followed Baisan Evid. Through an east that writhed in the travail of history, and writhing, shed great gouts of blood, he passed. Through Lur he passed as the olives ripened and smoke blackened all the northwards sky from burning homesteads. The Yellow Raiders were there. And, wrapped in his quest, his spirit-eyes on the far lands of India to which the Wanderer had fled, Evid passed unharmed of beasts and men. For the wind came over his footprints, blotting out his tracks that none might pursue, and in desert wastes the birds brushed him with their wings, leading him to hidden wells. In Hyrcania it was summer and they dressed the vines, and up the long hill-slopes he saw the dark groves of olives stir in a restless beauty each nightfall as though spreading their cloaks for sleep. And he cut himself a fresh staff there, and passed, with winter and a cloud of rumour and surmise gathering and following behind. . . .

So across the land that was not yet Baluchistan and into the Hindu Kush he passed, and in Nerses' record vanishes from recognisable geography into a mythic mist of fabulous cities and races. Yet even in those faery lands the story of Cartaphilus drifted and whispered. And ever he fled the footsteps of the white dreamer who followed unfaltering.

Autumn with a storm of rains, hot and steaming, swept over the paynim, jungle lands. The hills

towered white and green, crowned with devil
images, at night uplighted with strange fires.
But they stayed him, neither fires nor devils, the
deserts of Golconda or the haunted vales of Argania
where dog-like men snarled from their mountain
caves. And at length, in Serendib, with its golden
clangour of bells, he met with one whose tale
ended his questionings and blazed a straight path
before his feet. For this man, a wandering trader,
a convert of some lost Nestorian mission, told how,
far to the south in Mailapur, lay the tomb of St.
Thomas, sleeping the coming of his Redeemer.
And wild certainty blazed in the heart of Evid.
To the refuge of that tomb had fled Cartaphilus.

XI

It was nightfall, says Nerses, when he came to
that mount in Mailapur and climbed through jungle
paths. At the top the ruined mausoleum flashed
its red granite walls in the dying light. Troops of
little grey monkeys swung and called and were
plaintively uncomforted amid the trees. Far below,
on the roads between the villages, the humped
cattle went to and fro and stopped to graze; and
the still smoke rose from distant hearths. And
Evid climbed and knelt at last in the shadow of the
ruined structure whereneath awaited the coming of
his Master that Doubter whom the Kshatriya slew
at prayer.

A crumbling ruin in the dying light, deserted, a

tenebrous place. The upward paths, long lost to human feet, were choked and faint. Here, centuries before, the Message had sprouted from an alien seed, waxed and flowered in the blood of the martyred Doubter, scenting the wilderness. And time and the green Paynim gods had strangled and smothered that flower, oiling its memory away below a green canopy of jungle.

So yet, the world over, might pass and vanish the Message. The years and birth and death and savagery : Reality. Cartaphilus ?—who was this pitiful dream he had sought ? Who the Christ Himself but a madman's dream ?

And then, in that moment of frozen doubt under the ruined mausoleum of the great Doubter, some impulse upraised for him his head. And he leapt to his feet, staring across the brow of the mount.

For not he alone had stood in the shadow of the ruin. Across the slopes, cloaked, bent of head, went a Figure, northwards. And as Evid stared, heartwrung, unmoving, the night gathered and blinded the still land with darkness.

XII

He lay all that night in a stupor of mingled despair and hope under the mastaba of the doubting saint. Beasts crept snuffling up the slopes in the moonlight, one coming so close that its hot breath blew upon him. But there were other beasts that he lay and fought the while the night went on and the stars grew white, and far in the villages of Mailapur the cocks began to crow.

Not to him had been given the glory of winning that wandering Figure from his age-old denial. How indeed might a man become God's Huntsman of the Wanderer but that he himself was Christ-like ? The Christ—and Baisan Evid !

Yet at dawn, with a strange serenity come upon him at last, he arose, slowly, and went north in the footsteps of that shadowy Figure. But no longer did he pass across the Hindu lands as the Baisan Evid of the southwards journey. As through the eyes of a wondering child he saw the coming of winter in the wild Golconda country. As a child, wide-eyed and questioning, he climbed the hills and entered the paynim temples he had shunned with horror. And he tarried long hours in the brown hut-villages of the Deccan, helping the peasants at their toil in the fields, comforting the old, stumbling with slow and bleeding steps in that Path of Life that a greater than the Buddha had shown.

Nearly twelve months after his first crossing the white-capped Roof of the World he saw it tower in the sky again. Spring was there again and the snows flooding in thaw the desert lands below. He joined with a caravan of yellow folk from the far land of Kin, traders in silk and porcelain, going homewards with laden oxen. And with them he fought and toiled up the narrow mountain corridors, gasping in the thin, dry air. By ledge and ravine, by razor-edged escarpment dizzily poised above the pleasant lowlands, they passed. The beasts laired ; Evid helped to drag them from tarn and snowdrift. The yellow men would have turned back ; but they looked in the face of the serene, white saint who companioned them and pressed on. Till at last, beyond the ultimate pass, where a great monastery crowned the unmelting snows, Evid turned and left them. They wept at parting with him, and the beasts of the oxen-team gazed up with troubled eyes and nuzzled at the hand that caressed them in farewell.

He sought a night's shelter at the gates of the great paynim monastery. The abbot, shrivelled and bird-like and ancient, peered at him with quick, appraising eyes.

' The ways are many,' he droned in an old, thin voice. ' And the Christ's is one. But what road is yours—you, his Denier ? '

Evid looked at him in gentle wonder. ' What road ? Who then am I, old man ? '

' Have we not heard of your journeyings in Ind ? Who has not heard of you, that Joseph of Armenia, Cartaphilus, whom the Christians call the Wandering Jew ? '

XIII

Himself the Wanderer ! He had smiled at that surmise of the old abbot's, Nerses tells, and betaken himself to the cell allotted him and next morning to the trackless ways into the sunset.

Himself the Wanderer!—he, God's Huntsman, Christ's follower——

And then, for the second time, he fell into an agony of doubt. But now there was terror in that doubt as well as despair. *Who was the Wanderer?*

The screaming eagles cried the question from their eyries above the dark granitic gorges. The rainstorms whispered it, sheeting westwards in his tracks. Who was the Wanderer?—Cartaphilus or——?

Through Luristan, with the coming of that summer, passed a wild figure, bearded to the waist, hatless, shoeless, a preacher, a dervish. Yet, when the multitudes gathered round him he voiced no hope or fear and preached no creed but that men must seek out the Wanderer. . . . And in desert camp and Persian town, throughout the length and breadth of that land so long the home of Muslim heresy, the whisper of his message went to and fro, his words acquiring a mystic significance and power. For it was believed that he spoke of himself. . . .

In Yezd the governor, urged to the act by the alarmed mullahs, sent to arrest him. But the dervish, without following or farewell, had again vanished westwards, into the deserts of Mesopotamia.

XIV

The Golden City of the River rose before his eyes, its minarets blinding blue, mosaic'ed with Koranic texts, dazzling in the hot sunshine. High in air, as though hung from the fabled gardens of that mythic Babylon that mouldered in dust and legend beyond the river, uprose palace and tower and citadel. And Evid stood and looked once more at the city, says Nerses, with wonder for its fairness and foulness. For at the great gate men hung dripping from brazen hooks set in the walls, crying in day-old torments. So were the city's malefactors executed.

Now, two of those criminals hung in a torment of which Nerses may not tell. And Evid saw that they were a man and a woman. Even as he looked the woman stretched out her arms to the man, and then fell back dead. Her hair fell aside from her face.

And it was the face of Miriam, the lost love of Baisan Evid in far-off Sîs.

And something rose hot and stinging in the heart of the lost, mad knight. His quest blurred and shrivelled like a mirage-picture. Wrath white and terrible poured from his lips as he stood under the great gate, his arms outstretched in denunciation of the Golden City, crying the people of that city themselves to end this shame and horror. Crowds gathered about him, deeper and deeper, a multitude of men whose cry was presently added to his, till the sound of it echoed across the city, a threatening roar, to the walls of the Citadel.

XV

They brought out the Janissaries to end the riot that threatened an uprising. Again and again the soldiers rode against the defiant throngs, till at last these broke and scattered and fled. But the gate guard lay dead ; from hook and beam and pointed stake the criminals hung silent and at peace, justice baulked of their torments—slain or saved as the white dervish in his criminal mercy had directed. He himself at last was beaten to the ground, discovered living, and dragged at a horse's tail to the prison pits below the Citadel. . . .

He woke there long hours afterwards. The dungeon inmates near at hand heard him wake, heard the moan of involuntary agony that issued from his lips. Then a long silence fell. But in that stifling darkness memories stirred and flared and flashed through the mind of Baisan Evid, and he bowed a shamed, bloody head. The Wanderer whose quest he had undertaken and foregone— never for him now to achieve that salvation of earth's agonies he had dreamt, never for him to see face to face that Forsaken whose footsteps he had followed half across the earth and returning again——

What was that ?

A mere sigh in the darkness. But he knew it again. He knew it ! He started upright, swaying, dying, praying to live—if but a moment. His stiffening lips strove into speech.

'It is you, it is you! Leave me not again! I have followed you so long——'

And then it seemed to Evid as he tottered and fell that a voice, distant as the stars, closer than his own faltering heart-beats, sweet as the cry of bugles, spoke to him, and, as once before, a hand was laid upon his forehead.

'I will not leave you.'

And then light fell on Baisan Evid. Clear and wondering and awed his voice rang through the Citadel cells of Baghdad in that last cry that another prisoner and priest heard and remembered and heard cry, undying still, through all the years of his life.

'. . . Oh, blind that I have been! Cartaphilus he who wanders the earth unresting? Ah, no! . . . *Master, it is Thou!*'

VI

DAWN IN ALARLU

I

IT was summer of the year 1266.

Rustling their dusty carpetings of grass each morning the Persian lands swung eastward into the sun ; behind, clouded and glistening with globose mirages, rose the deserts of Iraq. Thick and tremulous on burdened trees that oozed a sun-weary sap clustered the fruits of the second date-harvest. In moments of the noontime hours the world quivered and reeled as if poised on the rim of a flaming furnace. And up towards Sar-i-Mil the millet harvest, betaking to itself the likeness of a mirror, flung high each afternoon a great green radiance against the red copper sky——

So, tinted in sudden colours, opens the last fragment of that record penned by the priestly historian of Alarlu. One knows it the Bishop's last, unrelated, unnumbered though it lies amid the leaves of that great Chronicle he wrote and loved and left to moulder through seven long centuries in the Monastery of Mevr. Here wide, blank spaces intersect the yellowed pages. Here that fine angular penmanship grows weaker. Groupings of notes erupt and stray and cease, for, listening to the long, wild song of that summer it seems that the pen of the Bishop fell idle often enough as the fierceness faded from the daylight, and night in its glistening sables came striding down from the peaks of the Kablurz Beg.

But high in his palace tower above the plateau—sleeping through nights that were presently silvered with the coming of a moon that seemed unsetting —no peace came to him, as he tells.　Instead, an aching unease.　He would sit long hours at his table, watching the winking lights across the Persian uplands, hearing the soft sounds of the night— the cry of a bird, the far baying of a watchdog in some corridor of the plateau, even, were it very still, the cough of some distant lion aprowl in the foot-hills of the Kablurz Beg.　And under his hand and the gleam of the single taper that lighted his tower-chamber the pages of his golden Chronicle would rustle forgotten and put by. . . . Summer!　He who had seen so many to watch in agony the passing of this last !

Realisation of himself as that watcher—it had come on him in a day and a night.　Yet forewarn-ings enough there had been.　For that spring the sharp, keen air had torn at his throat as he rode Alarlu's boundaries, seeing to the keeping of the little Nestorian diocese poised as a storm-beaten eyrie above the pagan lands of Persia.　That strange, cold hand at his throat !　Nor that alone.　There had come in a single hour, as it seemed, a dimming of eye and a faltering of hand with bow and bridle and hunting-spear.　And in dark, quiet hours he would wake breathless, coughing, with uncertain heart-beatings, and see above his bed the pictured Crucified gleam agonised in the moonlight.

Old.　But he kept to himself the secret of that

red coughing in the night-time hours, the while he
sought to think and plan for the little community
that was his care. . . . Think! And with an
aching contempt he found he could think of nothing
more than that he would never see another summer,
red-ochred in dawn and sunset, lighten the hills and
harvests of Alarlu.

Not see—the multitude of things he would never
see again! In an age and a century that walked all
unaware of sky and sea and sun, all the miracles of
birth and death and the white of the apple-blossom,
there rise from Nerses' pages, fore-dreaming the
Renaissance, a passion and a pathos that is almost
Tuscan. . . . And the fervid summer nights would
fade while he looked with eyes of memory at the
glint of winter beacons' rise across the deserts
from Baghdad, heard the drum of winter rain on the
palace roofs, smelt the keen iron tang of an autumn
morning so that his lungs ached like those of an
unquiet ghost. The joy of the chase and the whirl
and call of the wind! Never to know them again.
The music of words in a strange, wild tale! Never
to heed to them again on the lips of a strayed wanderer—as to so many he had heeded. Never to slip
for a day from his age and its cares into the dim,
musk worlds of the scripts that half-filled his tower
—scripts in vellum from besieged Byzantium, in
silk and scented tree-leaf from Ind and Kin, their
characters still but puzzles half-deciphered; scripts
in fine sheepskin, lambskin, the first of paper—
even, if his evidence reads aright (for the thing itself

has long crumbled to dust), an agave-leaf parchment strayed by some miracle of tide and trade from the faery Toltec lands beyond the Utmost Seas. . . .

A little wind came that midnight he wrote. It tapped a tendril against the window-ledge of his tower and he sat and listened, he who has left no portrait or portraying of himself, though one thinks of him tall and thin, wrapped in his dark priest gown, with the high forehead of his Persian blood and the great grey eyes he tells of in his daughter Amima. The tendril tapped again. A stranger awaited him there in the darkness.

Stranger? For him, a priest, a bishop? Nerses sighed and covered his face with his hands. Even were that Stranger a Friend, as he believed yet—yet out there in the night, as at last he must go, he would turn back, if he might, to the lights and scents of that world from which the Hand guided his footsteps!

II

Cockcrow aroused him and the feet of his daughter Amima running up the stone stairway to the door of his tower-chamber. In male hunting-gear, young and dark and vivid and unstill, she stood in the doorway, making a despairing gesture at sight of the seated Bishop.

' O father ! This again ! ' She came and dropped
to her knees beside him, and with tired, amused
eyes he watched the impatient look she cast on the
scrolls half-unwound from their cylinders, the pen
yet upright in its stand. ' How may you ever
regain the strength you lost this spring if you
never sleep ? '

' It may be I steal upon that lost strength while *it*
sleeps.' He took her face in his hands, looking
down into her eyes, the humour fading from his
own, one guesses, so that Amima suddenly stiffened
and gazed at him in frightened question. . . .
Amima ! What lot would fall to her when he had
gone, what fate of blood or terror or shame in this
country that cowered still from the impress of the
Mongol's feet ? How long in peace abide the
Nestorians in their little plateau above the dust and
din ? How—things beyond his foreseeing or
deciding.

Yet—and ah ! now so quickly—decide he
must !

His hands fell away from that caress that had
grown a passionate clasp. Morning in the trees of
Alarlu, morning in the eyes of Amima, the flow of
dawn on the mountain bastions, on the hair of a
known head——

' Father ! What ails you ? What is feared by
you ? '

' Eh ? ' Slowly he came out of that dreaming into
which he now fell so readily. Amima : the future :
winter : decide. . . . ' Fear ? What fear ? ' He

touched the short Mongol bow slung on her back.
' And why the bow ? '

' I go riding the marches with three from the
village. Wolves or a bear, they say, come up
from the eastern foothills each night and each
night steal a kid. But it may be they lie, for they
speak of stolen millet also, which sounds unwolfly.'
She was on her feet again, glancing vexedly from
the window. ' And I am late. It is almost full
light. Father——'

But they heard now other footsteps ascending
the tower stairway. They knew those footsteps.
Cut short in that brief scolding the Bishop guessed
she had been about to administer him, Amima
grimaced.

' Eidon, the chaplain, doubtlessly filled with
account of his night-time visions—for he ate
greatly of plums at supper ! '

III

One has met him before in Nerses' pages, the old-
young chaplain of Alarlu, pale and plump, with the
lowered head and unwinking eyes and the passionate
piety that was—in him, astoundingly—no pose.
He had never loved Eidon greatly, the Bishop
tells, but the amused tolerance of early years had
merged at last in a wondering respect. To the
simple all roads were plain—albeit their simplicity
and stupidity might be indistinguishable !

Eidon knelt for blessing in the morning-lit room
—a little gaspingly he knelt, because of that un-
ascetic plumpness, and kissed the Bishop's hand.
Then, even before the hasting clatter of Amima's
footsteps had died in the lower distance, he had
raised his head and was speaking astonishing
words, his narrow, unswerving eyes fixed on
Nerses.

' My lord, I desire to retire to the Monastery of
Mevr.'

' Retire ? ' Nerses stared at him. This was
unexpected enough. ' Retire ? Become a monk ? '

The chaplain bowed his head. The Bishop,
puzzled and amazed, sat erect, surveying
him.

' But this is surely a hasty decision, my
Eidon ? Retire ? Your labours here are of
moment, your place firm in the hearts of Alarlu's
folk——'

' And my soul enchained by these snares of hell.
O my lord, at last I have seen it ! Last night the
revelation came to me——' (the bishop started and
turned away his head)—'that I am denying my
God and denying my soul in these tasks and loves
I have cherished.' Suddenly he seemed no longer
ridiculous, kneeling ungraceful there. His eyes
on the Bishop burned with belief. ' I have filled
myself with conceit and worldly pride and only in
the silences of the cell may I expiate that pride—
and escape the hell of the lost.'

The Bishop rose to his feet. ' You are unstrung.

What sin is yours ? What denial of God have you made ? '

' I have blinded my eyes to that one enduring task set for us here—each to save his own soul from hell. Mine I have overlaid with prides and hopes that stifle it. . . . Lord Bishop, I pray that you will let me go.'

IV

' *What shall it profit a man*——'
Eidon had gone, his plea still unanswered. The Bishop sat and stared into the opal distances of Alarlu, in his heart a sudden guest whose name was surely terror.
' *What shall it profit a man*——'
Was not the case his own ? His soul forgotten, secreted, hid away below love of the colours and smells and voices of this world he feared to leave ! Eidon, fantastic and foolish, overwhelmed in a night by a glutton's supper to self-awareness of the little sinnings and the little regrettings of complacent stupidity—yet he sounded the trumpet-call of God. World and soul—the conflict eternal—and what part did he play in it now but that of renegade ?

Conflict—was it indeed unescapable ? Day at spring and the morning flaunting vermeil up from Mesopotamia, the calling of young goats in little fields, the touch of vellum under his hand— must his soul hate these to reach to God and peace ?

How else? So, not his alone, but every Faith since the world's beginning had affirmed. How else reach to that serenity when these things would crumble to dust in his sight and the Stranger come welcome and bidden? Instead—instead as now these things that tore at his heart like loved children lost in a forest at night. . . .

' *What shall it profit a man though he gain the whole world and lose his own soul?* '

He groaned and laid his face in his hands again, and the crumbling centuries leave uncrumbling question and naked agony alike in that morning seven hundred years put by. Below: the morning he might not look at, lest he cower from answering himself. Below——

Below rose the ringing clatter of a halted horse. A moment later the tower stairway rang yet again under hasting feet. Then the door was flung open and Amima stood fronting him, impatient, flushed, exultant.

' Father—we have caught the thief! No bear, but a man. Father, it is the escaped monk Petros Ishay! '

V

He was waiting, bound, in the courtyard, the three Nestorian villagers warily at hand. They sought as little contamination as seemed needful. Petros Ishay—the rebel monk of Mevr, who had assaulted its venerable abbot, resisted and almost slain three of its lay brothers who had sought to arrest him, and then broken from the monastery walls and disappeared into the hills. . . . News of him had travelled far and wide from Mevr, and with a stern curiosity the Bishop looked on this wolf of God. The wolf, bound, yet upright, returned his gaze with a nonchalant insolence—the nonchalant insolence of a boy.

He was little more, as Nerses realised in wonder; tall and young, with a clearer eye and a broader brow than was wont to companion criminality, with the pale face of privation and the rags of much mountain-wandering. He stood with uncovered head and after a moment, unfrightened, uninterested, looked away from the Bishop's face across the changing fields in sunshine to the far mountains shining their unmelted snows.

'You are the monk Petros?'

'I am Eskandar Eremie.'

The Bishop was patient. 'You are a Nestorian, who entered the Monastery of Mevr as a novice and there received the name of Petros?'

'Some such clownish rechristening I underwent.'

'You broke the rules of your order and assaulted your abbot to the danger of his life?'

'To no such danger—he is a corpse already. Always, I should think, he has been a corpse——'

He ceased abruptly, turning his head. It was at the sound of a blackbird whistling in the greenery of a terebinth. The anger of the old priest-historian of Alarlu kindled a little, as he confesses, at that fresh defiance.

'In a land which is under no law there is no secular power. That we of the Church take now upon ourselves. To-morrow a party will take you across the hills to the monastery. There are cells there where they may curb your insolence.'

'I doubt it.'

The Bishop made an impatient gesture to the peasants to lead the boy away. And then that happened which he was afterwards to remember in detail. The prisoner, turning, halted, looking over his shoulder. The Bishop himself turned then, with the slowness of the years that had come so swiftly upon him dragging at his feet. He looked where the prisoner looked.

Amima stood in the palace doorway, whip in hand, the black hair blown in little tendrils across her cheek, still in her unseemly hunting-garb, her young, grey eyes on the renegade monk. Contempt and curiosity her eyes had held, but now, slowly, that look changed, as one gazing on a face lost and forgotten and remembered. A strange pallor came on brow and cheek. Nerses glanced back at the prisoner.

Insolent? Bent on Amima his was again that strange, dreaming gaze that had come on him when the blackbird whistled in the terebinth.

VI

The Bishop shrugged aside monk and insolence and the whole irrelevant episode. That afternoon he went out and paced the paths amid the dyked millet fields, where his Nestorians toiled in long, back-bent rows and the smell of the tended earth rose ammoniac in his nostrils. So slowly now he walked—he who had been wont to cross and re-cross the plateau in hasting meditation on a single phrase or curlicue of his Chronicle! Children ran and tumbled in the paths, smiling up at him shyly as he blessed them, absently, with extended fingers and gaze remote. Not alone his child, but these children—all the folk of Alarlu—how would they fare when he had gone?

Was it his concern? His soul his concern, the orders Religious cried, for him the humbling peni-tence of self. So Eidon would have said—Eidon intent on refuge in that monastery from which the monk Petros had fled. . . .

If he himself went with Eidon? Out across the hills to Mevr, behind the shelter of its stern walls to await that end that now came so swiftly? Fear and love and hope and the smell of the earth— these to brush aside as evil phantasmata the while in darkness and prayer he climbed with faltering steps and naked soul up the stairway of everlasting salvation——

How heavy hung the dates this harvest! . . .

He found Amima awaiting him on his return.

'Father, we have locked Eskandar Eremie in the cellar——'

'Whom? . . . Ah, the monk Petros.'

'But he is no longer a monk. And he sent for

me as you had gone to the fields. He asks that he
may be chained all night in the courtyard, in the
open air, not under the ground.'

Nerses paused to consider this. 'Now what is
in the mind of the renegade?'

'Renegade?' He was aware, surprised, of a
doubting disbelief in Amima's face. She flushed
and looked away from him, impatiently. 'We do
not know. We had heard only the story of the
abbot.'

'And you have heard the other story?'

His query, one guesses, was too gentle for her to
find in it the offence she was prone, in youth and
quick temper, to imagine and challenge so readily.
She turned back to him.

'O father, we do not know! He was a prisoner,
there in Mevr. He was a boy when the monastery
took him; he did not know what it would be—
prison and silence and his life ended——'

'So to avenge his own inconstancy he sought to
end the life of the abbot?'

'That was a lie. The abbot beats the monks——'

'So would he beat me were I a monk. Could
not this Petros submit to the common discipline?'

'The abbot was beating another monk—an old
man whose screams were ringing through the
monastery. And Eskandar but took the whip from
the abbot.'

It rang with a certain truth. But the Bishop was
weary. So readily he wearied these days!

'Let be, let be! Had you no other task than

listen to the tales of a monastery criminal? Send to me Eidon, Amima. Now it is too late to return the renegade to Mevr to-morrow. But the day after——'

VII

Looking out from his evening meal, eaten alone as the shadows fell, the Bishop saw in the court-yard the figure of a man who stood looking sky-wards with such intensity that Nerses raised his own eyes. On the red roofs of Alarlu grew and changed a garden of unearthly blooms : Flowers of gold and flowers of fire sprang and blossomed and died and merged at last in one great blossoming western glow as the night rose impatient in the east. . . . In the courtyard was a muffled clink of metal. Nerses lowered his eyes and saw that the sky-gazer had moved. Reaching out to his bell, a little Buddhist bell, worn and far-travelled and clear-toned, the Bishop rang it and sent for Amima.

'By whose authority was the monk Petros chained in the courtyard?'

'By mine, father. Surely he was long enough robbed of air and starshine in Mevr? He says there are no trees there in the monastery—no trees!—and the walls so thick——'

'What he says is no matter. You will not speak with him again. You understand?'

She stood half in darkness, for the room was now flooded with shadows. He heard her breathing quicken, and sighed for the loveliness of that sound in a body that was young and passionate and rebellious. The loveliness of youth, its sleep and wakenings, its world that was there so fresh to mould beneath its impatient fingers! He said again, albeit wearily and half-idly, 'You understand?'

She said, low-voiced, but with an unwonted intensity in her voice:

'I understand. . . . Yes, I think—at last I understand.'

VIII

He sat thinking of her then when she had slipped away like a shadow from the room that the shadows had now made their own. What should he do with her?—he could not leave her in Alarlu when he had passed from it. Better some nunnery—if one unsacked were still to be found—that would quench her pride and impatience and mould her soul to God than leave her to the wild chances of these years and lands. A nunnery—that was the solution when he himself went into Mevr, behind those walls where the light of day never penetrated, where renegades dreamt of the starshine and the whistling of black-birds in a terebinth——

Eidon came to him then, returned from the far end of the plateau.

'You sent for me, Lord Bishop? Shall I bring a lamp?'

A faint waft of irony from other years tinged the Bishop's speech. 'You bring one in yourself, my

Eidon. Sit with me. Now, this is what I plan to do : You may retire to Mevr in a fortnight's time. . . . And I retire to it also.'

' Thou ? ' The intimate address was startled to Eidon's lips. The Bishop nodded, trying not to look from the window at the night that came, soft-footed, to listen.

' I also—and with better need than you, Eidon. To-night and to-morrow I will write letters to the Patriarch, and the day after to-morrow they must be despatched with the company which carries the monk Petros back to Mevr. See you to it. Within two weeks at least our successors should be in Alarlu.'

The chaplain flung himself on his knees, podgily, to kiss his Bishop's hand. His face glowed with approbation.

' My lord, this retiral of yours, honouring mine— it will be a call and a challenge to every Christian man ! '

The old historian moved uneasily, his eyes drawn unescapably at last to the night-stilled fields beyond the palace windows. Harvest so close. How better might the grain be stacked this winter against the storms that had half-destroyed the last ? . . . ' Eh ? I fear I was dreaming, my Eidon, and did not hear. And now I would be alone. Yet, stay——'

The chaplain had risen to his feet. He stood waiting on that last word, unaware of the impulse that had brought it to the lips of Nerses. Alone ? So soon he would be alone for ever that surely he might snatch for a little while at speech and hearing and the nearness of another. . . . The impulse died away. Eidon ! This careful soul so husbanding his soul ! What comfort was in him ?

' You may go.'

IX

And through that night, prisoned and sleepless, two watched the circling stars from the palace of Alarlu. In the courtyard Nerses would hear the chink of chain-links as the monk Petros moved and rose to his feet and prowled softly the length of his chains. Once, rising from penning a note on the nunneries to which he might send Amima, the Bishop went to the window and looked out and saw the prisoner, his white, boy's face upturned in the white radiance of the moon, standing rigid while far down the plateau-ravines some night-bird called in the darkness. . . . Sleepless as himself, the renegade, and with better cause. For was not his own future of prayer and silence and unlingering death assured enough—while punishment and stripes and long, grey years of expiation awaited the boy ?

But spite those assured to-morrows of his and the weariness that lay heavily upon him, sleep came hardly at all to the Bishop even when he had retired to another courtyard chamber. Dozing uneasily, he fell into a dream that soft footsteps passed and repassed his door in the darkness, that out in the night voices whispered and wept and were glad—

Love and the Stranger kissing one the other in the darkness that he had feared! . . . He coughed redly, wakening from that, and far off hearing some startled pony neigh in the stables of Alarlu.

Near morning, gasping for breath in the darkness that precedes the dawn, he found himself at the window again. The courtyard lay pitch-black below; Alarlu slept under the white kindling of the morning star. In the air was the soft sighing of the dawn-wind—that sound he had known in so many mornings, known and loved while he raised his eyes, surprised, from crowded pages, and planned a mind-clearing gallop with his bow in the reaches of the foothills!

And now, as the light grew, his eyes went down to the courtyard again, idly, tiredly. But the idleness presently kindled to keenness. He leaned and peered closely from the window into that pit of shadows now faintly suffused with the morning's fore-radiance. It was a plain and open space, lacking in alcove or shadowing balcony. There was no concealment possible there.

The Bishop caught up the Buddhist bell and sent its clangour through the sleeping episcopal palace of Alarlu. Petros, the renegade monk who called himself Eskandar Eremie, had disappeared.

X

Eidon the chaplain it was who roused the palace. Nor it only. In a few moments the village itself

echoed with the calling of tidings and commands·
Parties of the Nestorians set out, running swiftly
to the confines of the plateau to intercept the
fugitive. Nerses went back to his couch and
there waited for the news of the renegade's
recapture.

So might he have remained, but that a servant
burst in upon him excitedly.

'The Lady Amima—her room is empty! It is
feared that the monk——'

The same fear gripped the old Bishop, white-
faced, struggling to his feet. He called for his pony
and with Eidon and half a dozen others galloped
to the crest of the main ravine that led down to
the plain. There one of the Nestorian peasants, on
the scene a moment before, gestured to him eagerly.

'See there, my lord!'

The Bishop saw. The fugitive and his hostage,
both mounted, were but half-way down the gorge,
evidently unsuspecting of pursuit thus early. Two
of Nerses' party had bows. At a sign from the
Bishop they strung them, then the pursuit clattered
down the pass.

The renegade and his prisoner heard and turned
their heads. Eskandar beat his pony into action;
uncomprehending, the Bishop saw Amima do the
same. But Eidon's thin cry echoed down the
morning in warning menace.

'Stay! You are within bow-shot!'

They reined in at that, and half-wheeled round.
It was scarcely yet full light, but the Bishop saw

on the face of the boy the sudden ferocity of a
trapped animal. He reached down to the stolen
scimitar at his saddle-bow, but Amima's hand fore-
stalled him—gently and easily enough, it seemed.
She leant towards him, seeming to whisper something, her hand still in his. So, in that strange
attitude, they fronted the Bishop's party. Eidon
gestured forward the ready bowmen.

'So you would have added abduction to your
other crimes, renegade ? '

Amima rises clearly enough then through the
mists of the years, young and scornful as she faced
her rescuers, trembling like a plucked bowstring,
her hand yet clasped in that of the renegade
monk.

'Abduction ? Fool, it was I who freed him and
go with him willingly.'

'Amima ! '

She blanched a little at her father's voice, at
sight of the horror on his face. Then the quick
blood flooded her cheeks.

'So it is, my father. Eskandar is mine though
you kill him now or send him back to Mevr to be
done to death. He's mine for ever, though you
prison me also among the unliving of a nunnery—
as you have planned to do.'

Nerses started, remembering those notes that
had lain all night in his tower-chamber, remembering a dream of hovering footsteps in the darkness.
The bowmen closed in about Eskandar and one
of them drew a knife. The renegade smiled at

them, at Nerses, at the plump white righteousness
of Eidon.

' So now you kill me, priests, and carry the story
to the aching abbot of Mevr ? May it soothe his
unquiet hide ! And tell him I sent a message :
that I lost the monastery——' his eyes went to the
plateau heights, tinted with amethyst, to the face of
Amima, ' —and gained the world.'

Eidon thrust forward a blazing, fanatic face,
the phrase that had haunted Nerses on his lips.
' What shall it profit a man, O renegade, though
he gain the whole world and lose his own
soul ? '

' O eunuch who has never known the world ! '
The boy's dreaming face could blaze with another
faith. ' *What shall it profit a man if he gain his own
soul and lose the whole world?* Have I not known ?
Soul—the world's essence and fragrance as each
man distils it ! . . . I went into Mevr with a living,
troubled soul ; I lost it there, a blinded beast. I
came out and sheltered in holes like a fox and stood
chained in a courtyard—and found my soul again.
. . . Kill me now, then. Amima, turn you
away.'

But Amima, sitting white-faced while the renegade spoke, had seen the strangest changings in
the face of Nerses. She spurred forward her
pony and dismounted and knelt by the Bishop's
stirrup.

' Father ! *You* know, *you* understand Eskandar's
truth. . . . Father, I know ! And I love him—

and oh, we are out to see strange lands together !
You will let us go ? '

XI

Before the Bishop's eyes, surgent, unfaltering, the
dawn. Light in a flow of foam swept up from the
dun deserts of Iraq. Tern cried above them in lost
mountain pools, and the morning wind went out
from Alarlu into places as yet untouched by
the sunrise. Eidon made an impatient motion to the
bowmen.

' Bind the renegade.'

' Stay.'

All waited. The boy's face turned towards
the Bishop, wonder in the dreaming, defiant
eyes. Amima gazed at him with trembling lips.
Serene of soul at last in the wild heresy heard
on the lips of a renegade monk, the Bishop
motioned to the desert track where the sunlight
flowed.

' Your road.'

' Father ! '

Gladness and tears in the cry. But he did not
look at her, for strength had come with serenity.
Peace was his, as yet in the world's strife that shaped
their souls it would be theirs. Love whom he had
known, the Stranger whose face he had scarcely
glimpsed—they rode out of his life together. But
they would return. Might his heart weep its farewells when not a thing that passed from the earth

but knew again, far off, some day, some season, a morning that again cried ' Ave ! '

He pointed again to the desert road, and turned away his eyes, and heard them depart. And far above the plateau of Alarlu the banners of the sunrise marched their undying quest across the sky.

FELICITER

EGYPTIAN NIGHTS

I

L'Allegro

AMBER IN COLD SEA

I

*C*AIRO. *Outside the café awning the noon-blaze of the sun in the Place of the Green Step was almost liquid. A sakkah, his dripping goatskin slung on his back, slouched through the dust. Then a string of donkeys. A Ford car. A gendarme, with carbine and tarbouche, came loitering along the middle of the street. The trees of the Esbekieh Gardens lifted their branches to peer over the roof-tops towards us, or to gaze in vegetal surprise at the windows of Sednaoui's great clothing emporium opposite, where flaunted great notices of the delectable* mise-en-vente *within. My eyes blinked in the sunlight shimmer.*

A car hooted in the distance. Sergei Lubow, grinning with up-curling moustaches, fluttered the last leaf of my latest story, and chuckled.

'And *this* is life to the modern wise? A love-story—this drabness! Ah God, I prefer your out-moded Swinburne. "The Leper." You have read it? It goes so——'

'My nurse used to sing me to sleep with it.'

'So? And sleeping you dreamt such nightmare as this—realism?'

Sergei paused. The car heard in distance had drawn up opposite Sednaoui's with a scattering of liquid sunshine and powdered sand. A man got out, helping a veiled woman to alight. He did it ceremoniously, as might an old-time bridegroom his bride, and then turned to give some order to the driver. As he did so he caught Sergei's eye. So did the veiled woman. Both of them nodded, hesitated, glancing at me, and then turned and passed in through the swinging doors of Sednaoui's. I interrogated Sergei.

'Clients ? Newly married tourists ? '

He disregarded the question. He chuckled again. His eyes came back from the car and rested on me. My magazine on the table crumpled under the sudden impact of his elbow.

'A story.'

'Eh ? '

'A story for you. A fairy-tale.' Still seeming obscurely amused, he consulted his wrist-watch. 'A quarter of an hour of a story. The story of a romantic. The story of Gavril Dan.'

II

It is ten years (said Sergei) since I met the little Dan on the Krimea side of the Sivash Boloto. The Reds had driven the last White army into the Peninsula. Snow fell, it was very dark and cold that night. Because our men were weary and mutinous Andrei Bal'mont and I walked sentry, growing hungrier and hungrier with the passing hours, and chill with sleet and sadness. Over beyond the northern marshes we could see Perekop ;

all the northern horizon was specked with the lights of the Red Army besieging Perekop. The little thin autumn wind, the veter, screamed overhead, and sometimes died away for a moment so that the sound of the bombardment would deafen the marshes. Once that sound seemed drawing nearer. Bal'mont went into the night to investigate. I never saw him again.

Towards midnight I went back to the White lines and discovered that my troop had deserted *en masse*. I turned about at that discovery and set out to cross the Sivash to Perekop. But before I regained even the track of my sentry-beat a man staggered out of the snow-whirl and the front-ward darkness, mad and singing and waving a knife.

' Comrade, I will cut your throat ! '

He waved the knife foolishly and then fell at my feet. I peered down at him, seeking for light enough to shoot him, when suddenly the guns pounding the life out of Perekop rose into such clamour as threatened to crack the night. I raised my head and saw the threat fulfilled. The night cracked. It split apart, it and the horizon there in the north, in two great red-specked segments. The tovarishi had blown up the French-built fortress. . . .

III

I knew it was the end. Being a little dazed, and still seeking a good light in which to shoot him, I picked up the foolish man and walked away south-wards towards Dzhonkai. Presently behind us arose a great screaming and shouting and the sound of galloping horses. It was the Red cavalry crossing the marshes on the track of fugitives. But they missed us and passed unseen. None sought to stay our going except one straggler on foot, who suddenly appeared on the path, obtruding out of the darkness a bulging stomach, a cloth helmet, and a querulous revolver. Without questioning his purpose or political creed I kicked him hard in the stomach, into the night, and out of this story. Then we went on.

All that night it snowed. Our leader fled like a hare to Sebastopol and took ship to Stamboul. Our army followed at the excellent pace. I myself would have run as fast as any, but that the foolish man with the knife was weak and exhausted. For a fortnight, abandoning thoughts of Dzhonkai, we crept towards Kerch, hiding in hay-ricks and barns in the day-time, holding by the frost-rimed stars at night. Kerch illumined the southern darkness one night, and we reached the quays.

There a fishing sloop of eclectic opinions still lingered, sniped at from the shore and sniping in reply. I asserted in the loud voice that I was a Sovyet kommissar going to Stamboul. The captain took me on board, and instantly became a secret White. Still he waited outside Kerch, taking aboard other refugees, hoping that these would kill me.

While we waited there in alternate storms of sleet and snow, with the heaving of the Black Sea tides greening the faces of exhausted refugees, the foolish man with the knife, being by then a little less mad, babbled many things. He was Gavril Dan, an engineer of Melitopol, who had hated Reds and Whites, and manufactured motor-cars and loved his wife. When Budenni's cavalry came to Melitopol he was absent at Bero ; when he returned the tovarishi were abolishing God, parcelling out the motor-cars and women, and firing the town. The little Dan found his house in ruins and its doorstep much bemessed with blood and the rags of a dress which had once been his wife's.

So he had gone mad, and borrowing a revolver and a knife from a fellow-citizen who had for ever ceased to impassion himself in defence of private property—his head being permanently jammed in a drain-pipe—he had shot quite a number of the tovarishi and been chased out of the town by a company of enthusiastic, but fortunately inebriated, riflemen. These on his heels, he had strayed southward, raving of his lost Irina, whose soul was either in heaven or her body in hell. Being dark he had missed the besieging lines, wandered across the frozen Sivash Boloto ahead of the Reds, mistaken me for a tovarish, and——

IV

This was the tale the mad little Dan told me while we waited for the fishing sloop to leave Kerch. All this while White refugees—soldiers and sailors, merchants and peasants, beggars and boyars—crowded on board. Towards the end of the second day the good people of Kerch, suddenly converted to Communism with the appearance of a troop of Red cavalry on the skyline, turned a machine-gun on us from the shore.

The captain, very angry, pulled at the sails. The little Dan and I flung ourselves flat on the deck. The sloop began to move out into the pounding rollers of the Black Sea. Just then a last boat put out from the shore.

In it sat a man with clothes much travel-stained, and head and face be-bandaged. Rowing the boat was a girl, who ducked now and then to escape the bullets of the Marxian converts. Our ship moved so fast that it seemed they could hardly make it in time. But we waved to the girl, urging her on, and she caught a rope I flung to her, and we drew them on board with the last of the light, and faced to the darkness for Stamboul.

There was no food on board, but the girl who had come with the bandaged man—her name was Darya Martov—and I boiled much water, which everyone drank. It was an unmirthful voyage in bitter winter hours. Even the White generals on board ceased to dispute how they would divide our

little Russia when all the Reds were dead or repent-
ant. The little Dan would sit on the deck, staring
at the black coast-line, sick at heart with memory
of that Melitopol doorstep. Beside him Vasil
Ferapont, the bandaged man whom Darya had
brought, would lie and whisper like a hoarse ghost,
for the roof of his mouth was gone. He had been
through the Perekop explosion, this Ferapont,
Darya told me while we boiled the water ; he had
strayed, maimed and bleeding, into her house in
mid-Krimea while she herself was preparing to hide
before the Reds came. So she had bandaged him
and loved him and fled with him. . . .

She did not tell me she loved him, but at night,
when the Black Sea sleet smote the crowded ship,
they would lie on deck in each other's arms, and
Ferapont would whisper and mumble in his sleep,
and Darya rouse to soothe him and tuck their
ragged blanket more tightly about him. Pitiful
to see. Hateful to see. Beside them the little Dan,
who from the first had liked Ferapont as much as I
detested him, would sit and stare at them and brood
on the night and sea and his lost Irina. But I,
because I might not bear to look on them, would go
and boil more water.

After weary days—four of them, I think, though
I lost count because of the drifting we had in a storm,
and a time when a Sovyet gunboat chased us through
hours of driving mist—we came past Therapia to
the Corne d'Or, and by the landing-stage the little
Darya, with the sea-rain in her hair, held up her

face for me to kiss her farewell, the while Ferapont, blind and bandaged, stood near, whispering to Dan. It is only our custom, this kiss, but I thought of the lips of Ferapont, and turned away, like the fool I was. Her eyes grew troubled.

' What is the matter, Sergei Nikitich ? '

' Nothing,' I said. And then : ' Where will you go now ? '

' To Cairo. There are many Russians in Egypt, and Vasil and I have only enough money to take us so far.'

Now, having some French money, I had given half of it to Dan on the boat, and we had agreed to go together to Cairo. Darya's words sent a sad-glad ache through me.

' Then we do not part. The little Gavril and I go there also.'

She seemed but little surprised, yet looked at me with such gladness that I felt foolishly happy until I heard behind us the ghost-whispering of Ferapont. I nodded back towards him.

' You love Ferapont ? You will marry him ? '

Her face grew so tender and sad as no face of woman had ever grown for me. ' Love him— yes. But we may not marry. He—he is married already.'

So, after many delays and the unpadded journey-ings on cheap coasting steamers, we came to Cairo. At Manchiet el Sadr, in the Street of the Five Black Cats, Darya and Ferapont rented a room, and the

little Dan and I another on the opposite side of the
street. Then, all our francs being gone, we looked
for work.

v

Within a week the little Dan, who, though mad,
knew much of motor-cars, had employment in the
workshops of a great French garage, and Darya
was sewing white sun-dresses at the slave-rate of
three a piastre. Only Ferapont and I were idle—he
because it seemed he could do no work, I because
I could not find it.

Ah, God, it is a city of languages, this. Babel
Tower, I thought in despair those first days, must
here have been builded and the builders never
departed. And languages had been my only trade
in the days before the Revolution—the days when
I had taught in the Gymnasium of Kazan. No
school—and I tramped the miles of them between
Shoubra and Heliopolis—hungered to hear me
impart the French or English colloquialisms with
an authentic Russian accent. Almost I had des-
paired, and would have bought the tray of postcards
and ribbons and paraded the Esbekich Garden as a
hawker, when an old-time colleague of mine, one
Anton Saloney, by then a dragoman, came to my
aid and inducted me as the neophyte to his new
profession.

So I, Sergei Lubow, sometime Grand Prix of
Leipzig, became what I have been ever since—a
dragoman, guiding parties of sun-hatted tourists

to the Sphinx, of which I knew nothing, and to the Pyramids, of which I knew less, and to Citadel, of which I desired to know nothing. I spent my days chartering donkeys and arranging time-tables, hiring arabiyehs and holding sunshades. Within three weeks I had wandered as far afield as Memphis and Heluan, expounding at each locality incidents of such history as it seemed to me seemly for the ancient Egyptians to have possessed. I became a favourite because I knew so much.

February then. At the Manchiet the little Dan and I still lived in our one room. Though with better cause, seeing it had been his original work, he was proving as satisfactory a motor-maker as I a dragoman. Yet still he remained the man obsessed by that awful memory of the blood-specked doorway in Melitopol. It might have passed in time but for the new belief that grew in him—the belief that Irina was still alive ; that, lost as himself, she was wandering and seeking him. . . .

Spectator there, on the fringe of his life, I watched this common and commonplace little man transform into monomaniac. The type common enough he had been, I guessed—the commonplace man who had possessed a beautiful wife, whose pride in that wife's beauty had been a property instinct, though he had believed it love. Something of her character also it seemed to me I glimpsed—one who had loved him, but a little aloofly, perhaps always with a little of heartache because of the shallow depths from which his eyes had looked their pride at her. . . .

VI

The little Dan! The common man whom not I alone had viewed with the gaze of the purblind realist! A sleepy gaze often enough those days and nights. For under pressure of the fantastic belief that his Irina still lived and sought him he had turned again to his early faith. Hour-long at night he would kneel before a Coptic ikon; often in a morning I would find him stretched cramped and asleep in front of that ikon. Wearied with long trampings across the Ghizeh sands, I would fall asleep in the midst of his devotions and be bitten awake by mosquitoes, hours later, and find him still kneeling.

It palled in time. There is no pool of sympathy but dries in the parch-glare of unceasing pain. This wife of his—if not dead, she must be praying to be.

'I know she is alive,' he would aver. 'I can't lie down to sleep but I know it—terribly, in the stillness. I can't talk with our Russian friends here in Cairo, but it seems, in a moment, if they grew silent, I'd hear her speak. . . . And once, one night on that Black Sea boat——'

He would stare at me, white-faced. 'I heard her weeping in the darkness.'

I would yawn with sleep. 'How did you know it was she who wept?'

'Know? Have I not heard her weep before? . . . Long before, the moment of shame to me. Wept— as though God had died—once——'

I would turn to the wall and try to sleep. Love—
to be remembered by its tears! Love, with its
servitude to pain——

For I had grown to hate the bandaged, whispering
Ferapont those days. We went to see him and Darya
each evening, the little Dan and I, and the maimed
man would sit on the bed and whisper while Darya
crouched by the window and sewed and sewed till
her bright eyes grew red and strained in the failing
light. Her lips had taken to droop sadly at each
corner, and one night, seeing that strained tiredness
of her face, I turned on Ferapont in anger, asking
him how long he required a slave as well as a
mistress.

At that the little Gavril cried out at me and there
was the unpleasant scene, and Ferapont stared
through his bandages and whispered, whispered.
Only Darya said nothing, but sewed on in the dim
light with dim eyes. She looked up at me with
quivering lips as I rose to go, and down at the foot
of the railless stone stairs, standing there hesitating
in the swift Cairene twilight, I heard her come
behind me. She was weeping openly then, but I
looked at her with a dead heart.

'You are cruel—cruel, and you've lied, Sergei
Nikitich.'

'Lied? When all the Manchiet knows! Is it
not true that you slave for this bandaged fool, that
you are his mistress?'

She ceased to weep and began to laugh, weeping
and laughing in the same moment, so that I thought

it hysteria. Then she ceased from that, sobering to determination. She laid her hands on my shoulders.

'Look at me, Sergei. You believe—*that?*'

Believe it? I knew it. And I looked down into the laughing misery of her eyes, and felt sick at heart, and kissed her hands, and lied to her.

'No, I do not believe it,' I said.

And, ah! I hated Ferapont!

That same night—it was the eve of Easter Day—the little Dan awoke me, crying out in nightmare and getting up from his bed. Irina, his Irina, she was alive—calling for him, out there in the night. He would go to her.

He made for the door. But I caught him and held him and put him back in bed, bored and wearied of this lunacy. Then I waited until he seemed to sleep again. But it was only the seeming. At intervals all through the night he started up with mad eyes, raving the name of his wife in such voice that I doubted if ever the usual morning sanity would come on him again. In the street below, as I noted with sleep-heavy eyes, the moonlight lay white like ghost-snow, and across, in the room of Darya and Ferapont, a light still burned, and a shadow sometimes moved swiftly or stood blackly against that light. I knew it for Darya tending her sick lover, and my night was the longer for the knowledge.

VII

Easter Day.   But the spring's trumpets blow not in Cairo, and by noon it was eighty-five in the shade. The little Dan, by then a foreman and favourite at his workshop, had planned to drive the four of us down to Memphis and its sights and the coolness of the Nile that afternoon, in a car lent him by his company.   In spite his night of sleepless raving, he went off to his workshop, and by two o'clock I heard the horn of his car sound in the street below our room.   I went down and looked at him—the cool and efficient driver, the haggard-faced monomaniac.

'You had better go to bed,' I told him.

He shook his head, staring beyond me.   'It is so strange.   Last Easter Irina——'

But I had had enough of Irina.   I ran up the stairs to the room of Ferapont and Darya, and entered, to find Darya weeping again, very silently, while Ferapont stood with his back to her, fumbling with the loosened bandages about his head.   Ferapont again . . .

Darya tried to stop me, but I put her aside. I caught him by the shoulder and swung him round, and then stopped in my half-intention, and stared at him. . . . What wounds indeed could have required all those months to heal?

'You cheat,' I said.

He moaned and staggered, as though my light grip on his shoulder was a hurtful thing.   I dropped him on the bed, and then, in a revulsion from anger to wondering contempt, heard myself apologise to him. I would have retied his bandages for him, but he pushed me away, pettishly, and Darya came to his help, and I turned and left them.

Gavril had sounded his klaxon more than once before they descended to the street. They got into the car and I took the wheel and drove. Presently we were clear of Cairo, the rushing air tempering the heat, and I saw that the little Dan had fallen asleep. Once I glanced back into the seat behind me. Darya had her arm round Ferapont, and he had leant his head against her, and was fast asleep as Dan.

At Memphis I parked the car and we got out and tramped amidst the stones the while I acted the dragoman, and Ferapont whispered his wonder, and Dan stared about him dully, and Darya's tired eyes brightened with interest. But it was very hot. I turned my party about.

' We will go to the Whispering Cave,' I said.

VIII

The old sheykh of the cave knew me, and let us enter alone with a candle. It was hardly yet the show place it now is, and quite deserted, the ancient tomb that Arab grave-robbers had broken into and villagers spoiled for stones with which to line their dykes. The wind-currents played with our candle flame the while I upraised my arm to show the wall-paintings on either side the entrance, and the petrified boastings of the ancient dead further within the corridors. Dan wandered away a little in the region of shadows, while Ferapont lagged behind. At the entrance to the Whispering Corridor itself Dan, a little ahead of us, stopped and called to me.

'There are other people here. Listen.'

The place was filled with innumerable faint patterings and whisperings. I had shown it to many a tourist, and in the moment was droning my dragoman jargon.

'The sounds are caused by wind-currents playing through cracks in the cave-wall. But the natives call it the Corridor of Lost Voices. If you listen long enough you will hear your dead speaking here, they say——'

I stopped, and to myself cursed myself as a fool. 'We had better go back, I think. The draughts will blow out the candle in a moment——'

The candle went out.

I felt in my pocket for matches, calling to Dan and Ferapont to stand still until there was light again. But in that moment in the darkness I touched Darya, who was standing near me, and I forgot them.

I took her in my arms. She did not resist me, but put her own arms round my neck, and kissed me. So for a moment we stood, kissing, till a strange sound made us stop and listen.   And then, with memory of the little Dan's babblings, the blood grew cold about my heart.

Far off it sounded, at first, then came nearer, awful, unmistakable in the darkness—the sound of a woman sobbing, drearily, heart-brokenly.   I gripped Darya and shuddered, heard Gavril cry out, heard him rush past us, heard the sound of someone fall. . . . Then, after a long silence, the noise of stumblings towards the entrance.

I took Darya's hand and tried to run also.   But she held me back, speaking urgently, wildly.   I thought her more frightened than myself, and put my arms about her again.

'Listen, Sergei.   No, I'm not mad. . . . We followed you to Egypt when we heard you and Gavril on the Black Sea boat plan to come here. We tried to be near you, yet she would not tell him —because. . . . Oh, if he does not love her still ! She fled to Perekop from the tovarishi in Melitopol, and was maimed when the Reds blew up the French fortress, and I dressed her in a man's clothes when she came to me, because she could not bear ever to seem a woman again—after Melitopol. . . . How much can a man understand, how much can he love ? '

' Sh ! ' I held her very close.   My brain whirled. ' Ferapont ! ' I called through the blackness. Nothing but echoes.   Darya shook me in impatience.

' Don't you understand ?   Now Gavril does.

He caught her when she fell—he knew her sobbing.
. . . Don't you understand ?   Vasil is Irina, his
wife.'

IX

' And that was that, my friend.'
Sergei had finished.   I nodded.   ' There was an
almost similar case in China lately.   A Kwangsi
woman missionary and her husband. . . . I'd
guessed about Ferapont.   And it leaves me more
of a realist than ever.'
' Eh ? '
' Romantics, all of you, and with romantics'
luck.   Gavril Dan put Melitopol out of his mind,
no doubt—as a man can.   But if Ferapont's bandages had covered something real and hideous, if
they hadn't been just a disguise——'
' You think——? '   He was scarcely listening to
me.   He was scrawling idle pencil-words across
the top of my realist magazine-story.   I shrugged,
and glanced across at Sednaoui's.   So did Sergei.
' Watch.'
The little man and the veiled woman had come
out.   As she stepped into the shelter of the car the
woman drew aside her heavy veil——
I shuddered and turned away my eyes.   Sergei,
one hand on my shoulder, got to his feet.   He pushed
my magazine in front of me.
' The out-moded Swinburne—remember him ?
And now——'

He strode across the street towards Sednaoui's.
I looked after him, then turned to the looping
pencil-scrawl obliterating my realist story-title :

> Nothing is better, I well know,
>   Than love ; no amber in cold sea
> Or gathered berries under snow :
>   This was well seen of her and me.

II

Il Penseroso

REVOLT

I

BOOM! Hardly had the distant reverberations ceased before the sunset wind blew in the greenery of the city palms. It was as if Cairo sighed audibly. Day was officially dead. Crowned in red, squatting in the colours of the west, the Moqattam Hills peered down, perhaps to glimpse a miraculous moment on the surface of the Nile.

The Nile flowed red like a river of blood.

Rejeb ibn Saud, squatting in the Bulaq hut by the Nile bank, looked at his wrist-watch, at the face of the unconscious boy on the string-bed, at the fall of light on Gezireh across the river. But for one insistent whisper, the startling sunset was now a thing woven of silence.

'*The sea! The sea!*'

It was the whisper of the homing Nile. Gathering, hastening to fulfilment and freedom, joining its thousand voices, all the yearnings of its leagues of desert wandering, in that passionately whispered under-cry: '*The sea!*'

All that afternoon the cry had haunted him. Now, as the boy on the bed tossed and moaned, ibn Saud shook himself, stood up, and bent over the bed.

' Oh, Hassan . . .'

The hut door opened of a sudden. Out of the
sunset glare, into the dimness of the hut, Sayyiya,
ibn Saud's sister-in-law, entered. She was a Sudanese, young, full-faced, thick-lipped. At the tall
figure of ibn Saud she glanced enquiringly, then also
went to the bed and bent over it. The boy Hassan
seemed scarce to breathe.

' In an hour we shall know, master.'

' In an hour I shall not be here.' The man looked
away from the string-bed. The chill on his heart
had chilled his voice. Even at that moment, only
by an effort could he keep from listening to the
insistent whisper of the river.

' You go to the Khan Khalil to lead the Jihad ?
It is to-night ? '

Ibn Saud nodded. It was to-night. An hour
after the fall of darkness the Warren hordes, poured
into the Khan il Khalil, were to be mustered and
armed. Police and gendarmes, half of them active
adherents of the insurrection, would have with-
drawn from all western and central Cairo. The two
native regiments had been seduced from allegiance
to the puppet Nationalist Government : were
enthusiastically for the rising : themselves awaited
only the signal from the Khan il Khalil, the lighting
of the torch.

And it would be lit. That was to be Rejeb ibn
Saud's part. Golden-tongued, first in popularity
of the rising's masters, he was to be the last to
address the brown battalions in the Khan. For

them he was to strike fire to the torch that would, ere another morning, light the flames of vengeance and revolution across the European city from Bulaq to Heliopolis.

The song of the Nile—such the cry—of fulfilment, of freedom attained—that would to-night rise on the welling tide of the Black Warrens, from thousands of throats, from all the pitiful Cohorts of the Lost, the Cheated of the Sunlight . . .

' Master, if you come not back——'

Ibn Saud started. In his cold ecstasy he had forgotten the hut, Sayyiya, even Hassan.

' That is with God. But if Hassan—— Listen, woman. You will come to me at the Khan. When the change, one way or another, has passed upon my son, come to the Shoemakers' Bazaar, by the south side of the Khan, and send word to me. You will find your way ? '

' I will come.'

Something in her glance touched him, stirred him from his abstraction.

' The time has been weary for you since Edei died, Sayyiya. If I live through this night——'

Suddenly the woman was crouching at his feet on the mud floor. Passionately, scaredly, she caught at the long cloak he had wrapped about him.

' Master—Rejeb. . . . Those English whom you lead against to-night—they are ever strong, ever cunning. If you die, what will happen to Hassan and to me ? Master——'

Ibn Saud's cold eyes blazed. He flung the woman from him, flung open the hut door. Beyond, seen from the elevation of the Bulaq bank, the Cairene roofs lay chequered in shadows.

' And what of the folk—our brothers, our sisters—who die out there in their hovels and hunger ? Thousands every year.' He blazed with the sudden, white-hot anger of the fanatic. ' What matters your miserable life—Hassan's—mine—if we can show the sun to those who rot their lives away in the kennels of the Warrens ? We miserable " natives "—unclean things with unclean souls— to-night we shall light such a candle in Egypt as no man——'

He halted abruptly. The fire fell from him. Speaking in Arabic, he had yet thought in a famous alien phrase. Under his dark skin there spread a slow flush. Without further speech he bent and kissed his son, and then walked out of the hut into the wine-red gloaming.

Sayyiya crouched dazed upon the floor. Then a sound disturbed her. From the throat of the boy Hassan came a strange, strangled moan.

The small, fevered body tossed for a little, then lay very still.

II

Darkness was still an hour distant. European Cairo thronged her streets, cried her wares, wore her gayest frocks, set forth on evening excursions to

Saqqara and the Sphinx. John Caldon, seated on the terrace of the Continental, awoke from a sunset dream and turned towards his brother-in-law, Robert Sidgwick.

' Eh ? '

' . . . the edge of a volcano.'

' Where ? '

' There.' Sidgwick waved his hand to the brown driftage in the street below them. ' The political situation's the worst it has been for months. The Cairenes have been propaganda'ed for months by Nationalist extremists. Trade and employment are bad. The native quarters are seething.'

' Very proper of them.'

Caldon smiled into the lighting of a cigarette. An artist, he was making a westward world-tour from England. Together with his wife and daughter, he had arrived from India, via Suez, only the day before. Sidgwick's statement left him unimpressed. He had never yet encountered a white man, settled amongst brown, who was not living on the edge of a volcano. It was the correct place to live, just as it was the correct thing for a volcano to seethe pleasingly upon occasion.

Sidgwick had the monologue habit. Through the quiet air and the blue cloud from his own cigarette Caldon caught at a number of phrases.

' This damn self-government foolishness began it all. . . . Treat a native as a native.'

' Why not as a human being ? '

' That's what we've done here. Look at the result.'

Caldon was boredly ironical. ' Self-government —with an army of occupation ! An alarum-clock with the alarum taken away ! '

' It's advisable—if you give it to a native. . . . Take it my sister's never told you about young Thomas O'Donnell ? '

Caldon shook his head. Sidgwick nodded, without pleasantness.

' Well, the telling won't hurt you. He was a half-caste—an Irish-Sudanese, of all grotesque mixtures. His father had had him sent to a school in Alexandria ; some kind of irrigation engineer out here the father was, and pious to boot. He died when his son was seventeen, leaving instructions for the latter to be sent to a theological college in England to train as a missionary. All very right and proper. To England young Thomas O'Donnell came. To Bleckingham.'

Caldon, with some little show of interest, nodded. Sidgwick resumed.

' You know—though your people didn't settle in Bleckingham till about a year after the time of O'Donnell—the lost tribes the Theological College spates over the country-side to tea and tennis on spare afternoons ? One of these tennis-do's I met O'Donnell. He was a tall, personable nigger— not black, of course. Cream-colour. But it wouldn't have worried me in those days if charcoal had made a white mark on him. He was interesting. I liked him, invited him to tea. Clare was young also, in those days, you'll have to remember.'

'Why?' A tinge of red had come on the artist's cheekbones.

'Oh, Cæsar's wife is stainless enough. But a young girl hardly knows herself—or the stuff she handles. Had it been a white man, of course . . .

'Yes, Clare became fairly intimate with O'Donnell. Flirted with him, no doubt. Mother was then the same invalid as you knew ; I was supposed to be my sister's protector. But I suffered from attempting the assimilation of indigestible theories on the brotherhood of man. I admired O'Donnell. Oh, he fascinated.'

The light all down the Sharia Kamil had softened. Caldon sat rigid. It was Sidgwick who dreamt now.

'The outcome of it all was what I'd expect now. O'Donnell and Clare went picnicking on Bewlay Tor. . . . The nigger attempted to act according to his nature. Clare's screams saved her—attracted some students mountaineering. O'Donnell went berserk amongst them. You see, he wasn't a white man.'

'What happened to him?'

'God knows. He didn't wait to be kicked out of the College. They traced him as far as Southampton, where it was supposed he'd managed to get a job on board some ship. . . . Hallo, here's Clare. Good Lord, what's the——'

A woman was running up the steps from the taxi which had stopped below the terrace—a woman with a white, scared face. Behind her, weeping, came trailingly the ayah of Caldon's daughter.

' Jack, Jack ! . . . Little Clare—we lost her down in the bazaars, in the horrible Warrens. Jack —they stoned us when we tried to find her. . . .'

III

Never had it all seemed so secure.

But Rejeb ibn Saud, far out of the direct route from Bulaq to the Khan il Khalil, and striding down the Maghrabi with his *'aba* pulled close about his face, saw signs enough that were not of the olden times. Few native vendors were about ; no desert folk, sightseers of the sightseers from foreign lands, lingered by the hotels. Here and there, making way for the strolling foreigner, some dark Arab face would grow the darker.

Ibn Saud had sudden vision : Fire in the Maghrabi, massacre and loot ; the screamings of rape, crackle of revolver fire, knives in brown hands . . .

In three hours—at the most.

Ibn Saud half stopped in his stride ; the Maghrabi blurred before his eyes. Slave of the faith which had bound him these many years, he was yet compounded of so many warring hopes and pities that his imagination could suddenly sway him, to gladness or to despair, from a long mapped-out path. . . . The Green Republic of Islam—attained by those means—was it justified ?

A stout Frenchman and his wife moved off the sidewalk in order to pass the crazed native who had suddenly stopped in their path, muttering. Looking curiously back at him, they saw him move on slowly, dully, with bent head.

So, with none of his former pace and purposefulness, he went, in a little turning northwards into the deeper dusk of the Sharia Kamil. The whimsical intent that had originally led him to diverge through the European quarter still drew him on, but he followed it in a brooding daze. At the entrance to the bookshop of Zarkeilo he was jarred with realisation of his quest.

Nevertheless, he entered, and, disregarding the assistant's question, passed down into the interior of the shop to the section that housed Continental editions of English fiction and verse. With an almost feverish eagerness he began to scan the titles. About, the walls were here and there decorated with sham antiques—bronzes, paintings of Coptic Virgins, and the like. To a small red volume ibn Saud at length outreached an unsteady hand.

Rememberingly he turned the leaves. Ten years since this book had lain in his hands, but he had

remembered it—remembered because of those lines
which haunted him, which had inspired him since,
a homeless vagrant, he had landed at Suez to his
dream of Egyptian Renaissance, to the years of toil
and persecution in which he had built up this night's
insurrection. . . . With their music and their magic,
haunting as ever, the words leapt at him from the
printed page :

> ' One man with a dream, at pleasure
>   Shall go forth and conquer a crown ;
> And three with a new song's measure
>   Shall trample a kingdom down.'

Rejeb ibn Saud replaced the book, straightened,
stood upright with shining eyes. Doubts fell from
him. Outside, in the night, his dream went forth
to conquer . . .

His eyes fell musingly on a sham antique crucifix.
Last of the gloaming light upon it, the tortured
Christ fell forward from the cross. Upon his head,
each carven point a-glitter, shone the crown of
thorns.

IV

' Stone her ! Stone her ! '

Nightfall ; in the fastnesses of the native
quarter—the maze of the streets that radiate
around the eastern sector of the Sharia el
Muski ; a girl running—a child of nine, English,
with a flushed, scared face ; behind, peltingly,

laughingly, dirt and stone hurling, a horde of native children.

Such adults as were about turned amused glances to follow the chase. The hunt was up !

Ibn Saud halted and watched. Nearer drew the child, casting terrified glances to right and left. Then she caught his eye. Straight as an arrow towards him she came, clutched his cloak, and clung to him, panting.

The pursuing children surrounded them. One, a ragged hunchback, caught at the girl's dress. Ibn Saud spoke.

' Let be.'

' Why ? She is English. We are to kill them all to-night.'

Hate and curiosity in their eyes, the children drew closer. Two loafers joined them, and one addressed ibn Saud.

' It is so, brother. Let the children have their sport. Who are you to stop it ? '

' I am ibn Saud.'

At that name the children, cruel no longer, but shy and worshipping, drew away. The loafers, whose hatred of the English had apparently not induced in them any desire to join the army of the insurrection in the Khan il Khalil, slunk aside. Ibn Saud touched the girl's head. She had lost her hat.

' How did this happen ? ' he asked in English.

' Mother and nurse took me to the bazaars. I saw a shop I liked, and went into it. It had lots of doors.

Perhaps I came out at the wrong one. When I did I couldn't see either mother or nurse. Then I walked and walked. And those children struck me and cried things and chased me. I ran. Then I saw you.'

Thus, succinctly, the little maid. Ibn Saud stared down at her, a wonder in his eyes.

'But why did you think I would help you?'

The girl raised clear, confident eyes. 'Oh, I knew you would because—because you are different.'

An odd flush came on the face of the insurrectionist. He stood thoughtful. Folly, in any case. He was only saving the child for——

Oh, inevitable. He glanced impatiently round the dusking street. Then:

'What is your name?'

'Clare.'

He stood very still and then bent and stared into her face. For so long did he remain in that posture that the child's lips began to quiver. As in a dream ibn Saud heard himself question her.

'Where is your mother staying in Cairo?'

'At the Continental. If I could get a taxi——'

She was calm and methodical and very grown-up now. Ibn Saud took her hand.

'Come.'

He hurried. Through a maze of odoriferous alleys and walled-in corridors—the kennels of the Cheated of the Sunlight—he led her till on the dusk blazed a long sword of light. It was the Sharia el

Muski, strangely bereft of traffic. With difficulty ibn Saud found an *'arabiyeh.* When directed to take the child to the Continental, the driver blankly refused. Not to-night. Then ibn Saud drew aside the folds of his head-dress and spoke his name, and the driver saluted to head and heart. In Cairo that night that name was more powerful than the Prophet's.

What would it be by dawn?

'Thank you very much.' The earnest eyes of the child looked up into ibn Saud's dark face. With a sudden thought: 'Please, what is your name?—so that I can tell mother.'

Child though she was, she was never to forget him, standing there in the lamplight as he answered her:

'I am Thomas O'Donnell.'

V

Brugh! Boom! Brugh!

In a great square space, ringed about by the bulking of the bazaars, three bonfires burned, shedding a red light on the massing hundreds of the Black Warrens. Against the Khalil wall was up-raised a giant platform. At the other side of the square, curious, antique, a thing of the ages and with the passion of all Man's sweated travail in its beat, was mounted a gigantic drum. Out into the night and the lowe, over the heads of the massing insurrectionists, over the hastening chains of Cairenes converging on the Khan from alley and gutter, its challenge boomed, menacing, stifled, a gathering frenzy.

Already, eastwards and northwards, curtains of scouting insurrectionists, awaiting the final word, hung as self-deputed guards upon the heart of the revolt. But there was little need of guard. The gendarme had laid aside his uniform, kept his rifle, and was now mingling with the mobs of the Khan il Khalil. The petty official, long European-clad, was in burnous and kuftan, uplifting his voice in the wail of chanting which ever and anon rose to drown even the clamour of the drum. Spearhead of the revolt, the Cairene Labour Union massed its scores of rail and tramway strikers.

The hour was at hand.

' Brothers——'

From amidst the notables on the platform, one had stepped forth. High and dim above the Cheated of the Sunlight he upraised his hand.

Es-Saif of El Azhar. An echo and an interpretation of the savage drumming, his voice beat over the silenced square. He had the marvellous elocutionary powers of the trained Egyptian, the passion of the fanatic, the gift of welding a mob into a Jihad.

Presently, at the words rained upon them, long Eastern wails of approbation began to arise. Other speakers followed Es-Saif. The great bonfires, heaped anew, splashed the throngs and the grisly walls with ruddy colour. Quicker began to beat the blood in heart and head. Clearer and louder arose the pack bayings of applause.

Jammed in the midst of the vast concourse below the platform, Rejeb ibn Saud stood listening to the voices of his lieutenants. As if deafness had crept upon him, they sounded incredibly remote. . . .

That child . . . By now she would be safe. And to-morrow, somewhere amidst charred beams and smoking rafters, he might stumble over her bones. . . .

Surely the square and the bodies around him steamed with heat? What was Es-Saif saying? ' Our starved children who have died, who have cried in the darkness and held out their dying hands——'

Children crying in the darkness. . . . What was all history but a record of that? Hundreds, this night. Clare weeping in terror, the terror-filled mites of the Warrens, Hassan . . .

' Ibn Saud ! '

In a long lane that was closing behind him, a man had forced his way from the foot of the giant platform.

' We thought you lost or captured. We would have torn down your prison with our bare hands. Come, it is near your time to speak.'

He spoke in the commanding voice of a worshipping disciple, and then turned back towards the platform. Through the opening throng ibn Saud followed him. . . . Near his time. In a few minutes now he would stand forth on that platform and fire the blood-lust in the maddened horde whose wrongs he had stressed and nourished all those long years.

He found himself climbing to the platform. Dim hands guided him on either side, faces, red-lit, grotesque, profiled and vanished in the bonfires' glare. Abayyad was speaking now. At sight of ibn Saud, Es-Saif leapt up, and kissed him and led him to a seat, wondering a little at his lack of greeting, and the brooding intentness of the dark, still face.

Wave upon wave, a sea of faces below him. As one looking out upon his kingdom ibn Saud stood a moment, and suddenly his eyes blazed, aweing to silence the murmured questionings of Es-Saif.

Clare—Hassan—all the children of the Warrens and of all the warring races of men—*With them lay the world*. Not with his generation—white and brown alike, they had failed. He sought to poison the unguessable future that was not his : he sought to murder it now in death for the hearts and hands that might save the world. Never his generation, but some time, it might be, *theirs*, would yet win a wide path through all the tangles of breed and creed and race, reach even to that dream that might yet be no dream—the Brotherhood of Man. . . .

Below him the mist that was the mustering insurrection quivered. What was that?

He stared across to the far side of the Khan. Through the throngs, from the direction of the Shoemakers' Bazaar, a Sudanese was slowly forcing his way towards the platform. With the force of an utter certainty, Rejeb ibn Saud knew him for what he was.

He was Sayyiya's messenger.

VI

Abayyad's voice rose and fell in penultimate peroration. Behind him, ibn Saud, watching the approach of the messenger, stood with a sudden fire alight in his chilled heart.

For the sake of that his vision of the World of Youth, he would stake all on Chance and the mercy of God. If Sayyiya's note told of Hassan's recovery, he would violate every enthusiasm of his life in the Warrens, would speak peace to the mobs, cry on them to desist, preach to them the vision of the world that had arisen before his eyes. So, if there was a God, if he had but spared Hassan, he would speak. . . .

The lights in the Khan il Khalil flung a glow upon the heavens. Ibn Saud looked up. Beyond the glow, clear and cold, shone the stars. Infinitely remote, infinitely impersonal. . . .

Clare—Hassan—the saving of the near and dear to one—how pitiful!

' Ibn Saud ! ibn Saud ! '

The shouting of his name beat in his ears. Urgently upon his sleeve he felt the hand of Es-Saif. Abayyad had finished. Following the shout, upon the Khan fell a vast hush, broken only by the sound of a throaty breathing as Sayyiya's messenger reached the platform.

Ibn Saud took the note that was handed up to him, unfolded it, and read.

VII

Then a strange thing happened. About him, on the platform of the insurrectionists, they heard him. Ibn Saud laughed—a low, clear laugh, and glanced up again at the stars.

Infinitely remote.

The note slipped from his hand. To the edge of the platform he stepped forward and spoke.

For a full minute, sonorous, golden, the voice beloved of the dim brown multitudes of the Warrens rang clear. Then, obscuring it, began to rise murmurs of astonishment, counter-murmurs for silence. The stillness that had held the massed insurrection vanished. The crowds wavered and shook.

' Traitor ! '

A single voice spoke from the heart of the mob. A hundred voices took it up, a hundred others — those of ibn Saud's personal following—shouted to drown the word. Pandemonium broke loose.

Men screamed and argued, and over the whole
Khan swung and wavered the hand of an in-
credible fear.

'Infidel! Englishman!'

Face distorted, Abayyad sprang forward upon
ibn Saud. As at the touch of frost, the hand
of that fear stilled for a moment the tumult
below.

In that moment Abayyad, with gleaming knife,
struck home.

Ibn Saud shook him off. Crowned in his purpose, infinitely humble, he outreached both arms
to the mob. . . .

With a roar as of the sea, the hordes rose in a
wave and poured upon the platform.

VIII

Es-Saif wanders an exile in the land of the Senussi.
The secret history of that night in the Cairene
Warrens—that night which saw the insurrection
fall like a house of cards in the wreckage of the
stormed platform of the Khan, which saw the rebel
battalions, heart-broken and in despair, break up
and scatter to hut and hovel—is as dim to him as
to any who heard the traitorous speech for which
Rejeb ibn Saud paid with his life.

Yet from the platform Es-Saif salved a curious
relic—the crumpled note sent by Sayyiya to the
leader of the insurrection. Reading it, who can

guess the dream for which ibn Saud cheated himself of his bargain with God, or what crown he went forth to conquer?

' To my master, Rejeb ibn Saud. The mercy of God the Compassionate be with you. Thy son Hassan died at the fall of darkness.—SAYYIYA.'

III

L'Allegro

CAMELIA COMES TO CAIRO

I

*O*UTSIDE *the café awning the noon-blaze of the sun in the Place of the Green Step was almost liquid. A sakkah, his dripping goatskin slung on his back, slouched through the dust. Then a string of donkeys. A Ford car. A gendarme, with carbine and tarbouche, came loitering along the middle of the street. The trees of the Esbekieh Gardens lifted their branches to peer over the roof-tops towards us, or to gaze in vegetal surprise at the windows of Sednaoui's great clothing emporium opposite, where flaunted immense notices of the delectable* mise-en-vente *within. My eyes blinked in the sun-shimmer.*

Coincidence (said Sergei Lubow) is the mother of Necessity, Necessity the mother of Invention, and the children of Invention—they are Gossip and Glamour.

You saw the red-haired girl drive off from Sednaoui's in the runabout? You paid her no heed? My friend, you did well: she is outside and beyond the province of likelihood. For *her* mother was Coincidence and her children even those I have named. . . . You would prefer to sanction their pedigree yourself? But certainly! Why else this tentative story-approach?

II

It is nearly a year ago since I met her. I had been in the Red Desert for a moist three weeks, geologising, my friend Freligrath called it, but I had consulted perspiringly in my vocabulary and called it other things. Just as the fountains of my body-moisture dried, leaving me as a well-cured skin, the expedition came to an end and we returned to Cairo, Freligrath to *his* love, I to mine, domestic souls of rigid pattern the pair of us. Darya fed me and fanned me and read me the latest gossip from Russia, and no clients were in view, and I had no need of them. So I lazed and loved the world and slept in the shade of the eucalyptus tree that fronts our flat.

Till, a week after my return, I received one day a note from the English doctor, Adrian, the friend of my friend Saloney, then newly gone home to work with the sovyets.

I took a tram-car down to his house in Shoubra, finding him in, or it may be out in, his garden, a peaceable place, with every plant perspiring and fainting back on the leaves of its neighbour. Adrian himself was the one energetic object, fauna or flora, in view. With a letter clasped unaffectionately in his hands he strode to and fro the paths, endangering the lives of those roses that are his pride, scowling now at the wall, now at the house, now down at the missive in his hands. But at sight of

me he crumpled the paper and uncrumpled the
scowl.

'Thank God you've been able to come,
Lubow! I've been nursing this letter, off and
on, the last three days since I got it. Have a
drink?'

'Undoubtedly,' I said. 'And this letter—it is
a delicate matter?'

'Eh?'

'Else hardly it would need this nursing.'

'Kate delicate? Hell!' He carefully uncrumpled the letter again, folded it into the shape of
a crinolined female, and proceeded to wring its
neck. From my seat on a nearby flower-bed I
regarded this by-play in mild appreciation.

'Kate?'

'Kate. The one and only of her species ever
suffered to afflict the planet. My sister. From
England.' He began to stride again up and down
the paths of the garden. 'I've to be out on my
rounds in ten minutes again, but I'll explain you
the business first. Did you say you wanted a
drink?'

I said I might now want two, and Adrian shouted
for his servant. While we drank I gathered the
reason for his perturbation. His two sisters were
coming from England to pass the season in
Cairo.

'Not that I object to Helen. Nice little thing—
or was. Must be eighteen or nineteen now. Five
years since I saw her. But Kate——'

'She is a spinster?' I enquired with sympathy, and memories of Miss Austen upon me.

Adrian stopped and grinned upon me lopsidedly. 'Eh? Starched and under-done and wearing boots? That what you're thinking, Lubow? Nothing so pleasant. She's just—Lord, the most unpleasant female I've ever met! And I've met a few.'

I said that this sounded peculiar from a doctor whose speciality was the curing of women's unease. 'I have heard our friend Freligrath call you the best gynæcologist in Cairo.'

'Oh, they've the rottenest job on earth, women. It was the ghastly time that one of them had made me specialise.' He scowled at the garden. 'I'd rather go through hell in celluloid slippers than be a woman. One can excuse them anything—almost. But sister Kate's beyond excuse—or any reason for it. Why the devil hasn't Egypt stricter immigration laws?'

He swallowed his drink in a single ungrateful gulp and banged the glass upon the table. 'And if she expects—or Helen either—a round of entertaining and sight-seeing with me in charge, she's mistaken. She'll have to take you as second-best, Lubow, God help you. You'll wish you'd never escaped from Perekop. . . . That is, if you're free of other engagements and can take it on?'

My bones, remembering the stresses of the Red Desert and my promise to rest them, groaned silently one upon the other. But I had grown interested in this second incursion of the plagues of Egypt that Adrian so feared.

' I shall be pleased—if Miss Kate will consider me a suitable guide ? '

' She'll damn well have to. I'm no guide and I've no time. Work enough on hand to keep a college of surgeons going. Especially now that Lésdiguieres leaves in a fortnight.'

' Lésdiguieres ? '

' My partner. Never met him ? Middle-aged Breton chap. He's due for return to France on retirement ; good job, too, in some ways. Kate'd terrify him. He never took a course in pestology. . . . As it is, he's finding Cairo more and more shocking every day. His latest : some young woman has set up as a doctor out Heliopolis way— a German, he thinks, and a protégée of Citadel Hospital. Haven't met her myself, but Lésdiguieres did the other day—at the house of your friend Freligrath. He'd been attending the Freligrath baby, and of course his methods are rather obsolete. Time he retired. Anyhow, Mme Freligrath wasn't content with his ministrations and called in this young woman from Heliopolis.'

' Well ? '

Adrian chuckled, strolling to the garden end to call loudly that his automobile might be got ready. ' Some unsmacked young Bosche from a Frankfort college, I gather. Certainly Bosche, according to Lésdiguieres ! . . . She met him in the hall of the Freligrath house, told him his methods were antediluvian and appears to have hinted, without any modest reserves at all, that it was indeed time a woman doctor had come to Cairo—*Cairo*, shades of the harem! . . . Coming round with me?'

III

I slept until nearly next Thursday at noon, making up as much arrears of sleep as the noise of the tourists thronging into Heliopolis would allow me. The season had opened. So, towards noon on the Thursday, did I also, and remembered that Adrian's sisters would now have arrived. So I arose and set out to call at the Nile-bank house, as I had promised.

It was a cool, clear afternoon, I remember, the air a little bitter as though the taste of kvass was in it, and I sighed at memory of that taste, myself an exile in this land of sweet, sick wines. There was no traffic visible all the wide curve of the road to Cairo, and I decided to test out my rested bones by walking as far as Abbassieh. In three minutes' time I was regretting the decision in companionable sympathy with my still-unconvalescent thigh-joints, and half was minded to turn back for a tramcar when the burring approach of a motor-cycle behind me made me climb the sidewalk in an aching speed to avoid the dust. I was the only person in view, so when the sound grew and increased behind me, but did not pass, I turned about.

'Jump in, will you?' said a voice. 'Going to Cairo?'

It was neither a motor-cycle nor a car, but a vehicle of three wheels, the first runabout I had ever seen. So I goggled upon it my surprise. It was painted a brilliant yellow and quivered as the door was flung open, and ensconced within, as though fitted in a glove, was a girl.

'I *am* going to Cairo,' I agreed, 'but——'

She squeezed herself against the far side of the vehicle, which emitted a panic-stricken creak. 'Lots of room!'

In face of such mendacity I had no choice. I climbed in, much gingered. The runabout shook as in a high wind, screeched angrily, and then shot down the white glitter of the road. I made to coil myself as tightly as possible.

'Lots of room.'

I decided that this was probably the battle-cry of her clan. She was English. She wore a green cap, a beret. Horn-rimmed spectacles bestrode with much elegance her short, straight nose. Below the beret was a hint of close-shorn hair, very vivid hair of a smoky red, but her eyebrows were almost black, fine brows which made me wonder as to the colour of her eyes; as Darya's have taught me to wonder. Her face was less young than at first I had thought: it was less a girl's than a woman's, though not the latter either in a manner satisfactory and conclusive. Then I noted her hands upon the wheel —intensely white hands, with blunt-trimmed nails.

'Where do you want to go? I'm running into Shoubra myself.'

'That is my objective as well. If you will drop me in the Sharia el Anwar——'

'You must point it out to me. I don't know Cairo very well yet.' She turned her head and smiled at me, to the imminent danger of the nearing loom of the Abbassieh traffic. 'Except some of its notabilities. You're M. Lubow, aren't you?'

I admitted this. 'But how did you know?'

'Fame.' She depressed the exquisite brows as we entered the traffic. 'Why are all Cairene donkeys so morbidly suicidal?'

We out-manœuvred a straying string of the moody beasts, amidst the loud outcries of their driver. Thereafter she paid all her attention to the streets. In a moment I was explaining 'El Anwar is the next turning. The house on the corner is where I—decant.'

She had pleasant laughter. ' "Decant" is the word I've been searching for myself. This one?'

Out on the pavement I turned round to thank her. She had pushed up the horn-rimmed spectacles, and I said to myself, *en passant*, that it had been more than a shame to keep secret the colour of such eyes.

'. . . Nothing at all, M. Lubow. Besides, I know a friend of yours who is always singing your praises—Mme Freligrath.'

I looked down at the pale hands that had puzzled me, remote from both their century and the Shalimar. But now I had sudden enlightenment. ' Why, then you are the new doctor——'

But our conversation proceeded no further than that. The runabout abruptly disgorged its remaining occupant into the embrace of a girl who had come running from the courtyard opening of Adrian's house.

' Camelia ! ' cried this girl. ' How ever do you come to be in Cairo ? Noel ! Kate ! It's Camelia Carson ! '

IV

So, mothered by Coincidence—or was it sired ? I forget the metaphor—that meeting. In a quarter of an hour all of us sat drinking tea in the courtyard of Adrian's house, and I looking over my dish with some interest at the three strangers to that garden. Dr. Camelia Carson was by Adrian's favourite rose bush, the Misses Adrian, Kate and Helen, grouped near her. Adrian himself I saw sit toying with an empty cup, or occasionally glancing from his sister Kate to the new Heliopolitan doctor and indulging in a sardonic twitching of eyebrows.

' But how did you know where *we* were, Camelia ? Oh, of course, you didn't. It was pure luck your giving M. Lubow a lift '—with a smile at me and a plunge into seriousness. ' And if it hadn't been for that we might never have met again ! You didn't write me once in five years—and wherever have you been all that time ? '

This was Helen, you understand, very young and naïve, somewhat, it seemed to me, like a pleasingly early, be-tinted edition of Adrian himself. Very obviously she was a worshipper of the mysterious Dr. Carson, in spite of neglect.

' But I did write—once—after I left London,' said the guest who had brought me. ' It was you who never answered.'

Now Miss Kate intervened, smilingly. ' Ah, but it was to me you wrote, wasn't it, Camelia ? I remember I received your letter and was too busy to answer it at the time. Then it must have slipped my memory. . . . Of course you remember, my dear ? '

Adrian's younger sister turned on Miss Kate. ' But you never told me——' and then stopped, glancing from one to the other. Camelia Carson smiled into her cup.

' Was it to you I wrote, Miss Adrian ? Perhaps. Anyhow, it was rather a mixed time. I spent the next year in the South of France and the next four in Germany, where I took my degree. Then I came out here at the invitation of the Citadel Hospital people, as there wasn't a woman doctor in Cairo, and they said—quite truthfully—that one was badly needed.' She glanced across the court. ' Do you know a man Lésdiguieres, Dr. Adrian ? '

I looked at Adrian. He was leaning back in

his chair, surveying the sky. 'Intimately. He is my partner.'

'Oh.' Though she did not continue, she seemed but little taken aback; rather, I thought, amused and a little contemptuous. Miss Adrian poured tea.

'And you're a doctor now, Camelia? How interesting! Must be *so* convenient! . . . Remember what a wild young thing you were in college-time? Noel disapproved of you very much that year he was in practice in London and you became Helen's friend. He said you would never take your degree.'

All this, you must know, she said smilingly, and I began to understand the peculiar quality of her Englishness. Adrian, I thought, had been right. She was a small woman, neat and pleasantly garbed, with a constant pleasant smile and a constant flitting eye. Only after a little had I noted that no warmth ever came in her eyes, and only now did I realise that our tea-gathering was developing into a duel between her and the owner of the runabout.

I had heard her last remark without comfort, as evidently had the young Helen. But Adrian himself continued surveying an entirely uninteresting sky, and on Camelia Carson's face was merely amused indifference.

'Let's hope he's a better doctor than prophet . . . Well, I must go back. Prescriptions and things to make up. Why, yes, Helen, come often.'

She stood up and the rest of us rose also. Miss
Adrian, with screwed-up eyes and smile unwaveringly pleasant, regarded her from head to
foot.

' And that illness that made you leave London ?
You never suffer from it now, do you, dear ? *So*
unpleasant ! We were never quite sure what it was,
either.'

' No ? Oh, a very common complaint. Can I
give you a lift anywhere, M. Lubow ? '

I had no indecision over that. For the one thing,
it seemed to me there was more than mere courtesy
in her offer ; for another, Adrian had intimated to
me that my duties would not commence until the
morrow, and in the acid Miss Kate I found no
inducement to stay in gossip.

' If you will.'

V

We collected then various small packages from
her chemist's in the next street, and drove back
through the evening traffic, both of us silent and I
in a queer expectancy of I knew not what. I saw
Camelia Carson peer ahead with a little wry smile
upon her comely lips, and of a sudden heard myself
being questioned.

' Well, M. Lubow, do you like me ? '

I think I was commendably prompt. ' Very
much.'

She nodded. She was very frankly pleased. It

was to strike me very soon she was the frankest person I had ever met. ' Rather hoped you would. Mme Freligrath said we'd be friends. I'll need all I can find in Cairo. . . . Kate Adrian detests me, of course. You see, I'm not quite respectable.'

By an inch she avoided a gamin, we burred down the Sharia Abbassieh, she turned upon me brows whimsically upraised. ' So I'd better forestall her, for she'll hint to you and most Cairo about it, no doubt, till you suspect me of simony and hashish. The matter's a good five years old, but Kate hasn't forgotten. Funny. Something wrong with her glands, no doubt. . . . That illness she spoke about is a very common one, as I said, M. Lubow. I had to leave London because I was going to have a baby.'

She looked straight ahead, then started a little and turned her head questioningly.

' Always,' I said, ' I like to shake hands with those who are to be my friends.'

Lightly her disengaged hand reached to touch mine. ' Well——'

She had been an orphan in London, five years before; eighteen years of age, with an elderly guardian who had done but little guarding, I gathered. By the wish of her dead father she was also a medical student—a student very much bored and disgusted.

' Noel Adrian had good grounds for his prophecy, I suppose. Fun and excitement and—oh, well!— admiration was what I wanted. And had.' She

whipped betwixt a train of camels and a tramcar
here. 'Not that I still don't want them. Lovely
things. But that year : I was eighteen and very
young and unsmacked——'

'It was possibly your glands,' I suggested.

The smile of Camelia made devastation of the
grave groundwork of Dr. Carson. So we shot out
of the evening Abbassieh haze.

'Probably. I came to know the Adrians through
Helen. Adorable child. But the other two after a
bit I couldn't stick. Nor they me. Mutual. . . .

'And then I was disreputable—shockingly—and
had to go away. Rather a scared infant myself,
you know, though not so scared as my partner in
indiscretion. He was—oh, not nearly so much a
fool as myself, I suppose ! Goodness knows how
we ever came to either the intimacy of detail or
indiscretion. . . . He'd a reputation to consider,
and plainly imagined I'd trapped him somehow.
Generosities go very quickly in a business like that.
Mine did.

'We kept the matter as secret as possible. He
insisted on the usual convention, but didn't figure
in my farewells. A trying round, that, especially
with the three Adrians. Then I went away to the
south of France with an old German nurse. *He*
came south to see me, once—afterwards, when I
was recovering. I taunted him—hysterically—and
he went away. Never saw him again. Poor man,
how I detested him !

'Baby died, as I very nearly did. Clumsiness and

mismanagement. Funny how one awakens to life. Before that I'd never known there were women in the world—as women. It sent me to Germany for four years, and I studied—hard. Gynæcology. And now I've come out to Cairo to work.'

She laughed, this very cool and disciplined young woman, with the light of memory on her face. ' Though I don't suppose the Adrians will ever believe it ! '

Now for some reason I thought then of a wild night beyond Perekop when I had lain for hours in a gun-pit and heard a man screaming for water. And I had feared to go out to him : I had not gone out to him. Not a memory of which to be proud. But I do not think that since then I have either over-estimated myself or made hasty under-estimation of others. So I understood the new doctor who had come to Cairo.

' I do,' I said.

VI

Now, next day Lésdiguieres made his farewells and departed for France. So much I learned from Adrian himself, chance-met, hurrying, and over-worked.

' Helen alone wants to see you to-day, Lubow. Relief, eh ? Kate won't be in evidence. Out making friends—the Lord help *them* ! '

' You miss the good Lésdiguieres ? ' I enquired, sheering aside with a dragoman's tact.

'Confound him, yes. Time he went, but why just in the busiest season, when half the residents are insisting on propagating their kind, and half the tourists ululating for medical aid to stave off diseases incomparably less harmful than themselves —well!'

'You should take a new partner,' I advised. 'Dr. Carson, for example.'

'God forbid. I wouldn't trust her with a sick kitten. See you again.'

I reached the Adrian house and sent in word to the younger sister that I was at her service. Unfortunately, Miss Kate had returned earlier than was expected, and insisted on accompanying Helen and myself out to the Pyramids and back through feet-wearying miles of bazaars. Inimitably, she succeeded in making me feel both responsible for Cairo and ashamed of it. By good luck, however, she proved but a poor pedestrian, and in the Khan Khalil, very footsore, was compelled to summon a taxi and drive home. For the rest of the day I found compensation in the naïve enthusiasm of the younger sister, and here and there leant against the appropriate scenic effects and solaced myself with a short nap the while the appropriate dragoman patter rolled from my lips.

Next afternoon, however, when I arrived again at the Shoubra house to take Helen on a promised excursion up the Nile, I found her absent. Miss Kate smiled upon me, unwaveringly, instead.

'I'm afraid she's gone to see Camelia Carson in Heliopolis. The person rang her up this morning. So annoying! Most undesirable acquaintance. Not to be trusted as a doctor, you know, M. Lubow. I've already had to warn several of my friends in Cairo.'

I stared at her in astonishment and then for a moment was on the verge of such uncensored comment as employees but seldom use to their employers. I saw beyond her cold, smiling face, the brave, desperate head of Dr. Camelia. . . . Pain of restraint sent me forth in something like anger, almost into the arms of Adrian himself, about to enter the courtyard.

' Hello, Lubow.' And then, ' What's wrong ? '

' It is my sense of humour failing me, I think. Tell me, is it English professional etiquette to blackguard rival practitioners ? '

' Eh ? '

I told him of Miss Kate's conversing with her friends, and he stood and scowled and then grinned at me curiously.

' Pretty damnable. Yes, I know all about Camelia Carson. But how did you ? '

' She told me herself.'

He stared undisguised surprise and then shrugged his shoulders. ' She did, eh ? . . . Still the same ! Probably has a dozen lovers in Cairo by this time and told the lot of them. So why worry ? '

' But are you sure this disease is uncontagious inside the family circle ? '

' What ? '

' But scandal-mongering.'

He pushed me aside, half-angrily. ' Rot. She's only playing at being a doctor—as she once played at being a student. Gives her cachet. . . . As for such distractions as a quarrel with Sergei Lubow— I'm too busy.'

No such press of work drove Camelia Carson, I was to discover. Going home, she hailed me from the Heliopolis House Hotel terrace. We sat together and drank iced coffee and watched the sunset come over the desert while she puzzled on the failing demand for her professional services.

' Funny. I was getting on quite well, too. Not that I came out to Cairo to doctor decaying Europeans, but a practice is necessary among them before I can get at my real people—the Egyptians.'

I hesitated to hint at the cause and went home and debated the matter with Darya, who gave sage advice that strayed into a questioning for portrait-details of the new doctor's appearance. By the following evening, however, necessity for action on my part was overpast. The explosion had already occurred.

VII

I was myself no witness of it. Helen, the younger Adrian sister, very puzzled and dismayed, consti-tuted herself my reporter.

Adrian, it appeared, had but newly returned from a strenuous day when the runabout drew up in the Sharia el Anwar and Dr. Carson sent in word that she wished to see Dr. and Miss Adrian. Followed a very angry scene in front of Helen, whom they had forgotten : Miss Kate, still I imagine with the smile and the flitting eyes and an air of shocked remonstrance, Adrian louring, Camelia Carson in a white passion of wrath. The scandal-whispers had reached her.

'I don't expect fairness from either of you. I suppose it's your way to bolster up your practice. But if there's any more of this filthy gossip I'll report you to the medical council of Cairo.'

'There'll be no more gossip,' said Adrian. 'And, anyway, the remedy's in your own hands.'

'Whatever he may have meant by *that*,' related Helen. 'What, anyhow, could have been all this awful gossip of Kate's ? Camelia went out and banged the door and was gone in the runabout before I could catch her. . . . It's quite too beastly.'

Though less puzzled, I also agreed it was oppressively zoological. We were on the Nile while she told me this, down opposite the Geziret Roda, in the late afternoon and with a little blow of River wind. In despite the comicalities and distractions of the scene, Adrian's younger sister persisted in an unwonted low-spiritedness.

'Noel's temper gets worse and worse. I'll be glad—almost—when the season's over and we get back. Anyhow, he's off to Alexandria for a week to-morrow, and, whatever's happened, I'm going out to Heliopolis to call on Camelia again.'

She shivered, and I awoke to a good guide's cares. 'You are cold?'

'A bit. Feeling out of sorts. I think we'll turn the boat and go back.'

VIII

Next day she stayed in bed, with still the out-of-sorts feeling upon her. Adrian went up to her room to see her, and made brief diagnosis. 'Feverish a bit. Quinine. Don't *you* go and fall ill, for I'm off to Alexandria for that operation, and my patients'll get scanty attention from the Citadel Hospital people. Anything you want?'

'Yes,' she had said, sitting propped around with pillows and very bored. 'Collect M. Lubow when he comes, and ask him to come and gossip with me.'

'Good Lord,' was her brother's announcement of this proposal when I called. '*There's* a drago-man's job for you, Lubow!'

I had carried out many more oppressive and far less pleasant. I sat and told all the seemly lies I could call to mind from the literature of five languages, and the patient sat and called for more, and exacted from me a promise of a further supply on the following day.

That next day Adrian set out for Alexandria.

I did not reach Shoubra until late in the afternoon, meeting Miss Adrian about to drive away from the house in her brother's car. She smiled at me graciously.

'The dear child is all right again, though very peevish.'

'You have but newly come from her?' I asked.

'No, but I was in after lunch. Sleeping now, I think. One of the servants will show you up, M. Lubow. I must fly. I know you'll excuse me. Cairo—*so* interesting!'

I was shown up to the room, but after repeated knockings had no invitation to enter. Still, though in some hesitation, I went in. . . .

It was almost half an hour thereafter, before I could find Camelia Carson, and that at last through a chance telephone call to Darya, with whom she sat drinking a dish of tea and discoursing my lack of demerits. 'Will you come at once?' I said. 'Helen Adrian is very ill—in delirium, and has been unattended I do not know how long.'

IX

I do not cherish in memory details of that night nor yet of the following day. I stayed at the Shoubra house with the feeling that, in the absence of Adrian, it was somehow the concern of myself. In the forenoon Camelia Carson brought a nurse from the Kasr-el-Ain Hospital, and at two o'clock in the afternoon came and sought out Miss Adrian.

'Send a telegram to Alexandria and tell Dr. Adrian to come back at once.'

'But I thought *you* were a doctor, my dear? Do you need his assistance already?'

Camelia Carson disregarded this challenge. 'Helen's seriously ill and he's her brother. . . . And you must do your share of nursing. Nurse must rest sometimes and I've one or two other patients to see to.'

She was back again inside three hours. By then the younger sister was in delirium and worse. Miss Adrian was frightened and would have awakened the nurse, but I had stopped her from that and taken some little part in the nursing myself. Camelia Carson, her small face without expression, and upon it no sign that she had not slept for nearly twenty-four hours, evicted both of us, summoned the nurse, and closed the door of the sick-room.

I did not need to be told of the diagnosis. I had seen enteric fever before—acquired in Helen Adrian's case through the drinking of a chance cup of street-bought lemonade, we guessed. There came from that upstairs room sounds unpleasant to hear. Miss Adrian sat and listened with a face very drawn and scared by then, and minus its once unwavering smile. Darkness came down, long stifling hours of it, and still, with the very brief interludes of calmness, the unseen battle went

on. Half the night had gone before I heard the
noise of a taxi drive up and Adrian himself came
through the courtyard and into the house.

He delayed a minute with me in the hall, then
climbed to the sick-room, knocked at the door,
and vanished inside.

x

An hour later that door again opened. The
nurse came out and went to her room, and Camelia
Carson leant over the bannisters and beckoned.
'You may come up and have a peep. . . .' She
considered. 'You as well, M. Lubow. You
deserve it.'

So we climbed the stair and went in on the pussy
foot. Adrian was standing by the window, looking
out; Camelia Carson had sunk into a chair. Upon
the many-times smoothed pillows of the bed reposed
the head of Helen Adrian. The flush and perspiration had gone from her face and she was fast
asleep.

I looked from her to the doctor who had carried
on this long fight of thirty hours. In despite the
horn-rimmed spectacles she looked most absurdly
young and tired, her small body drooping there in
the chair, most sheerly weary. I sought in appropriate colloquialisms.

'You must be dead-beat.'

She smiled at me, repressing a sudden yawn.
'Nearly. Sleepy, at least.'

And then Adrian turned round from the window, and their eyes met, and the smile went from her lips.

XI

Suddenly I found myself staring from one to the other and realising impossible things. But they had no eyes for a spectator. They might have been strangers who had come through long miles of tunnel together and now saw each other in the light at last. The face of Adrian was white while Camelia looked at him.

Then her lips began to quiver. A faint smile came on them.

'Well, Noel, do I pass now?'

She held out a tentative hand, found her eyes closing involuntarily, and yawned again.

'Oh—Camelia!'

He had left the window. He smiled down on her, an unwonted twitching in his smile, and then put his hands under her arms and raised her from the chair.

'Lubow is right. Dead-beat you must be. I am, with half the cause. We'll go to bed. . . . Lubow, you'll be wanted in Heliopolis, I guess. Kate can keep an eye on Helen. Don't wake us unless it's anything urgent.'

'But——' It was an amazed twitter from Miss Adrian. 'Where are you going?'

'To bed. Both of us.'

The eyes of Adrian's elder sister appeared to be about to pop from her head. Camelia Carson turned round, drowsily, from the doorway.

' That coat of mine, there. Bring it, will you, Noel ? Ready ? ' She smiled at Kate Adrian with sleep-weighted eyes, and Adrian put his arm about her. ' Quite all right, you know. Noel and I were married in London five years ago. 'Night.'

Il Penseroso

DIENEKES' DREAM

I

TO see the face that launched a thousand ships peep from below a poke-bonnet at a street-corner confessional induces a sense of shock that speedily passes into irritation. Such face, you feel, no doubt had once its appropriate function and setting ; but in the twentieth century it is fantastic. Horatius kept his bridge well enough for the purpose of inspiring later ages to juvenile recitation ; reincarnated as a gangster with a machine-gun in a Chicagoan alley he loses charm. Leonidas and his Spartans, holding liberty and Thermopylæ against the hosts of Asia, were heroes, but——

And you stand, a strayed tourist in the unfrequented warrens of Cairo, and stare at that wall and inscription in the Sharia el Ghoraib.

It rises high, this street-wall that girds the rear of some ancient khan. It glimmers dour and brown and unremarkable, all the length of it—except at this one spot. For here, from a distance of three feet upwards, the dried mud is pitted and flaked as though, in its liquid state, it had been pelted with pebbles. Below those marks of an incomprehensible hail-storm, a great red stain is a dull blotch in the sun-shimmer, and carved into that blotch, in letters Greek and gigantic, is the single word

ΘΕΡΜΟΠΥΛΑΙ

You stare at it and transliterate Thermopylæ; you go closer and see a line of smaller lettering. A quotation—a familiar enough quotation.
A misascribed quotation.
Who really spoke it? You wander back in thought to forgotten pages of a forgotten history-lesson. Of course! Not Rhizos—whoever he was—but Dienekes of Sparta when they told him the Persian arrow-hail would darken the sun. . . .
Fantastic thing to find inscribed on the wall of a Cairene khan!

II

It stood a wall still uninscribed that night seventeen years ago when the weavers of Selitsa—over thirty of them, men, women, and children, clinging to pathetic and parlous packages wherein were shrouded their dismembered looms—tumbled out of the Alexandria train into the dark inhospitality of Cairo Central Station.
' Are you all here? ' roared Georgios Londos, a trifle mechanically, when they grouped round him outside the station gates. They chorussed a tired and optimistic yes. Londos ran his eye over them, scratched his head, considered the flowing

darknesses and jaundiced lightnings that were
Cairo, and seemed a little at a loss.

' Then—we're here, then.'

Here indeed at last they were—Sina, with his wife
and mother and two daughters ; the Latas ; the
Vasos ; the little thin widower with a single son and
a name like a battle-cry, Kolocrotoni ; these, the
others, and the two who were the group's actual, if
unnominated, leaders, little Trikoupi and the giant
Londos. Here in Cairo at last. . . .

' What shall we do now, Big Londos ? ' piped ten-
years-old Rhizos Trikoupi from the side of his
father, Elia. He voiced the silent questionings of
the party.

The giant of Selitsa yawned, ear-achingly, and
found solution in the yawn. His silhouette
vanished, materialising to view again as a dim
recumbency.

' We'll sleep. I haven't had a wink since we left
Dourale. . . .'

III

There was no moon that night, but presently the
coming of a fine frostiness of stars. In that starlight the Greek weavers huddled in an uneasy
rhythm of sleep beneath the bland bass snorings of
giant Londos.

The winter nights are cold in Cairo—as you may
have noticed from the terrace of the Continental.
And long—when you lie on damp cobblestones and

your body exudes heat and inhales rheumatism in enthusiastic accord with some mystic law of physics. Young Rhizos Trikoupi was never to forget the feel of those cobblestones under his insufficiently-padded hip : it was so bad he thought the cobbles must ache almost as much as he did. . . .

A late train chugged out of Cairo. He raised himself on his elbow and watched its wavering comet-tail of sparks grow dim and disappear. Perhaps on board it was some Greek returning to Greece—Cairo to Alexandria, Alexandria by un-ending discomforts of the trading boat to Dourale, Dourale to—perhaps someone on board that train would even journey up from Dourale to Mother Selitsa in the eparchy of Oitylos !

Once Spartic of the Spartans, Selitsa town. But its weaving community had fallen on evil days and were near to starving when Londos, a lumbering Moses, knocked from door to door and at each delivered his ultimatum.

' Stay here—and starve ; abroad—we may eat. Greece buys but the goods of the American machines ; Mother Selitsa has no need of us—but she's sent our reputation abroad. Such cloths as ours still sell well in Egypt. Let us go there.'

And here the most of them were—the last of their money gone in fares for their varied and un-easeful journeyings—sleeping on the Cairene cobble-stones, waiting for the dawn.

Rhizos laid his head down again, and again sought sleep. But, with a pallor upon the stars, the night

had grown colder than ever. He found young
Kolocrotoni awake near him, and they conversed
in whispers, looking at a sky that grew darker and
darker in the moment before morning, and then
was suddenly aflaunt, all along the flat roof-spaces,
with the blown streamers of a host of crimson
banners. The boys stared raptly, the cold forgotten.

'When we've beds,' averred young Kolocrotoni,
cautiously, ' it mayn't be so bad to live here.'

Rhizos remembered giant Londos's promise.
' Our Mother has a fortune waiting us here.'

IV

And then——

Were this still no more than prelude I might sing
you a very pretty Odyssey indeed of the wanderings
of those Selitsa weavers in search of a place in
Cairo wherein to lay their heads. Penniless, full
of hope, and much be-cursed by the Greek consul,
Londos and Elia Trikoupi tramped the streets while
the other males guarded the women and looms
and grew hungry and thirsty and were evicted
by carbine'd gendarmes now from one squatting-
place, now another. For Cairo declared itself over-
crowded and poverty-stricken already. ' Go back
to Selitsa,' said Cairo, literally and in effect. Whereat Londos, an uncultured man, cursed it forcibly.
' We'll stay in Cairo and set up our looms,' said he,
' on a midden—if need be.'

Not that they might not have found employment.
But they had learnt, they and generations before
them, tenacity in the bitter Peloponnesus.   They
were determined, with an altogether regrettable
archaic obstinacy, to erect their own looms, not to
work for others.   They found an archway under
which they were allowed to camp, and there
endured existence for three days until on the third
midnight giant Londos returned to them in some
excitement and shot the sleepers out of sleep, and
some of them nearly out of their wits, with his
shout :

' I've found it ! '

Dazed and drowsy, they packed up and set out
after him, tramping through the dark Cairene streets
for hours, a grotesque procession enough.   Until
beyond the Bab el Zuweiya, and at the foot of the
Sharia el Ghoraib, Londos halted and pointed.
And the place to which he had brought them was the
cul-de-sac wherein the sharia terminated, a waste
space of half an acre amid the high walls of the
surrounding khans.   Once it had been a rubbish
depository, but had been long abandoned for even
that purpose.   Yet still from the ancient buried
offal arose a sickening odour.

It troubled even the nostrils of the gentle Elia
Trikoupi, no æsthete.   ' Has it not—a little per-
fume ? ' he asked, turning diffident eyes on the giant.
Whereat Londos's immense laugh boomed out
over the sleeping Warrens, startlingly.   The other
Greeks took it up.   They stood and rocked with

laughter in that Cairene midnight, hungry, forsaken, light-hearted. The giant of Selitsa wiped his eyes.

' Little Perfume—what a name for our midden ! You have christened it, Elia ! '

V

They set to building sheds on the edge of it next day—the waste and odoriferous piece of land claimed by no one, the seeming haunt of half the pariah dogs and all the amorous cats of Cairo. They tramped to the edge of the town, to Nile-bank, to the Greek quarter, begging, borrowing and stealing stray pieces of timber and canvas. They delved out foundations at the edge of the waste—the smells that arose were dreadful—and drew up the huts at an angle fronting towards the Sharia el Ghoraib. In three days the huts were almost habitable. And then Londos procured a slab of wood and a piece of charcoal and, grinningly, scrawled a legend on the slab, and nailed it up above the angle hut :

' Little Perfume.'

They were on an island, the Selitsa settlers—an exceedingly dry island. There was no water nearer at hand than that in the public fountain at the far end of the Sharia el Ghoraib. From this fountain water had to be fetched—a task which fell to the children, for the older settlers from Selitsa, men and women, betook themselves to the looms as soon

as these were erected. On an advance of yarn
and silk they set to weaving the mantles that had
already won them reputation in Egypt, and the
straggling, hourly procession of children making
towards the fountain would hear the thump and
boom, rise and fall, behind them in every hut of
Little Perfume.

It seemed to them the only friendly sound in
Cairo. The sharia looked on them sourly, and at
the fountain itself they would find the Arab hosts
marshalled to give battle—children who threw
stones and dirt, and spat with some venom. Ring-
leader of this Asiatic opposition was a small,
ferocious and underclad girl whose favourite amusement was to drop dust-bricks into the fountain
just prior to the arrival of Rhizos and his companions. Rhizos bided his opportunity, found it
one afternoon, dropped his bucket, pursued the
damsel, tucked her head under his arm in a business-
like if unchivalrous fashion, and proceeded to
punch her with great heartiness. . . . But such
satisfactions were few enough, and wilted in retro-
spect on the painful return march to Little
Perfume, with small arms aching and small back
breaking and the conviction deep in one's heart
that some meddler had elongated the sharia in one's
absence. . . .

That was in late winter and for a time the locality
was endurable. But the summer drew on. Desperately engrossed as they were in the attempt to
find an opening for their wares in the Egyptian

markets, the Selitsa settlers had borne with their
strangely-odoured habitat uncomplainingly. They
rose with the first blink of daylight, into those fervid
Cairene mornings when the air is unthinkably pure
and the day for an hour has the hesitating loveliness
of a lovely woman, and cooked their scanty break-
fasts and set to work at their looms. They ceased
not even at the failing of the light, but took to the
coarser work under the glimmer of great tallow
candles, giant Londos and the gentle Elia leading
in feats of endurance. Sometimes it was midnight
before the humming of the looms would cease,
and Londos, a little unsteady, would lumber out of
doors to look up at the splendour of the Cairene
moon and chuckle tiredly ·as he caught the
glitter of moonlight on the notice-board of the
settlement.

But the summer drew on, and with it each morning arose from the waste of Little Perfume, as
though a foul beast hibernated underfoot, a mal-
odorous breath of a vileness unendurable. With
it came clouds of mosquitoes—insects rare enough
in Cairo—and hordes of flies. By midday the ancient
dunghill had a faint mist. In a fortnight two of
the Greek children were dead and half of the community was sick in bed.

The evening of the day on which they buried
the children Londos stalked to the door of the hut
where Trikoupi leant pallidly over his loom and
little Rhizos knelt by the heap of sacking on which
his mother slept uneasily.

'Come out, Elia.'

So Elia went out, and waited. Londos strode up and down in the evening light, debating with himself, once stopping and throwing out his arms hopelessly. Then he halted in front of the gentle Trikoupi.

'There is only one thing we can do, Elia.'

'Leave Little Perfume?' Elia had guessed this was coming.

'No, remove it.' Londos pointed to the waste hillock towering away behind the huts. 'We must shift that, and quickly.'

Trikoupi stared at him as though he had gone mad. 'Remove it? But how? And where?'

Londos indicated the louring of the Moqattam Hills in the sunset. 'There. It is two miles away, beyond the town boundaries.'

'But move this hill—It is a month's work for scores of men.'

Londos nodded. 'And we must do it in a fortnight—if our children are to live.'

VI

They did it. It turned in the telling of later years into an epic of struggle, a thing of heroism and great feats, intermingled with shouted laughter. The fatigue and horror and weariness the years came to cover with the tapestry of legend: how Londos, stripped to a breech-clout, dug and excavated and filled every one of the sacks and baskets for four days on end, the while the others bore them on their two-mile journey—Londos, gigantic, unsleeping, pausing now and then to drink the coffee brought him, and vomit up that coffee at the next nest of dreadful stenches and even more dreadful refuse his shovel uncovered ; how the gentle Trikoupi bore loads without ceasing, day or night, till he was found walking in his sleep, a babbling automaton ; how the women, laughed at and pelted by the Cairenes, bore load for load with the men ; how three died in that Iliad—one of them, the Vasos mother, by the pits beyond the walls—and there was no time to bury their corpses ; how the police descended on the excavators and gave them a time-limit in which to finish the work ; how in desperation the weaver Gemadios went to Citadel in the dark hours of one night and stole a great English Army handcart, and worked with it for two days (doing feats in the removal of offal) and then returned it, the theft still undiscovered ; how——

They did it. It was cleared at last. The burning Cairene sunshine smote down on ragged floors, once the floors of some Mameluke's palace, perhaps, in the days of Cairo's greatness. Underneath those floors was plentitude of bricks and stonework. And the odours died and passed, and the weavers, men and women, reeled to their huts and flung themselves down beside their looms and slept and slept, and woke and groaned with aching muscles, and slept again.

Little Rhizos Trikoupi, staggering to the fountain alone that night with an endrapement of pitchers, found seated on the coping the ferocious little female whose head he had once punched. She sat and regarded him without apparent hostility. He disregarded her, ostentatiously.

But as he lifted up the laden jars she came to his side.

'I'll help,' she said, friendly of voice.

She bore a jar to the confines of Little Perfume. There she set it down and smiled at Rhizos. 'My name is Zara,' she said, inconsequently. Then told him disastrous tidings, casually. 'They are not to allow any more of your people to carry water from the fountain to the Place of Stinks.'

VII

It was a crushing blow. Londos and Elia Trikoupi went and argued with the ward-masters. But they refused to be moved. All of them except Muslih, a Nationalist and father of that advanced feminist Zara, were quite openly hostile to the Greeks. The fountain was intended to supply the streets which surrounded it, not such carrion-grubbers as might settle in abandoned middens . . .

That evening Londos himself, bidding the children stay at home, went for water with two great buckets. He came back hatless and bleeding, but grinning, with a jeering, stone-pelting crowd behind him. But the buckets were full. He put them down, emptied them into the settlement's jars, and started out again. By the fountain-coping three men still lay and groaned where he had left them. He refilled the buckets.

But next morning Rhizos and young Kolo-crotoni, scouting, came back to tell that there was a policeman on guard at the fountain. Giant Londos swore at that information and scratched his head. It was one thing to crack the cranium of the stray and obstreperous Cairene, another to do the same to a gendarme. The Greeks collected to debate the matter, Elia Trikoupi, dust-covered from exploring the uncovered floors of Little Perfume, arriving last.

'Abandon Little Perfume now we will not,' swore Londos. 'Not though we have to carry water from the Nile itself. Those lawyers! Elia, we'll rear that son of yours to be one and defend our interests. Then we may drink in peace.'

'We may drink before that,' said Trikoupi, gently. 'If you will all come with me——'

They went with him. He led them to the middle of the waste of Little Perfume. In the ground was a circular depression filled with earth and building rubbish. Londos stared at it and then embraced Trikoupi.

'A well—once a well. And we'll make it one again.' He threw off his coat, groaned like a bull at an ache that leapt to fiery being between his shoulder-blades, and called for a spade. 'This will clinch for ever our right. We can start building. We can start making gardens.' He sighed, almost regretfully. ' The great tale of Little Perfume is over.'

VIII

But indeed, could he have known it, they had lived no more than its prelude. Almost unnoticed, yet weaving assiduously into the web and woof of Cairene life stray threads of story-plot from Little Perfume, the War years passed over Egypt. Demand for the products of the looms that had once hummed in Selitsa grew in volume and value. Nor did the aftermath bring any slump. The settlers flourished.

Yet out of its profits the little community succeeded in banking scarcely a piastre. Replacing the saving instinct of generations a new habit had grown upon the weavers—the enrichment and embellishment of Little Perfume. Its gardens grew famous throughout the Warrens. They even planted trees—quick-growing Australian trees procured by Rhizos Trikoupi when he learnt of those plants in botany lessons. A great shed, built of mud-bricks, airy and cool and flat-roofed, gradually rose to being in the centre of the one-time rubbish depository. This was the communal loom-shed. Round it, one by one, were built the houses of the weavers—twelve houses with much space and garden-room. Those houses at night were lighted no longer by candles, but by electricity. The long-tapped well brought water to each. . . . Londos, gigantic still, but bulkier, slower, than of yore, would sometimes walk away down the Sharia el Ghoraib and then wheel round abruptly, in order to shock himself into fresh surprise over the miracle of Little Perfume. He would stand and stare at it fascinatedly, and so was standing one evening in October when young Rhizos Trikoupi, the law-student returning from his studies in Cairo, hailed him as he came down the sharia.

'Dreaming again, *papakes?*'

'Eh?' The giant started. 'Ah, you, Rhizos. And how much have you learned to-day?' He chuckled. 'Apart from the shape of the ear of Zara Muslih, I mean.'

Rhizos coloured a trifle, and attractively. Daily, almost, he and Zara, both students at the University, travelled into Cairo together. Her father, the fervid progressive and friend of the Greeks, had deter-mined to give her such education as would shock her mother and every other veiled woman east of the Bab el Zuweiya. . . . She had certainly lovely ears.

Londos chuckled again, clapping an ungentle hand on the law-student's shoulder.

'And why not? But remember you are our Samson, and there must be no Delilahs.'

'There are no Philistines,' said Rhizos, tolerantly, and then nodded back towards the Sharia el Ghoraib, the street which had stood decaying ever since that midnight when the Selitsa settlers passed through it to the conquest of the ancient offal-heap. 'At least, not nearer than the sharia! What is happening there?'

'Eh? Oh, the house-breaking in the upper half?' Londos shrugged indifferently, his eyes on the night-shadowed peace of Little Perfume. 'Its owner following our lead at last—it has taken him ten years. Clearing away the huts and building houses, I hear. Site-prices are soaring high in Cairo.'

IX

Cairo, indeed, was advancing in Westernisation in great strides. Site-prices had doubled and trebled since the War. New buildings were springing up in every ward of the ancient city of the Mamelukes. Nor were effects unforeseen and numerous enough slow to erupt from all that causal activity. Title-deeds and land-rights were everywhere being questioned and overhauled, claim and counter-claim jostled one the other in every lawyer's office. And presently, from the midst of this maelstrom of modernisation, a long wave reached out and burst like a thunder-clap against the shores of Little Perfume.

Twenty-four hours after that talk with Londos, Rhizos returned to find his father, the giant, Vasos, and old Sina in anxious consultation over a long tri-lingual typescript. They cried out their relief

at sight of him, and Londos handed over the
document.

'It was wise to train this son of yours, Elia,'
he said, and wiped his forehead. '*He* will deal
with it.'

Rhizos took the crinkling sheets of paper and sat
down and read them, and presently was aware
of a deafening, sickening beat of blood around
his ears.

It was a notice to the effect that the site-property
of El Ghoraib, 'commonly known as Little Perfume,' was required by its owner for building
purposes, and that the Greek squatters at present
in occupation must vacate it within a month's time.

x

The Greeks took the case to the courts, Rhizos
engaging a lawyer on behalf of the settlement.
But even with this development Londos and the
older weavers refused to treat the claim seriously.

'An owner for Little Perfume?' said Londos.
'It must be the man in the moon. Or of a certainty
a lunatic.'

He proved less unharmful. They caught their
first glimpse of him as the case was being tried—
a *rentier*, a Parisian Egyptian of the new generation,
suave, sleek, and bored. His lawyers submitted
the claim with a casualness which was deceptive.
It covered certainty. El Ghoraib, together with the

nearby Sharia el Ghoraib, had been the property of
the Falih family from time immemorial. The title-
deeds were impeccable.

'Why did you not evict the squatters before?'
demanded the Greeks' lawyer.

Falih smiled. 'Because until recently I'd forgotten El Ghoraib's existence.' He added coolly :
'And I make no claim on the squatters now,
provided they leave the site undamaged.'

It was as heartless a case as had come within his
province, said the Egyptian judge in a curt summary.
Nevertheless, there could be no disputing the claim
of Falih.

Judgment was entered accordingly, and Londos
and Trikoupi, acting for the settlers, allowed to
appeal.

The appeal was quashed.

XI

The news was brought to Little Perfume.
Giant Londos, shrunken, rheumatism-crippled,
stared from Rhizos to his father, then around the
circle gathered to hear the news— all old men, bent
with toil at their looms. Rhizos could not meet that
stricken look in the eyes of the giant whose labours
in clearing the rubbish-waste were already legendary.

'But—it means we go out of here as we came!
It is impossible,' said Londos, and burst into tears.
. . . The old men sat silent, but Rhizos slipped out
of the gathering and walked the Cairene evening in

a red passion of anger. He found himself at length outside the door of the Muslih house, at the other end of the Sharia el Ghoraib. It was a familiar enough door to him and in a moment it was closing behind him the while he made his way to the room where Zara sat over books and lecture-notes. At sight of him she rose eagerly.

'The appeal?'

He laughed. 'Quashed. Falih can evict us when he chooses.'

She kindled from his own anger. 'It's a shame —oh, a damned shame! Those old men and women who have worked such a miracle. . . . Can't they claim compensation?'

'They can take away nothing but the looms they brought. We're liable to prosecution if we damage the very houses we've built.'

She looked at him in helpless pity. 'Surely something can be done? If only that Bill were passed in the Chamber!'

'What Bill?' he asked, indifferently.

He had been too busy heeding to the court cases to know of outside events that might affect them. He listened half-unlistening, until meaning of what she was saying penetrated the cloud of his anger.

'A Bill enforcing value-compensation for improved sites—to become law as soon as passed! That would mean Falih would never dare evict us from Little Perfume. It would cost him too much. . . . But when will it pass?'

' They are fighting it, my father says, but it is bound to pass. When ? Within the next week or so, perhaps.'

' Too late. If only——'

He began to walk up and down the room, Zara looking at him. He stopped and stared at her, absently. They had each the same thought.

' If we could keep off Falih till then——'

XII

That was on the Monday. Next day the Greeks of Little Perfume received a notice from Falih's agent to vacate the site within twenty-four hours.

They made no attempt to comply. Instead, Rhizos went and argued with the agents. Reluctantly, those agents extended the time-limit another forty-eight hours. But they were insistent that at the end of that period the site be left vacant. Later in the day they sent a note curtailing the extra forty-eight hours to twenty-four. The growth of support for the new Bill in the Chamber had alarmed Falih.

Meantime, Rhizos organised the inhabitants of Little Perfume. At a meeting they voted him to control the situation, with young Kolocrotoni his assistant. Then they retired to uneasy beds, wondering what the next day would bring.

It brought Falih's bailiffs, four of them, knocking at the door of Trikoupi's house. The Greeks gathered round the arrivals quickly enough, while a crowd of curious Egyptians flocked in from the far end of the sharia. Nor were they hostile to the Greeks, those Egyptians. The Greeks had won their place. Here were thieves come to dispossess them. . . . The bailiffs grew angry and frightened, beating upon Trikoupi's door. The gentle Elia opened it.

'This house must be cleared,' said the leader. He motioned forward one of the others. 'Carry out the furniture.'

Londos, who had been waiting for this, as instructed by the absent Rhizos, rose from a chair. They saw a tipsy giant behind a table littered with full and empty bottles. 'Drink first,' he invited, swayingly. 'Drink to our leaving this place of stinks. Sit down and drink.'

The bailiffs hesitated, but a growl came from the crowd pressing round the open door. Falih's men sat down and, not unwillingly, filled glasses from the bottles indicated. . . .

They passed down the Sharia el Ghoraib late that evening in two arabiyehs hired by Rhizos; they passed down it drunk and roisterous and singing improper songs. They had fallen mysteriously asleep after the first drinks, had slept until afternoon and had awakened to be again forcibly regaled with draughts of the potent Greek brandy. . . . Listening to their drunken brawling receding into the evening, Rhizos turned to Zara, who had come to see the day's *dénouement*. She was flushed and laughing at the stratagem's success, and he stared at the shapeliness of her ears.

'We've won the first skirmish, but to-morrow ——' and his face grew dark.

She suddenly kissed him. 'Luck for to-morrow!' And was gone, leaving him staring after her breathlessly, with flushed face.

XIII

To-morrow——

The papers bore news of the Bill. It had passed, after a fierce struggle, into the Egyptian equivalent of the committee stage. From there it had still to emerge, still to receive the King's sanction. Rhizos read the news from the sheets of *El Ahram*, he and young Kolocrotoni together.

'Falih's men will return long before then,' said Kolocrotoni.

'They'll return to-day,' said Rhizos, 'unless we go to them instead.' He had already planned his next move. Within half an hour, after canvassing from house to house in Little Perfume, he went down into Cairo with notes to the value of three thousand piastres in his wallet. Of what he accomplished on that journey he never told. But he returned with an empty wallet and Falih's agents did not come that day. Falih himself, indeed, had gone to Alexandria.

But Rhizos knew it was only a respite, that to

buy off subsidiary agents was not to buy off Falih's lawyers. He read the news about the Bill with growing anxiety. There were difficulties in the committee stage.

' It's hopeless to wait for it,' said Kolocrotoni, dark and young and fierce. They stood together in the sunset, looking at Little Perfume from Londos' ancient stance at the mouth of the sharia. ' Better that we leave it so that this Falih will wish it were a midden again.'

' How ? ' asked Rhizos.

' Burn it, blow it up.'

' Blow it up ? Where are you to get the explosives ? '

Kolocrotoni laughed. ' That would be easy.' And he told of a warehouse in Cairo where arms were stored before being smuggled through to the Senussi. ' It is from there that the Nationalist students get their arms.'

' Could we ? ' asked Rhizos.

Kolocrotoni stared. He had hardly meant to be taken so seriously. ' Revolvers ? '

' Yes.' Young Trikoupi seemed to be calculating rapidly. ' Or automatics. Thirteen revolvers and ammunition.'

XIV

Now, as I've told, there was only one street which led into the square of Little Perfume. Down this street the next morning came a body of men,

labourers and carpenters. With them was Falih's
own lawyer. Gemadios's youngest son brought to
the Greeks news of the invaders' approach. Giant
Londos, bending over the garden-patch in front
of his house, with a great hose in his hand, nodded.

The lawyer halted his host, glanced at Londos,
and then walked past him. Or rather, he prepared
to do so.

' I would not pass,' said Londos, in friendly tone.
And added, as an anxious afterthought, ' This is
the first time I have used a garden hose and I am
still inexpert.'

The little lawyer turned on him angrily, and at
that moment was lifted off his feet by a stream of
water hitting him in the chest. He rolled out of
Londos's garden, rose, and was promptly knocked
down again. The hose appeared to have gone mad
in the hands of Londos. He stabbed a beam of
water to and fro amid the heads of a lawyer's
following. They broke and ran for the sharia, and,
running, found themselves objects of suspicion to
the Egyptians of the sharia's hovels.

Cries rose : ' Who are they ? '

The answering cry came quickly. ' Thieves !
Stop them ! '

Thereat, apparently in a passion for justice, the
Sharia el Ghoraib emptied a multitude of pursuers
and assailants upon the followers of Falih's lawyer.
They were pelted with refuse, kicked, cuffed, and
finally driven ignominiously from the street. The
little lawyer, beyond the reach of the last missile,

turned and shouted. Zara Muslih, standing listening at the door of her father's house, heard him and went up through the laughing, excited street towards Little Perfume. Beyond the inhabited quarter, towards where the sharia terminated in the strange settlement of the Selitsa weavers, she found Rhizos Trikoupi staring up and down the two hundred yards of high, blank-faced street-wall.

'The lawyer has gone for the police.'

Rhizos nodded. 'I expected he would. But he'll take some time to change his clothes and get there. By then the police chief will be having his siesta. They'll not dare to disturb him very early in the afternoon. When they do, the lawyer will find that my father has arrived simultaneously with himself, lodging a counter-complaint for assault and damage.'

Zara's eyes sparkled. 'This is generalship. Oh, splendid!' Then her face fell. 'But how long can you keep it up—playing them off by tricks?'

'This is the last of the tricks.'

'And father says the King is almost bound to sign the Bill the day after to-morrow.'

Rhizos's eyes turned to the high, ravine-like walls about them. 'We shall keep Little Perfume until then.'

And then some realisation came to Zara of what he intended. She stared at him, sick at heart. 'But —it will be the gendarmes who will come to-morrow.'

He nodded. 'I know. And you must not come

again until—after. Not down into Little Perfume,
I mean. I don't want other people implicated or
arrested.'

' Am I " other people " ? '

He could smile at that. ' Always, for me. Apart
and adorable, my dear.'

But her momentary flippancy had passed. ' Oh,
it'll be madness.' Her eyes widened. ' And it's
not just a scuffle you intend. *That* is why Kolocrotoni has been buying revolvers—I heard of it.
. . . Rhizos—you who've always hated fighting
and laughed at the dark little melodramatics of
history ! '

His look almost frightened her. ' Do you think
I haven't hated the trickeries and treacheries of the
last few days ? Do you think I don't hate the dirty
little pantomime we're staging now ? But I'd
rather mime in the dark than crawl like a coward
in the sunlight.' He shuddered and passed his
hands across his eyes. His voice fell to a dull
flatness. ' And there'll be no fighting. Look here,
Zara, I must go back.'

They touched hands, not looking at each other.
She did not kiss him this time. Her eyes were
suddenly blind with tears.

XV

That evening the Greeks—thirteen of them,
young men between the ages of eighteen and thirty,

and all unmarried—moved out from Little Perfume
with pickaxes and shovels, and, a hundred yards
along the Sharia el Ghoraib, began to dig up the
roadway. It was very quiet, in that hushed Cairene
semi-darkness, and Rhizos Trikoupi, with knit
brows and a tape-line, went from side to side of the
street, measuring and calculating. It might have
seemed to the casual onlooker like an ordinary gang
of street workmen but for the silence that went with
its operations. Young men from the representative
families of the settlement—Kolocrotoni, Vasos,
Sina, the two young Latas, Gemadios, Zalakosta
and the others—they dug and hewed through the
dried mud and were presently excavating the ancient
paving-stones. From behind them there was silence
also in all the locked and shuttered houses of Little
Perfume. Even the looms had ceased to hum.

For a battle had been fought there over the paper
Rhizos had prepared and forced the Greek house-
holders—his father among them—to sign. This
was a document disowning Rhizos and his followers
as ' young hotheads ' whom the elders of the community were unable to restrain. Little Perfume,
it declared, entirely dissociated itself from them.

' I will not sign it,' swore Londos, in bed with
rheumatism, and groaning as he stirred indignantly.
But, like all the others, sign he did at last, and held
Rhizos's hand, peering up into his face. ' If only
I could come with you ! '

' You'll be less bored in bed, *papakes*,' Rhizos
assured him lightly. ' Probably we'll all catch

damnable colds. But our bluff will keep them off for a time—and they can only give a few of us a week or so in prison when it's over.'

But midnight saw a barricade, business-like enough and breast-high, spanning the sharia from side to side. Then, leaving the Latas, armed with cudgels, to look after it, Rhizos and his companions went back and slept in Little Perfume, a sleep that was broken in early dawn by one of the Latas coming panting to the door of the Trikoupi house with the news that Falih's lawyer was approaching with his gang of labourers. Evidently he expected to take the settlement by surprise.

Rhizos dressed hurriedly and went to the barricade. With the lawyer he saw two Egyptian policemen.

The party was evidently staggered at sight of the barricade. What happened then is not quite clear. For a little, while his young men ran up, Rhizos stood and parleyed with the lawyer, the gendarmes at first laughing and then losing their tempers in the quick, Egyptian way. One of them unslung his carbine—it was in the days when they still carried carbines—and, levelling it at Rhizos, ordered him to start demolishing the barricade. For answer Kolocrotoni, looking over the barricade, at some distance from Rhizos, called out:

'Drop that carbine!'

The gendarme looked up and found himself covered by a dozen revolvers. His carbine clattered to the ground. At the order of Kolocrotoni the

other policeman also disarmed. Sina climbed
over the barricade, and, in the midst of a queer
silence, went and collected the weapons. Then he
returned and the two parties looked at each other
undecidedly. Suddenly the first gendarme turned
round and hastened down the Sharia el Ghoraib.
His companion trudged stolidly after him. Falih's
lawyer, after a moment of hesitation, followed
suit, his gang behind him in straggling retreat.
The young Greeks at the barricade avoided each
others' eyes and beat their hands together in the chill
morning air. Somewhere a cock began to crow,
shrilly.

At ten o'clock a policeman came down the sharia,
surveyed the barricade and its defenders, and then
retired. Kolocrotoni brought Rhizos a cup of
coffee, and while the latter drank it, himself mounted
to the highest point of the defences and watched.
Suddenly he drew a breath like a long sigh.

' Here they come.'

XVI

How far those thirteen young Greeks had
imagined the affair would go it is impossible to say.
In the subsequent enquiry the police affirmed that
the Greeks fired the first shot. There can, at least,
be little doubt that the police at the beginning made
no attempt to shoot. The squad of twenty men
marched to within ten yards or so of the barricade,
and Rhizos called them to halt. For answer the

officer in command ostentatiously turned his back on the barricade, ordered his men to club their carbines and charge, himself turned round again— and came forward at a rapid run, swinging a loaded stick in his hand. The attackers were greeted with a hail of stones. Carbine and revolver shots rang out. The officer pitched forward into the dust, and for a moment the policemen wavered. But only for a moment. They came on again. And then Rhizos committed himself openly. He leant over the barricade and shot three of them in rapid succession. Thereat the survivors broke and ran. The Greeks did not fire, but glanced, white-faced, at their leader. Rhizos, white himself, calmly ejected the spent rounds from his revolver, and re-loaded it.

Then, with a glance down the empty sharia, he climbed the barricade and inspected the four uniformed figures lying in the dust. The officer and one other were dead. Two of them lived, one with a broken arm, the other with his skull slightly grazed. Rhizos bandaged the last one, helped the man with the wounded arm to his feet, and pointed down the sharia. Holding to the wall, like a sick dog, the policeman shambled out of sight. Rhizos was turning in perplexity to the other bodies when his companions called to him urgently. . . . He gained shelter just as the rifle-fire opened.

None of the defenders had any experience of warfare, and it says much for the skill with which the barricade was constructed that in the first few

minutes only two of them were killed. Kolocrotoni was shot through the shoulder. Rhizos,
calling to the others to keep their places, crawled
to him and bandaged him. Presently the rifle-fire
ceased for a moment, but after another abortive
charge opened again. . . .

By evening there were eight Greeks, including
Rhizos, left alive. In spite of threats and entreaties
on the part of those who held the barricade, non-
combatants—the gentle Elia among them—crawled
out from Little Perfume and took away the bodies
of the dead. But with the evening the gendarmes
withdrew (in futile search of a way over the khan
walls, as was afterwards told), the stretch of street
in front of the barricade was left deserted, and,
staring at each other unbelievingly, the young men
ate the food brought them from Little Perfume.

They seemed unending those evening hours.
Rhizos had two bonfires lighted at a distance of fifty
yards or so down the sharia, so that there might be
no surprise attack. A tarpaulin had been brought
from the settlement and erected behind the barricade
in the form of a hut, and what dark thoughts assailed
the outlaws till they dropped exhausted in its shelter
no one will ever know. But long after midnight
some of them awoke and heard Rhizos, alone wakeful and guarding the barricade, singing in a strange,
shrill voice snatches of a song they had never heard
before. It was a frightening thing to hear in the
listening silence of the sharia, and Kolocrotoni
prevailed on him to go and lie down. Utterly

weary, he swayed to the shelter, staggered—and
was asleep before Kolocrotoni's arm caught him
and lowered him to the ground.

Near three in the morning, eluding somehow the
police-picket at the upper end of the Sharia Ghoraib,
Zara Muslih reached the barricade and whispered
the news to Kolocrotoni : the Bill was to be signed
and issued in the morning. The story of the affray
in the Warrens had hastened the signing.

'And you must all get away at once,' she urged.
'Throw up rope-ladders over the khan walls.'

Kolocrotoni shook his head. 'We cannot leave
here until the Bill is definitely signed, Rhizos says.
If we abandon the barricade now the police may be
in possession of Little Perfume before morning.'

'Rhizos—he doesn't know what he's done!
You people were in a searchlight of sympathy before
he started this resistance—no one has a scrap of pity
for you now. . . . Oh, tell him I *must* see him!'

The young Greek shook his head again, looking
at her with narrowed eyes. 'He's asleep. This isn't
a woman's business.'

A moment they looked at each other, Kolocrotoni
implacable, Zara desperately pleading. Then she
glanced at that tragic barricade for the last time,
and went back through the dying light of the bonfires and never saw either Rhizos or Kolocrotoni
again.

For at starset, in the lowering darkness that
precedes the Egyptian morning, they shook Rhizos
awake. The police were approaching again, and

in considerable force. He started up as he felt their hands on his shoulder, and looked at them, Kolocrotoni and the younger Latas, remotely, alertly.

' *What is it? The Persians?* '

They stared at him, stumblingly attempting to follow strange rhythms and accentuations in his speech. 'It's the gendarmes,' said Kolocrotoni. 'And we'll hardly be able to make them out. There's not a gleam of sun yet.'

Rhizos laughed, jumping to his feet, speaking again in words they barely understood—albeit they might have been direct answer to Zara's passionate denunciation. . . . Then he shuddered and passed his hands across his eyes, as though awakening from an inner sleep.

' What is it? What have I been saying? I had a dream. . . . The gendarmes? '

Far down the sharia came the steady tramp of disciplined feet.

XVII

They sent an armoured car against it eventually, that flimsy erection behind which a dwindling band of Greeks defied the hosts of the Orient. It crashed through, indifferently, half an hour after the promulgation of the Bill, and it was then that Rhizos and Kolocrotoni were killed. Three of the defenders, Sina and the two Latas, escaped back into Little Perfume, their ammunition exhausted. There they managed to scale the khan walls and were

R

seen never again in Cairo. But before they went they told the tale of those last few hours. . . .

The historian pauses, his theme in diminuendo, himself standing in the bright Cairene sunshine, lost in fantastic speculation as he sees again that misascribed quotation graved below the word ΘΕΡΜΟΠΥΛΑΙ on the dusty wall of the Sharia el Ghoraib :

> ' *So much the better. We shall fight in the shade.*
> —Rhizos of Sparta.'

L'Allegro

SIWA PLAYS THE GAME

I

*O*UTSIDE *the café awning the noon-blaze of the sun in the Place of the Green Step was almost liquid. A sakkah, his dripping goatskin slung on his back, slouched through the dust. Then a string of donkeys. A Ford car. A gendarme, with carbine and tarbouche, came loitering along the middle of the street. The trees of the Esbekieh Gardens lifted their branches to peer over the roof-tops towards us or to gaze in vegetal surprise at the windows of Sednaoui's great clothing emporium opposite, where flaunted immense notices of the delectable* mise-en-vente *within. My eyes blinked in the sun-shimmer.*

Ask (said Sergei Lubow) with but a sufficiency of persistent stupidity, and ye shall receive. Seek, with eyes but sufficiently myopic, and ye shall find. Where prayers may leave the Gods unmoved the clownish clamour of reiterated conviction may bore them to the compliance of exasperation. As witness the tale of George Menteith Elvar de Selincourt.

You have heard of George Menteith Selincourt—with the Elvar de thrown in? Alas, and who in your English world has not? And, had you but cast your eyes across at the façade of the good Sednaoui's some three minutes ago, you would have seen him in the flesh vanish within these portals in the tow of his lifetime's dream and desire. He is the dreaded warning : he has found what he sought. Heaven lies about us in our infancy.

II

It is some two months ago when I first met him —or rather, was summoned to his presence in the Continental. He had heard of the two best guides in Cairo, he told me—Anton Saloney and Sergei Lubow. Anton had gone, therefore, did I prove satisfactory on examination, he would engage me.

All this he told me with a pompous assurance, his small form, padded and pink, bulging from the depths of a basket chair, his small eyes, padded and pink in like manner, bulging from the depths of his almost featureless face.· I looked upon that face in some astonishment, and, being without clients at the time, repressed my ribaldry and paid him my thanks. He beamed with a fatuous complacency. There may be fauna on this unfortunate planet gifted, when complacent, with a greater fatuousness than the average Englishman, but so far God in His mercy has spared me the horror of encountering them.

'That's all right,' he said. 'Now, look, this is what I want. You've heard of me, of course?' he broke off.

I expressed my regrets. 'I am but little acquainted with the English aristocracy.'

'Fourth Estate,' he corrected, and waved his hand to the bookshelves in the room. Three tiers there were crowded with volumes still encased in their paper jackets. 'I am a novelist.'

'May I inspect?' I asked, and he nodded with a pleased graciousness.

But you have heard of him and will guess what titles I inspected in that room in the Continental. *Purple Sands*, I saw, had reached its fortieth thousand. *A Dahlia in the Desert* was in its tenth printing. *The Yellow Silence*—I forget the staggering sales of this work, but I turned my eyes upon its author with renewed surprise.

'Then you have been much in Egypt? I had gathered that this was but a first visit.'

He smiled, complacent as ever. 'So it is. I have never been in Egypt before. Imagination'—he waved again to the astounding shelves—'these are the fruits of. They are, I think, the best proof of how sheer intuition may reach to awareness of a life never actually lived. . . . That, however, is now over. I have come to Egypt to gain a deep personal acquaintance with that mysterious East whose life I have hitherto known only intuitively.'

Some secret doubts stirred then in me, but I merely nodded, and the good George proceeded with his explanations. He wished to journey to Sollum and from there take a camel train down to Siwa in the Red Desert—'The oasis of Jupiter Ammon, in the footsteps of the Great Alexander. I've heard rumours there's a tribe of a lost white civilisation in that neighbourhood '—his eyes made a further unseemly pop from his head, '—and there at least the True East still lives unchanged. I want to hear the singing from the harems at night, see the veiled, dusky beauties go by through silent lanes at noon, listen to the tom-toms beat at a native wedding.   Cairo '—he   glanced   disparagingly around his gorgeous apartment—' is not the East. And I want a guide to take me into those haunts where civilisation has not yet penetrated.'

All this he delivered with his fat legs crossed in repose, his small pig-face glinting with assurance. I said, ' But I know nothing of Siwa. It is far from here. You had better employ a native who knows the district. Doubtlessly such can be found in Cairo.'

He nodded. ' That is what I want you to do, arrange the—expedition, shall we call it ?—generally, employ a guide who knows Siwa, and spare me all the details which an artist must avoid if he is to concentrate on his art. I will pay you well, of course.'

I considered him for a moment and then the gods played upon my weakest point, my sense of humour. I saw far off in the depths of the weeks a twinkling mirror reflecting oddities innumerable, and if I refused employment I should assuredly miss the sight of them. Darya could live with the Dans while I was away. I nodded.

' Very well, I will come at the salary you offer.'

III

Three weeks later we were approaching Siwa, an unclean blot on the south-western landscape. I remember the afternoon very well, because it was then that the Khawaga George (I had reached to the stage of calling him by his first name, as well you may do when you have also reached to the stage of anointing a man's saddle-sores and holding his head the while he is sick) turned towards me and groaned at the movement in the saddle of his camel.

'Good God, is *that* Siwa ?'

'Such,' I said, 'I understand from Selim Hanna to be the case.'

The Khawaga George groaned again and then Selim, our Siwan guide who had halted *his* camel, struck in with that unfortunate flow of unauthentic colloquialisms which was his passion. 'By God, yes, sirs, that's him all right, all right. Much plenty colour of East, no ?' and he peered at our employer ingratiatingly, the while I drew forth my handkerchief and in its depths concealed side by side with many a companion of the past three weeks another of those laughs which had saved me from combustion or collapse.

I think that the good George had had doubts of Selim from the first. For our guide was neither taciturn nor sinister, as were all good guides in the books of George himself. Instead, he had the ingratiating geniality of a leech and something of its blood-surfeited odour. Large and perspiring, his head in the past two weeks since we had left Sollum, had bobbed assuredly in the van or was deep-bent over his passion—a copy of *The Descent of Man* by the German savant, Haeckel. This was Selim's Bible. At frequent intervals he would draw rein by the side of the long-suffering Khawaga George.

' By God, sirs, he is some fine chap, this Sheikh Haeckel! Him show God and Muhammud and Isa ben Miriam—them all damn muck. Damn fine!' And Selim would beam again the while George's eyes goggled like those of a crab in the throes of colic. But for some remote spark of genuine pride, coupled with a kind of pig-like obstinacy, it was plain to me that he would long before have cancelled the whole expedition—despite the hope that Siwa itself might be different, more in accord with the stirring pages of *The Yellow Silence*, a copy of which I had purchased in Cairo and wept over in silent laughter through many an hour of our southwards trek.

For, if you comprehend the mentality of *The Yellow Silence's* author, he felt actually insulted. He had come to the East in the fullest expectation that he would find it faithfully reposing as portrayed in his own books—written mainly, I believe, in a London suburb called (unaccountably) Balham. And, in the unamazing, disgusting world of the actual desert, there must have grown upon him a thing equivalent to the belief that some malignant

deity had seized and changed and transformed the
landscape for the sole purpose of vexing his soul !

For Arabs were neither hawk-nosed nor handsome ! instead, they had generally the appearance
of having been violently dropped upon their faces
by careless nurses in their early youth. They were
neither taciturn nor abstemious nor fanatic ; instead,
they behaved, as he told me, like drunken dock-
labourers on a charabanc tour. And there were no
ruins or signs of them. No beauteous maidens
wept at eve beside the pillars of a civilisation long
buried in the sand——

' Ah ! You will listen, no ? '

Selim Hanna had halted again, his finger upraised
to his ear. Siwa lay closer now, its unclean walls
offset by the tarnished greenery of its palms.
And in the air throbbed and whined a strange noise
—a noise like that which one might hear from an
amorous cat supplicating its mistress. I glanced
at the Khawaga Geor;e and again sought my handkerchief. Unburied in the sands, unwept at eve,
civilisation had penetrated to Siwa. From the
Southern Gate a gramophone was wailing forth
the haunting transpontine strains of ' Ma Baby's a
Wow.'

IV

For the time being, at least, it seemed that had
broken the spirit of the Khawaga George. He
allowed himself, almost in silence, to be led by Selim

and myself to a tumble-down hotel that had less pretensions at being a caravanserai than has the average public-house in unwarranted Balham. There we found him a room, arranged for his supper, and left him to the mysteries of the Eastern night. Selim had invited me to visit his home.

Also, he had told me something of his personal and family history. His father was the Sheikh Ohmed, keeper of a sweetmeat stall by the Southern Gate, and very early in life Selim had displayed those qualities which were later to stand him in such good stead. His was, I think, a good Siwan example of the kind of career which your Samuel Smiles would have loved to brood upon and adorn with comely epithet. Becoming bored with life in Siwa he had, at the age of sixteen, stolen a camel and set out for Cairo. Since then, and after selling the camel, he had never looked back. Neither had he ever come back. However, a delayed correspondence had smoothed things out, the original camel-owner had died, and he now expected, so he told to me in his exceptional English, 'Some booze and a dance of welcome, God damn it, no?'

He received even more. Behind the closed doors of the Southern Gate dukkan we found the whole of the Hanna clan, or so it seemed to me, assembled to honour this Siwan prodigal. I enjoyed myself considerably and without reservation. Old men and young men, women veiled and women unveiled, crowded around Selim. The gramophone played the Hanna's single surviving record, 'Ma Baby's a

Wow '; and whenever it ceased from playing some thoughtful soul would rewind it and start it afresh. There was arrack to drink and honey-cakes to eat. And presently Selim, who had no Oriental reticences, led a woman through the throng and introduced her to me.

' This my sister Zoo. You like her, yes ? Perhaps you sleep with her ? Virgin.' And he regarded me and the sister with a speculative eye.

I also looked at the woman and a little shock of surprise came on me. She was much lighter in colour than either Sheikh Ohmed or the disreputable Selim. Her face, indeed, would have been lovely but for its defiant sullenness. But at me she smiled slowly, consideringly, and beneath the layers of grime I saw the possibility of a charming woman emerge.

' Your sister? But surely she cannot be ? ' I said to Selim, the while the girl sat down beside me, and, unaware of a word of English, turned on me her large, brooding eyes. Selim explained rapidly and without hesitation. She was his half-sister. Her mother had been a Greek woman sold from bidder to buyer, a mere girl, in the days of the Mahdi and at length, in her old age, had reached the Sheikh Ohmed's possession. Then, surprisingly, she had given birth to Zoo, and died when the latter was a year old. . . . I caught at the name.

' Zoo ? Ah, her name is Zoë.'

' That's right, all right, khawaga. Damn bitch she is. Won't marry mens come for her—scavenger

he offer to buy. Won't marry. Third wife for old
sheikh that makes shoes. Won't go. Says she only
marry white. You like her, yes ? '

I shook my head, ' But I am married already,'
and looked into the eyes of Zoë Hanna in some pity.
And there, deep in their depths, was a look and a
dreaming desire such as I had thought Siwa incapable of bearing outside the novels of the good
Khawaga George, now seeking his sleep in the unauthentic caravanserai by the Eastern Gate.

V

Of that sleep we heard more than a little next
morning ; and then it was that the absurd George
misbehaved in such fashion as for me put him
beyond the pale of the merely humorous.   I
gathered that his supper on the preceding night had
consisted mainly of goat-gut and garlic.   That on
top of his desert-aches, he had retired to bed with an
aching head and a stupefied stomach, but even so
had found no rest.   For he was in the Glamorous
East.   Bugs in battalions infested the strings of the
bed, and all night long, horse, foot, and artillery,
insisted on practising their annual desert manœuvres
across the novelist's small and shuddering chest.
To cap it all, far into the romantic Eastern night a
gramophone played again and again on one maddening record and apparently one maddening needle,
the refrain of ' Ma Baby's a Wow.'

So perhaps the good George's awakening condition was in some measure understandable, if but slowly forgivable. Myself, I had slept with some relish and the after-affects of the Sheikh Ohmed's arrack, and awoke next morning more than hungry. Having breakfasted, I sent for Selim, and together, as two good employees should, we betook ourselves to the room of the Khawaga George to demand his instructions for the day.

The voice that bade us enter might have served as forewarning. But it was not until we stood in front of him—he raised the popping eyes of fury above a riddled suit of pyjamas, for some mischance had led him to occupy the worst room of the hotel—that he released upon me the full blast of his indignation. I stood and regarded him in an amazement of great blankness, for hitherto I had taken to myself no blame for the unseemly condition of the fauna and flora encountered in our desert expedition.

But now I learned that I was to blame for most of the happenings since our encounter in Cairo. What did I mean by saying in the Continental that Siwa was the last oasis where the genuine East was still to be found? How had I the impudence to stand before him as now I did when I had led him into the beastliest hole on earth, out on an expedition in which he had suffered nothing but disgust and discomfort? And where were the ruined cities I had promised to show him, the relics of the lost white race I had said inhabited Sahara?

It was a farrago of nonsense. But I had seemed to hear it before, in a different context and setting. And then I recollected : these were the things of which he himself had spoken in his room in the Continental ! . . . Very suddenly he ceased to amuse and merely bored me.

' You are being slightly more absurd in fact than your books are in fancy,' I said. ' What orders have you for me or Selim to-day ? '

He was almost in a hysteria of weeping disappointment by then. And from the midst of the hysteria he issued his ultimatum. ' This : find me some of the things I was led to expect, or I'll sack the pair of you—here on the spot—and you can find your way back to Cairo as you like.'

It was an absurd enough threat, and did not greatly worry me. The good George apparently forgot that he would also have to find *his* way back to Cairo. But Selim took the matter much to heart and broke loudly into expostulation.

' God damn it no, not do that. Much to-day show you, wazzas, girls dance the Charleston, my father he have gramophone, in house of mullah's cousin is the radio, there is the new beer-shop where they make the cocktails, no ? No sack. Hell no.'

I dragged him away from the Khawaga George's curses, and together we went out into the winding, odorous lanes which twist amid the palms and dungheaps of white-walled Siwa. And there it was that a sudden idea came upon me. I halted and looked back at the crumbling façade of the hotel, looked at

Selim, and remembered a passage from the pages of
The Yellow Silence. The idea, a seed at first, ger-
minated, sprouted and burgeoned the while I stood
in the sun-glare and looked at the Sheikh Haeckel's
last, most faithful worshipper. I took him by the
shoulder.

'It seems there is nothing we can do at the
moment to please the Khawaga George,' I said.
'Now let us entertain ourselves. And as we go
you can tell me more of your family history and
dispositions.'

VI

That day the good George fretted through
all alone, never leaving the hotel in which he had
bedded so hardly during the previous night. By
noon, I imagine, he was already regretting his hasty
dismissal of Selim and myself. Siwa yawned and
gossiped and chattered beyond his windows. The
hours wore by. Still neither Selim nor I returned,
selfishly immersed in our own amusements, our
employer guessed. But Romance outrides all aids.
It was there in Siwa, as in great detail George afterwards made plain to me, and like called to like across
the bounds of creed and race.

For, just as the darkness fell, he had retreated
to his own room with a book, and there lighted the
paraffin lamp set for the convenience of guests.
No sooner had he done so than mosquitoes with
drones like the noise of twin-engined bombers

came pinging through the window and gathered about him in clouds : mosquitoes such as the hero of *Purple Sands* had never dreamt of, far less engaged in pitched battle. And just as George smote at them bitterly, Romance came flying through the window and hit him full in the face. Literally.

He gasped and bent gingerly to pick up the thing which had hit him. It was a woman's garment, extremely soiled and of so intimate a nature that George, all of whose books were exceptionally reticent, blushed with a very great vividness. But there was something else. Pinned to the garment was a note, and George rent it free and spread it on the table before him.

' Oh, my hero, my hero, come quick and save me ! I you in Siwa have heard be : I am prisoner in the white house by Southern Gate, and to-night to old Sheik am married be.

' My father was professor Hellene whom Arabs capture and now to one I am to wedded be unless you come. Oh, me come and save, for of you I have heard !

' This is my gage and bringing it you may be known. For me a faithful dying friend this write I have no english. Quick come.'

There was no signature. But, you will gather, none was needed. In a moment the Khawaga George was upon his feet. His eyes, popping enthusiastically forth from the perspiration that rivuleted his face, shone with the light that never was, to re-quote a phrase he had made his own.

Romance! Romance, even as he had written and dreamed, was out there in the glamour of the Eastern night. Romance and intrigue, a frightened maiden to rescue, were there in the night. Siwa —Siwa, in fact, in the phrase beloved of his books, was playing the game.

VII

His messenger fell in speedily enough with Selim and myself : we were returning towards the hotel when he came upon us. Fired by the urgency of the call, we coursed up to George's room at racing speed and there found him, in leggings and a revolver, abrim with the news and determined to sally forth in rescue of the daughter of the ' professor Hellene.'

I attempted to dissuade him. ' Even if it is not a trap to seize you and hold you to ransom, what can you do with this Greek girl when you rescue her ? '

But he had his answer pat for that, even as, while putting the question, I had known he would. And I stood and stared at him a moment with the astonishment of one who finds a piece of mechanism act as it is warranted to act, yet is of such peculiar action that your astonishment remains unquenched. ' Do ? We'll escape from Siwa. You and Selim must fix up the camels—an extra one for the girl— and have water and provisions ready. One of you come with me and help in the rescue—I'll do all the actually dangerous work—and we'll make for Sollum as soon as we're mounted.'

' But still you have not told me what you will do, even if you reach Sollum,' I persisted. ' What thing is to happen to this Greek girl, especially if she is young and comely ? '

It was then that Selim struck in, his eyes upraised to the sweating ceiling in reminiscence. ' By God, yes. Now do I remember, of her I have heard. She the beautiful girl, captive in old white house, with great dark eyes of perishing fawn, in Siwa call her the Desert Flower.'

' What ? ' It was, if I may so describe it, a bay of joy that came from the Khawaga George. Looking at him, I knew that necessity for further questioning was needless. That which he would do was plain to me. And I myself would be there to see that he did it.

VIII

And so as planned the rescue fell out, for was it not the Glamorous East ? While I and the cook awaited with five camels by the Eastern Gate, George and Selim, as they afterwards told me, crept on that white house at the other side of the town, flung the unmentionable gage in through a window, and had but a minute to wait when a door thrust open and a veiled figure glided from it. In the starlight the figure made for George and flung its arms about his neck. He choked and then employed his own arms to like effect. Then the veil slipped aside and George looked upon the face of the girl, and choked again, as might an overstrung cockerel. . . .

So all that night we fled northwards over the desert till at dawn we made camp, safe, in Selim's estimation, beyond temporary pursuit. Then we ate a swift breakfast and held a swift conference. Selim was despondent, and even the Khawaga George heeded to him, turning his glowing pop eyes a moment from the vision of the Grecian captive beside him, sitting in demure beauty and silence, eating the dates we had given her.

' Hell of row, oh yes, they raise, the Siwa Araba. Damn ignorant. They the abduction will call it, we will be tried and jailed in Sollum. Raise hell, the Siwa Arabs, oh yes.'

I suggested that perhaps they might be bought off —if George cared to buy them and Selim cared to go back to Siwa and make the attempt. Selim intimated his willingness. But—it was not the kind of thing that was done by the heroes in George's books.

' We have guns and camels. We are in the right. We'll fight it out if they follow,' he said, his fat cheeks glowing damply.

I glanced at Selim. He nodded, still more despondently, to George's remark.

'By God yes. But in the last abduction in Siwa the mans they caught oh yes, and split him open and put the salt and sand in his tum-tum. By God yes he screamed. . . .'

A short half-hour later we mounted our camels,

and turned to look south. Far off, a swift-moving dot, was Selim on *his* camel, hull-down, piastre-laden, returning on his hopeful mission to soothe the Siwan choler.

IX

They were married in Sollum, the Khawaga George and the Greek girl whom he had rescued. I acted as witness, and George bought me and himself the new and elegant drill as garb for his wedding. Then we got aboard the waiting tanker and came back to Egypt, from Alexandria to Cairo ; and I received my promised emoluments, and made them my bow.

Then I returned home to Darya, and laughed and wept, and grew sober, and laughed again, and grew solemn in wonderment as to how that odd jest that was yet no jest would turn out in the sequel.

But it was needless for me to have worried. But yesterday as I passed through the lobbies of the Continental a servant summoned me to a gorgeous suite and there I found the new Mrs. Selincourt seated at a table, brooding upon a letter she had written, very charming in her handsome clothes new-purchased in Cairo. We greeted one the other and she handed me the letter and I sat and read in the looping Arabic script :

' This is the last five hundred piastres I can send to you and to the Sheikh Ohmed. I have got it from Jorj, as with other sums. But soon he would begin to suspect, and, though he is a fool, I love him a little. He has not beaten me yet.

' Also, I need pay no heed to your threats for he would not believe you. You thought to win great wealth from the trick that you and the Russki played on Jorj, but you had forgotten that Egypt is not his land. In two day's time we leave for England, and I shall be far from you, away with Jorj, who, though a fool, I love a little.

' Kiss the saint's tomb by the Southern Gate for me, though I do not worship the Prophet now, being wife of Jorj, who, though a fool, I love a little. He has not beaten me yet.

' Your sister,

ZOE.'

X

One wonders if, after all, George Menteith Elvar de Selincourt has not the best of it !

Il Penseroso

THE CHILDREN OF CERES

I

THIS is a tale they tell in the little streets that glimmer and brood in the scent and stench behind the Tent-makers' Bazaar. A myth, a fable, or an idle fancy, this youngest of tales that already is old, El Kahira listens and nods and questions neither objective truth nor objective origins. For are not the great glass globes still there, plain for a man to view? And are not the thoughts of men known to God and made known to man once again?

So the tale begins with the great glass globes that were reared above the roof of the tall new restaurant overshadowing the entrance to the Wagh el Berka. By night they glowed their invitation in a spectrum of colour; by day the wheeling sun above the Cairene streets wheeled them upon the dusty walls and cobblestones of the dank, still entrance to the Prostitutes' Street. Ground and blown from the fine white sand of the Delta beaches, heritors of a million years of sun and sky, the voices of the earth and its waters, the great glass globes grew overnight a landmark above the bazaars.

And the tale tells on how it came one day that a gendarme stood at the entrance of the Wagh el Berka, and scowled on the streets, for his belly

pained him and his brain was an ache and despair
within his skull. The night before he had drunken
of arrack, and gamed, and drunken of arrack again,
and it seemed to him that the long daytime duty
hours would never pass, and allow him the ease of
the bed that his aches so craved.

And he raised his eyes to the wheeling lights of
the great glass globes and saw at last that it was late
in the afternoon. And he lowered his eyes down the
coloured spray of the sunlight shafts, and there,
in a blotch of prismatic shadow, he saw the woman.
She squatted by the left-hand corner of the Wagh
el Berka's entrance, and he stared at her in surprise
for he had not seen her come. For a while, in the
dazzle of light, he made little of her look or likelihood, and he shaded his eyes with his hand and
made a half-step towards where she crouched. A
strange lightness came in his head and veins.

But that passed. For he saw the crouching woman
with great clearness then, the dull, brute face and
jaundiced eye, and he turned aside and spat his
disgust. Some woman of the Street whose days at
her trade were overpast, he guessed, and meditated
a blow in her ribs with his carbine, and then spat
again. Involve himself in a brawl with a hag when
his duty drew at length to its end?

And the tale tells then that a young man drew
aside from the drift of pedestrians in the street
below, and looked at the entrance to the Wagh el
Berka, and looked at the gendarme, and peered
at the little watch which was strapped on his wrist,

He was young, he was comely, a Gentile, an artist. He saw the globes as the wheeling suns of the Dog Star, and life was good in his mouth, and women desirous under his hands. And he laughed as he saw that he stood at the entrance to the Prostitutes' Street, and looked again at his little watch, and went swiftly in towards the Wagh el Berka.

It was then that he too saw the crouching shape by the left-hand entrance. No more than a shapeless shape, a fusing of sun and shadow, he saw in his haste, and paid her no heed, and went whistling out of the sunlight into the dark, quiet shadows that mantled in warmth and stench the silent Street.

But hardly had he gone than along the street two women came, one a heathen woman from the island of Japan, one Italian, and harlots both of them from the great houses of the Wagh. In search of foods or of laces to deck their bodies, they had spent long hours away from their rooms, and returned exhausted now from the day's adventurings. And their feet were swollen with their wanderings and their minds made brittle by anger, for all men knew their trade and their lives, and called to them, jeering, and shamed them in unknown places. So they came with sly, quick looks at the face of the gendarme, and he saw them come, seeing them, it so was, at the moment they themselves cast eyes on the squatting woman of the left-hand corner.

And the gendarme, stilling the ache of his head, called them by jesting, obscene names, but for once

they paid no heed. And the Italian woman stared
and spat, as one moved to sickness, and cried :

' Look on the foul whore in the corner ! She is
shameful and diseased. Ah God, why is she not
gaoled ? '

And horror came also on the face of the
harlot from Japan. ' Her face ! Do you see her
face ? '

So the two of them stood for a frozen moment
and looked at the horror of that face, and then, near
to running, white and terrified, they sheered to the
right and plunged within the portals of the Wagh el
Berka. And the gendarme stared in their wake,
without understanding, and looked upon the sky,
and looked at the woman who squatted there in
the left-hand corner. And he spat again at that
sight.

And the tale tells then that the hour of sunset
drew near, and with its coming came two others, a
man and a woman from the great Giaour land of
wealth across the seas. Their youth was over and
the days of gladness when the blood sang as a song
in their veins, and peace and plenty, the untroubled
mind, were now their desires. So they came to the
entrance to the shameful Street, and stopped and
looked, with the little books held in their hands.
And they read in the little books that in this Street
women sold their bodies to the lusts of men. And
the twain from the land of wealth were displeased
and eager, and the man said, ' We have a little while.
Shall we go look ? '

So the woman said that they would, and they turned into the entrance of the Wagh el Berka. And as they turned the woman touched her man and cried, ' Look at the dear old one who is seated there ! '

Then the man looked, and saw her who squatted in the left-hand entrance. And he was troubled.

' She looks as one un-evil and respectable,' he said, and the woman whose bed he had ceased to desire nodded her head, and pointed again to the neatness of the clothes of the squatting figure. And she said, ' Throw to her money.'

So the man drew forth his purse and searched in it and as he and his woman moved forward into the Wagh el Berka the coin he had flung spun and rang about the feet of the squatting figure. But she paid it no heed. Hearing the ring of the coin the gendarme turned and watched, and he saw that the woman paid no heed, and he spat yet again, saying to himself, ' The drunken sow has not noticed they have flung her a piastre.'

Now an old man, a Greek, came shuffling then from the streets that led to the Sharia Muhammud. Nearly seventy years had passed since the day he had come to Cairo from forgotten Lemnos, and he walked dimly, in the painless stupor of the old, till he too neared that corner where squatted the woman in the shadow. And he looked at her, and, half-blinded though he was, saw her with clearness, albeit that he blinked and half-halted with the faintness that came on him then.

It was her beauty that brought the blood beating in such wise in his heart. That, and her youth, for under the veils he saw her face, so fair and young that a little cry came from his lips, and far back in the years of lost Lemnos he heard the singing of the ghosts of desire.

' Why stays she there? Awaiting the coming of someone?' And he sighed. 'Alas, not I!'

So he too went on, slowly, remembering, and the light waned fast above the streets, and the gendarme paced with aching head at the entrance of the Wagh el Berka. Sleep weighed upon him, and pacing, he glanced at the squatting woman and saw that she too nodded. And then he heard quick steps come sounding from the entrance of the Wagh el Berka, and turned and looked at the man who came.

He came and paused in the dying sunlight and set a match to the tip of a fine cigar. For wealth and respect and a clear, quick mind was his, the noted Fransawi of the Street. His was the task to procure fresh women for the Wagh el Berka, and as he threw the match from the lighted cigar his glance fell on the woman of the corner.

And he invoked his Faith, asking, ' Who can she be? Not of the houses—but surely not of the streets?'

And he felt angered and dismayed at the thought, for such life was a waste of the goods she might sell, and he stepped a quick step towards her and stood in wonder. Tall and long-limbed, with the painted face and eyelids he saw her, a harlot surely of value and experience, one such as brought him much credit and profit. And he thought of the third house up in the Street, where a new woman purchased a fortnight before had failed so signally to withstand the playful lusts of a giant client.

But he shook his head. ' No. She hunts the bigger game for herself. It were better to leave her now.'

So he too passed her, with the backward glance of regret, and went on, and found himself in the throngs that foreshadowed the coming of night. And as he went, tells on the tale, the new woman looked out and saw the sky and planned her escape from the third house up in the Street of Shame. She crawled from her bed then, in the dankness of her little room, and sought for her clothes, and found them, though she shuddered at the touch that they brought to her hand. And frightened as a child, as indeed she was, she stood and listened, and drew the garments about her, and staunched at nose and mouth the little foamings of blood that came. Then she found her shoes, and was shod, and slowly crept down the stairs to a doorway deserted and the Wagh el Berka beyond like a sharp-edged nullah with the sunlight aglow on its long, grey ledges. As yet she was safe, for the trade and thronging of the Street came after dark.

So this child who had looked on a woman's

terrors crept then away from that doorway, and with stealthy walk, clinging to the wall, made her slow way past house after house. Near to the entrance of the Street she raised heavy eyes, and they swam with little specks in her sickness, and she saw the light wheel from the great glass globes in a long, straight shaft that the darkness waited to devour. Beyond the entrance she saw the gendarme pace, and fear came on her again, but she might not stay, and crept by the wall in the shadow.

So she came at last to the entrance and stepped from it, and far off then in Abbassieh, tells on the tale, the sunset gun pealed forth its cry. And the woman started at the sound as a frightened fawn, and the blood that had sprayed from her mouth in a little foam became of a sudden a torrent. Staunching it then, and swaying in sickness, she raised her eyes and looked and saw the woman who squatted in the left-hand corner.

And she knew her at once, the face turned towards her, remembered, un-angered, compassionate. How had she known ? How was she here ? And fear went from her, and she made a last stumbling run.

‘ Mother ! ’

.   .   .   .   .

And the tale tells on how the gendarme heard that cry and wheeled round and looked. And he saw the girl who came stumbling from the Street of Shame, and he saw her fall and lie still, and he looked unmoved. And then he gasped and clutched at his carbine and was fearful.

Darkness was filming the streets, and the play of light from the great glass globes of the Delta beaches had gone. So had the Woman who waited.

MAKTOUB